Nine ships blasted off from Moon Base. Once in space, eight of them formed a globe around the smallest. They held this formation all the way to Earth.

The small ship displayed the insignia of an admiral—yet there was no living thing of any sort in her. She was not even a passenger ship, but a drone, a robot ship intended for radioactive cargo. This trip she carried nothing but a lead coffin—and a Geiger counter that was never quiet.

BAEN BOOKS by ROBERT A. HEINLEIN

Farnham's Freehold
Glory Road
The Menace From Earth
Podkayne of Mars
Revolt in 2100 & Methuselah's Children
Sixth Column
Take Back Your Government (nonfiction)
The Green Hills of Earth

Robert A. HEINLEIN

THE GREEN HILLS OF EARTH

THE GREEN HILLS OF EARTH

This is a work of fiction. All the characters and events portrayed in this book are fictional, and any resemblance to real people or incidents is purely coincidental.

Copyright © 1951 by Robert A. Heinlein

"Delilah and the Space Rigger" © 1949 by McCall Corporation for *Blue Book*. "Space Jockey" © 1947 by Curtis Publishing Company for *The Saturday Evening Post*. "The Long Watch" © 1949 by The American Legion Magazine for *The American Legion Magazine*. "Gentlemen, Be Seated" © 1948 by Popular Publications for *Argosy*. "The Black Pits of Luna" © 1948 by Curtis Publishing Company for *The Saturday Evening Post*. "It's Great to Be Back" © 1947 by Curtis Publishing Company for *The Saturday Evening Post*. " '—We Also Walk Dogs' " © 1941 by Street and Smith Publications, Inc. for *Astounding Science-Fiction*. "Ordeal in Space" © 1948 Hearst Publications for *Town & Country*. "The Green Hills of Earth" © 1947 by Curtis Publishing Company for *The Saturday Evening Post*. "Logic of Empire" © 1941 by Street and Smith Publications, Inc. for *Astounding Science-Fiction*.

A Baen Book

Baen Publishing Enterprises
P.O. Box 1403
Riverdale, NY 10471

ISBN: 0-671-57853-7

Cover art by Patrick Turner

First Baen printing, January 1987
Second Baen printing, February 2000

Distributed by Simon & Schuster
1230 Avenue of the Americas
New York, NY 10020

Printed in the United States of America

To My Parents

Acknowledgment

The phrase *The Green Hills of Earth*
derives from a story by C. L. Moore
(Mrs. Henry Kuttner), and is used here
by her gracious permission

R.A.H.

Contents

Delilah and the Space-Rigger   1

Space Jockey   21

The Long Watch   47

Gentlemen, Be Seated   67

The Black Pits of Luna   83

It's Great to Be Back   103

"—We Also Walk Dogs"   129

Ordeal in Space   163

The Green Hills of Earth   187

Logic of Empire   203

The Heinlein

Note: stories in brackets never written. See Postscript to *Revolt in 2100*.

DATES STORIES	CHARACTERS	TECHNICAL
A.D.		
Life Line		
"Let There Be Light"	Martin / Pinero / Douglas	
[Word Edgewise]		
The Roads Must Roll	Blekinsop	
Blowups Happen		
The Man Who Sold the Moon		
Delilah & the Space Rigger		
Space Jockey		Mechanized roads
Requiem	Wingate	
The Long Watch	Rhysling / Gaines	Helicopters
Gentlemen, Be Seated	Harper / Erickson	King / Lentz / Harriman
The Black Pits of Luna—	Sam Jones / Satchel	McIntyre / Cummings
It's Great To Be Back	Nehemiah Scudder	Interplanetary travel
"—We Also Walk Dogs"		
Searchlight		
2000		Douglas-Martin sun-power screens
Ordeal in Space		Commercial rocket travel
The Green Hills of Earth	Lazarus Long	
[Fire Down Below]		
Logic of Empire		
The Menace from Earth		
[The Sound of His Wings]	Novak	
[Eclipse]	Master Peter	Hiatus
[The Stone Pillow]		
"If This Goes On—"		
Coventry	Zeb Jones	
2100 Misfit	John Lyle	Developments in psychometrics and psychodynamics
Universe (prologue only)	Ford / Magelene / MacKinnon	
Methuselah's Children	"Fader" Randall / Persephone	resumed
Universe	The "Doctor" / Libby	
Commonsense	McCoy / Rhodes / Doyle	Limited use of telepathy
[Da Capo]		

Timeline

	DATA	SOCIOLOGICAL	REMARKS
Static submolar engineering — Uranium 235 - artificial radioactives, atomic cont.,	Transatlantic rocket flight Antipodes rocker service	THE "CRAZY YEARS" Strike of '76 The "FALSE DAWN" First rocket to the moon Luna City founded Space Precautory Act Harriman's Lunar Corporations PERIOD OF IMPERIAL EXPLORATION Revolution in Little America Interplanetary exploration and exploitation	Considerable technical advance during this period, accompanied by a gradual deterioration of mores, orientation and social institutions, terminating in mass psychoses in the sixth decade, and the Interregnum. The Interregnum was followed by a period of reconstruction in which the Voorhis financial proposals gave a temporary economic stability and chance for re-orientation. This was ended by the opening of new frontiers and a return to nineteenth-century economy.
	Bacteriophage	American–Australasian anschluss	Three revolutions ended the period of interplanetary imperialism: Antarctica, U.S., and Venus. Space travel ceased until 2072. Little research and only minor technical advances during this period. Extreme puritanism.
Growth of submolar mechanics,	The Travel Unit and the Fighting Unit Commercial stereoptics Booster guns Synthetic foods Weather control Wave mechanics The "Barrier"	Rise of religious fanaticism The "New Crusade" Rebellion and independence of Venusian colonists Religous dictatorship in U.S. THE FIRST HUMAN CIVILIZATION	Certain aspects of psychodynam-ics and psychometrics, mass psychology and social control developed by the priest class. Re-establishment of civil liberty. Renaissance of scientific research. Resumption of space travel. Luna city refounded. Science of social relations, based on the negative statements of semantics. Rigor of epistemology. The Covenant.
	Atomic "tailoring" Elements 98–416 Parastatic engineering Rigor of colloids Symbiotic research Longevity		Beginning of the consolidation of the Solar System. First attempt at interstellar exploration. Civil disorder, followed by the end of human adolescence, and beginning of first mature culture.

Delilah and the Space-Rigger

SURE, we had trouble building Space Station One—but the trouble was people.

Not that building a station twenty-two thousand three hundred miles out in space is a breeze. It was an engineering feat bigger than the Panama Canal or the Pyramids—or even the Susquehanna Power Pile. But "Tiny" Larsen built her—and a job Tiny tackles gets built.

I first saw Tiny playing guard on a semi-pro team, working his way through Oppenheimer Tech. He worked summers for me thereafter till he graduated. He stayed in construction and eventually I went to work for him.

Tiny wouldn't touch a job unless he was satisfied with the engineering. The Station had jobs designed into it that called for six-armed monkeys instead of grown men in space suits. Tiny spotted such boners; not a ton of material went into the sky until the specs and drawings suited him.

But it was people that gave us the headaches.

We had a sprinkling of married men, but the rest were wild kids, attracted by high pay and adventure. Some were busted spacemen. Some were specialists, like electricians and instrument men. About half were deep-sea divers, used to working in pressure suits. There were sandhogs and riggers and welders and shipfitters and two circus acrobats.

We fired four of them for being drunk on the job; Tiny had to break one stiff's arm before he would stay fired. What worried us was where did they get it? Turned out a shipfitter had rigged a heatless still, using the vacuum around us. He was making vodka from potatoes swiped from the commissary. I hated to let him go, but he was too smart.

Since we were falling free in a 24-hour circular orbit, with everything weightless and floating, you'd think that shooting craps was impossible. But a radioman named Peters figured a dodge to substitute steel dice and a magnetic field. He also eliminated the element of chance, so we fired him.

We planned to ship him back in the next supply ship, the R. S. *Half Moon*. I was in Tiny's office when she blasted to match our orbit. Tiny swam to the view port. "Send for Peters, Dad," he said, "and give him the old heave ho. Who's his relief?"

"Party named G. Brooks McNye," I told him.

A line came snaking over from the ship. Tiny said, "I don't believe she's matched." He buzzed the radio shack for the ship's motion relative to the Station. The answer didn't please him and he told them to call the *Half Moon*.

Tiny waited until the TV screen showed the rocket ship's C.O. "Good morning, Captain. Why have you placed a line on us?"

"For cargo, naturally. Get your hopheads over here. I want to blast off before we enter the shadow." The Station spent about an hour and a quarter each day passing through Earth's shadow; we worked two eleven-hour shifts and skipped the dark period, to avoid rigging lights and heating suits.

Tiny shook his head. "Not until you've matched course and speed with us."

"I *am* matched!"

"Not to specification, by my instruments."

"Have a heart, Tiny! I'm short on maneuvering fuel. If I juggle this entire ship to make a minor correction on a few lousy tons of cargo, I'll be so late I'll have to put down on a secondary field. I may even have to make a dead-stick landing." In those days all ships had landing wings.

"Look, Captain," Tiny said sharply, "the only purpose of your lift was to match orbits for those same few lousy tons. I don't care if you land in Little America on a pogo stick. The first load here was placed with loving care in the proper orbit and I'm making every other load match. Get that covered wagon into the groove."

"Very well, Superintendent!" Captain Shields said stiffly.

"Don't be sore, Don," Tiny said softly. "By the way, you've got a passenger for me?"

"Oh, yes, so I have!" Shields' face broke out in a grin.

"Well, keep him aboard until we unload. Maybe we can beat the shadow yet."

"Fine, fine! After all, why should I add to your troubles?" The skipper switched off, leaving my boss looking puzzled.

We didn't have time to wonder at his words. Shields whipped his ship around on gyros, blasted a second or two, and put her dead in space with us pronto—and used very little fuel, despite his bellyaching. I grabbed every man we could spare and managed to get the cargo clear before we swung into Earth's shadow. Weightlessness is an unbelievable advantage in handling freight; we gutted the *Half Moon*—by hand, mind you—in fifty-four minutes.

The stuff was oxygen tanks, loaded, and aluminum mirrors to shield them, panels of outer skin—sandwich stuff of titanium alloy sheet with foamed glass filling—and cases of jato units to spin the living quarters. Once it was all out and snapped to our cargo line I sent the men back by the same line—I won't let a man work outside without a line no matter how space happy he figures he is. Then I told Shields to send over the passenger and cast off.

This little guy came out the ship's air lock, and hooked on to the ship's line. Handling himself like he was used to space, he set his feet and dived, straight along the stretched line, his snap hook running free. I hurried back and motioned him to follow me. Tiny, the new man, and I reached the air locks together.

Besides the usual cargo lock we had three G. E. Kwikloks. A Kwiklok is an Iron Maiden without spikes; it fits a man in a suit, leaving just a few pints of air to scavenge, and cycles automatically. A big time saver in changing shifts. I passed through the middlesized one; Tiny, of course, used the big one. Without hesitation the new man pulled himself into the small one.

We went into Tiny's office. Tiny strapped down, and pushed his helmet back. "Well, McNye," he said. "Glad to have you with us."

The new radio tech opened his helmet. I heard a low, pleasant voice answer, "Thank you."

I stared and didn't say anything. From where I was I could see that the radio tech was wearing a hair ribbon.

I thought Tiny would explode. He didn't need to see the hair ribbon; with the helmet up it was clear that the new "man" was as female as Venus de Milo. Tiny sputtered, then he was unstrapped and diving for the view port. "Dad!" he yelled. "Get the radio shack. Stop that ship!"

But the *Half Moon* was already a ball of fire in the distance, Tiny looked dazed. "Dad," he said, "who else knows about this?"

"Nobody, so far as I know."

He thought a bit. "We've got to keep her out of sight. That's it—we keep her locked up and out of sight until the next ship matches in." He didn't look at her.

"What in the world are you talking about?" McNye's voice was higher and no longer pleasant.

Tiny glared. "You, that's what. What are you—a stowaway?"

"Don't be silly! I'm G. B. McNye, electronics engineer. Don't you have my papers?"

Tiny turned to me. "Dad, this is your fault. How in Chr—pardon me, Miss. How did you let them send you a woman? Didn't you even read the advance report on her?"

"Me?" I said. "Now see here, you big squarehead! Those forms don't show sex; the Fair Employment

Commission won't allow it except where it's pertinent to the job."

"You're telling *me* it's not pertinent to the job *here?*"

"Not by job classification it ain't. There's lots of female radio and radar men, back Earthside."

"This isn't Earthside." He had something. He was thinking of those two-legged wolves swarming over the job outside. And G. B. McNye was pretty. Maybe eight months of no women at all affected my judgment, but she would pass.

"I've even heard of female rocket pilots," I added, for spite.

"I don't care if you've heard of female archangels; I'll have no women here!"

"Just a minute!" If I was riled, *she* was plain sore. "You're the construction superintendent, are you not?"

"Yes," Tiny admitted.

"Very well, then, how do *you* know what sex I am?"

"Are you trying to deny that you are a woman?"

"Hardly! I'm proud of it. But officially you don't know what sex G. Brooks McNye is. That's why I use 'G' instead of Gloria. I don't ask favors."

Tiny grunted. "You won't get any. I don't know how you sneaked in, but get this, McNye, or Gloria, or whatever—you're fired. You go back on the next ship. Meanwhile we'll try to keep the men from knowing we've got a woman aboard."

I could see her count ten. "May I speak," she said finally, "or does your Captain Bligh act extend to that, too?"

"Say your say."

"I didn't sneak in. I am on the permanent staff

of the Station, Chief Communications Engineer. I took this vacancy myself to get to know the equipment while it was being installed. I'll live here eventually; I see no reason not to start now."

Tiny waved it away. "There'll be men and women both here—some day. Even kids. Right now it's stag and it'll stay that way."

"We'll see. Anyhow, you can't fire me; radio personnel don't work for you." She had a point; communicators and some other specialists were lent to the contractors, Five Companies, Incorporated, by Harriman Enterprises.

Tiny snorted. "Maybe I can't fire you; I can send you home. 'Requisitioned personnel must be satisfactory to the contractor.'—meaning me. Paragraph Seven, clause M; I wrote that clause myself."

"Then you know that if requisitioned personnel are refused without cause the contractor bears the replacement cost."

"I'll risk paying your fare home, but I won't have you here."

"You are most unreasonable!"

"Perhaps, but I'll decide what's good for the job. I'd rather have a dope peddler than have a woman sniffing around my boys!"

She gasped. Tiny knew he had said too much; he added, "Sorry, Miss. But that's it. You'll stay under cover until I can get rid of you."

Before she could speak I cut in. "Tiny—look behind you!"

Staring in the port was one of the riggers, his eyes bugged out. Three or four more floated up and joined him.

Then Tiny zoomed up to the port and they scattered like minnows. He scared them almost out of their suits; I thought he was going to shove his fists through the quartz.

He came back looking whipped. "Miss," he said, pointing, "wait in my room." When she was gone he added, "Dad, what'll we do?"

I said, "I thought you had made up your mind, Tiny."

"I have," he answered peevishly. "Ask the Chief Inspector to come in, will you?"

That showed how far gone he was. The inspection gang belonged to Harriman Enterprises, not to us, and Tiny rated them mere nuisances. Besides, Tiny was an Oppenheimer graduate; Dalrymple was from M.I.T.

He came in, brash and cheerful. "Good morning, Superintendent. Morning, Mr. Witherspoon. What can I do for you?"

Glumly, Tiny told the story. Dalrymple looked smug. "She's right, old man. You can send her back and even specify a male relief. But I can hardly endorse 'for proper cause' now, can I?"

"Damnation. Dalrymple, we can't have a woman around here!"

"A moot point. Not covered by contract, y'know."

"If your office hadn't sent us a crooked gambler as her predecessor I wouldn't be in this jam!"

"There, there! Remember the old blood pressure. Suppose we leave the endorsement open and arbitrate the cost. That's fair, eh?"

"I suppose so. Thanks."

"Not at all. But consider this: when you rushed Peters off before interviewing the newcomer, you cut yourself down to one operator. Hammond can't stand watch twenty-four hours a day."

"He can sleep in the shack. The alarm will wake him."

"I can't accept that. The home office and ships' frequencies must be guarded at all times. Harriman Enterprises has supplied a qualified operator; I am afraid you must use her for the time being."

Tiny will always cooperate with the inevitable; he said quietly, "Dad, she'll take first shift. Better put the married men on that shift."

Then he called her in. "Go to the radio shack and start makee-learnee, so that Hammond can go off watch soon. Mind what he tells you. He's a good man."

"I know," she said briskly. "I trained him."

Tiny bit his lip. The C.I. said, "The Superintendent doesn't bother with trivia—I'm Robert Dalrymple, Chief Inspector. He probably didn't introduce his assistant either—Mr. Witherspoon."

"Call me Dad," I said.

She smiled and said, "Howdy, Dad." I felt warm clear through. She went on to Dalrymple, "Odd that we haven't met before."

Tiny butted in. "McNye, you'll sleep in my room—"

She raised her eyebrows; he went on angrily, "Oh, I'll get my stuff out—at once. And get this: keep the door locked, off shift."

"You're darn tootin' I will!"

Tiny blushed.

I was too busy to see much of Miss Gloria. There was cargo to stow, the new tanks to install and shield. That left the most worrisome task of all: putting spin on the living quarters. Even the optimists didn't expect much interplanetary traffic for some years; nevertheless Harriman Enterprises wanted to get some activities moved in and paying rent against their enormous investment.

I.T.&T. had leased space for a microwave relay station—several million a year from television alone. The Weather Bureau was itching to set up its hemispheric integrating station; Palomar Observatory had a concession (Harriman Enterprises donated that space); the Security Council had some hush-hush project; Fermi Physical Labs and Kettering Institute each had space—a dozen tenants wanted to move in now, or sooner, even if we never completed accommodations for tourist and travelers.

There were time bonuses in it for Five Companies, Incorporated—and their help. So we were in a hurry to get spin on the quarters.

People who have never been out have trouble getting through their heads—at least I had—that there is no feeling of weight, no up and down, in a free orbit in space. There's Earth, round and beautiful, only twenty-odd thousand miles away, close enough to brush your sleeve. You know it's pulling you towards it. Yet you feel no weight, absolutely none. You float.

Floating is fine for some types of work, but when it's time to eat, or play cards, or bathe, it's good to feel weight on your feet. Your dinner stays quiet and you feel more natural.

You've seen pictures of the Station—a huge cylinder, like a bass drum, with ships' nose pockets dimpling its sides. Imagine a snare drum, spinning around inside the bass drum; that's the living quarters, with centrifugal force pinch-hitting for gravity. We could have spun the whole Station but you can't berth a ship against a whirling dervish.

So we built a spinning part for creature comfort

and an outer, stationary part for docking, tanks, storerooms, and the like. You pass from one to the other at the hub. When Miss Gloria joined us the inner part was closed in and pressurized, but the rest was a skeleton of girders.

Mighty pretty though, a great network of shiny struts and ties against black sky and stars—titanium alloy 1403, light, strong, and non-corrodable. The Station is flimsy compared with a ship, since it doesn't have to take blastoff stresses. That meant we didn't dare put on spin by violent means— which is where jato units come in.

"Jato"—*Jet Assisted Take-Off*—rocket units invented to give airplanes a boost. Now we use them wherever a controlled push is needed, say to get a truck out of the mud on a dam job. We mounted four thousand of them around the frame of the living quarters, each one placed just so. They were wired up and ready to fire when Tiny came to me looking worried. "Dad," he said, "Let's drop everything and finish compartment D-113."

"Okay," I said. D-113 was in the non-spin part.

"Rig an air lock and stock it with two weeks supplies."

"That'll change your mass distribution for spin," I suggested.

"I'll refigure it next dark period. Then we'll shift jatos."

When Dalrymple heard about it he came charging around. It meant a delay in making rental space available. "What's the idea?"

Tiny stared at him. They had been cooler than ordinary lately; Dalrymple had been finding excuses to seek out Miss Gloria. He had to pass through Tiny's office to reach her temporary room, and Tiny had finally told him to get out and stay out. "The idea," Tiny said slowly, "is to have a pup tent in case the house burns."

"What do you mean?"

"Suppose we fire up the jatos and the structure cracks? Want to hang around in a space suit until a ship happens by?"

"That's silly. The stresses have been calculated."

"That's what the man said when the bridge fell. We'll do it my way."

Dalrymple stormed off.

Tiny's efforts to keep Gloria fenced up were sort of pitiful. In the first place, the radio tech's biggest job was repairing suit walkie-talkies, done on watch. A rash of such troubles broke out—on her shift. I made some shift transfers and docked a few for costs, too; it's not proper maintenance when a man deliberately busts his aerial.

There were other symptoms. It became stylish to shave. Men started wearing shirts around quarters and bathing increased to where I thought I would have to rig another water still.

Came the shift when D-113 was ready and the jatos readjusted. I don't mind saying I was nervous. All hands were ordered out of the quarters and into suits. They perched around the girders and waited.

Men in space suits all look alike; we used numbers and colored armbands. Supervisors had two antennas, one for a gang frequency, one for the supervisors' circuit. With Tiny and me the second antenna hooked back through the radio shack and to all the gang frequencies—a broadcast.

The supervisors had reported their men clear of the fireworks and I was about to give Tiny the word, when this figure came climbing through the girders, inside the danger zone. No safety line. No armband. One antenna.

Miss Gloria, of course. Tiny hauled her out of the blast zone, and anchored her with his own safety line. I heard his voice, harsh in my helmet: "Who do you think you are? A sidewalk superintendent?"

And her voice: "What do you expect me to do? Go park on a star?"

"I told you to stay away from the job. If you can't obey orders, I'll lock you up."

I reached him, switched off my radio and touched helmets. "Boss! Boss!" I said. "You're broadcasting!"

"Oh—" he says, switches off, and touches helmets with her.

We could still hear her; she didn't switch off. "Why, you big baboon, I came outside because you sent a search party to clear everybody out," and, "How would I know about a safety line rule? You've kept me penned up." And finally. "We'll see!"

I dragged him away and he told the boss electrician to go ahead. Then we forgot the row for we were looking at the prettiest fireworks ever seen, a giant St. Catherine's wheel, rockets blasting all over it. Utterly soundless, out there in space—but beautiful beyond compare.

The blasts died away and there was the living quarters, spinning true as a flywheel—Tiny and I both let out sighs of relief. We all went back inside then to see what weight tasted like.

It tasted funny. I went through the shaft and started down the ladders, feeling myself gain weight as I neared the rim. I felt seasick, like the first time I experienced no weight. I could hardly walk and my calves cramped.

We inspected throughout, then went to the office and sat down. It felt good, just right for comfort, one-third gravity at the rim. Tiny rubbed his chair arms and grinned, "Beats being penned up in D-113."

"Speaking of being penned up," Miss Gloria said, walking in, "may I have a word with you, Mr. Larsen?"

"Uh? Why, certainly. Matter of fact, I wanted to see you. I owe you an apology, Miss McNye. I was——"

"Forget it," she cut in. "You were on edge. But I want to know this: how long are you going to keep up this nonsense of trying to chaperone me?"

He studied her. "Not long. Just till your relief arrives."

"So? Who is the shop steward around here?"

"A shipfitter named McAndrews. But you can't use him. You're a staff member."

"Not in the job I'm filling. I am going to talk to him. You're discriminating against me, and in my off time at that."

"Perhaps, but you will find I have the authority. Legally I'm a ship's captain, while on this job. A captain in space has wide discriminatory powers."

"Then you should use them with discrimination!"

He grinned. "Isn't that what you just said I was doing?"

We didn't hear from the shop steward, but Miss Gloria started doing as she pleased. She showed up at the movies, next off shift, with Dalrymple. Tiny left in the middle—good show, too; *Lysistrata Goes to Town*, relayed up from New York.

As she was coming back alone he stopped her, having seen to it that I was present. "Umm—Miss McNye. . . ."

"Yes?"

"I think you should know, uh, well . . . Chief Inspector Dalrymple is a married man."

"Are you suggesting that my conduct has been improper?"

"No, but—"

"Then mind your own business!" Before he could answer she added, "It might interest you that he told me about your four children."

Tiny sputtered. "Why . . . why, I'm not even married!"

"So? That makes it worse, doesn't it?" She swept out.

Tiny quit trying to keep her in her room, but told her to notify him whenever she left it. It kept him busy riding herd on her. I refrained from suggesting that he get Dalrymple to spell him.

But I was surprised when he told me to put through the order dismissing her. I had been pretty sure he was going to drop it.

"What's the charge?" I asked.

"Insubordination!"

I kept mum. He said, "Well, she won't take orders."

"She does her work okay. You give her orders you wouldn't give to one of the men—and that a man wouldn't take."

"You disagree with my orders?"

"That's not the point. You can't prove the charge, Tiny."

"Well, charge her with being female! I can prove *that*."

I didn't say anything. "Dad," he added wheedlingly, "you know how to write it. 'No personal animus against Miss McNye, but it is felt that as a matter of policy, and so forth and so on.'"

I wrote it and gave it to Hammond privately. Radio techs are sworn to secrecy but it didn't surprise me when I was stopped by O'Connor, one of our best metalsmiths. "Look, Dad, is it true that the Old Man is getting rid of Brooksie?"

"Brooksie?"

"Brooksie McNye—she says to call her Brooks. Is it true?"

I admitted it, then went on, wondering if I should have lied.

It takes four hours, about, for a ship to lift from Earth. The shift before the *Pole Star* was due, with Miss Gloria's relief, the timekeeper brought me two separation slips. Two men were nothing; we averaged more each ship. An hour later he reached me by supervisors' circuit, and asked me to come to the time office. I was out on the rim, inspecting a weld job; I said no. "*Please,* Mr. Witherspoon," he begged, "you've *got* to." When one of the boys doesn't call me "Dad," it means something. I went.

There was a queue like mail call outside his door; I went in and he shut the door on them. He handed me a double handful of separation slips. "What in the great depths of night is this?" I asked.

"There's dozens more I ain't had time to write up yet."

None of the slips had any reason given—just "own choice." "Look, Jimmie—what goes on here?"

"Can't you dope it out, Dad? Shucks, I'm turning in one, too."

I told him my guess and he admitted it. So I took the slips, called Tiny and told him for the love of Heaven to come to his office.

Tiny chewed his lip considerable. "But, Dad, they *can't* strike. It's a non-strike contract with bonds from every union concerned."

"It's no strike, Tiny. You can't stop a man from quitting."

"They'll pay their own fares back, so help me!"

"Guess again. Most of 'em have worked long enough for the free ride."

"We'll have to hire others quick, or we'll miss our date."

"Worse than that, Tiny—we won't finish. By next dark period you won't even have a maintenance crew."

"I've never had a gang of men quit me. I'll talk to them."

"No good, Tiny. You're up against something too strong for you."

"*You're* against me, Dad?"

"I'm never against you, Tiny."

He said, "Dad, you think I'm pig-headed, but I'm *right*. You can't have one woman among several hundred men. It drives 'em nutty."

I didn't say it affected him the same way; I said, "Is that bad?"

"Of course. I can't let the job be ruined to humor one woman."

"Tiny, have you looked at the progress charts lately?"

"I've hardly had time to—what about them?"

I knew why he hadn't had time. "You'll have

trouble proving Miss Gloria interfered with the job. We're ahead of schedule."

"We *are?*"

While he was studying the charts I put an arm around his shoulder. "Look, son," I said, "sex has been around our planet a long time. Earthside, they never get away from it, yet some pretty big jobs get built anyhow. Maybe we'll just have to learn to live with it here, too. Matter of fact, you had the answer a minute ago."

"I did? I sure didn't know it."

"You said, 'You can't have *one* woman among several hundred men.' Get me?"

"Huh? No, I don't. Wait a minute! Maybe I do."

"Ever tried jiu jitsu? Sometimes you win by relaxing."

"Yes. Yes!"

"When you can't beat 'em, you jine 'em."

He buzzed the radio shack. "Have Hammond relieve you, McNye, and come to my office."

He did it handsomely, stood up and made a speech—he'd been wrong, taken him a long time to see it, hoped there were no hard feelings, etc. He was instructing the home office to see how many jobs could be filled at once with female help. "Don't forget married couples," I put in mildly, "and better ask for some older women, too."

"I'll do that," Tiny agreed. "Have I missed anything, Dad?"

"Guess not. We'll have to rig quarters, but there's time."

"Okay. I'm telling them to hold the *Pole Star*, Gloria, so they can send us a few this trip."

"That's fine!" She looked really happy.

He chewed his lip. "I've a feeling I've missed something. Hmm—I've got it. Dad, tell them to send up a chaplain for the Station, as soon as possible. Under the new policy we may need one anytime." I thought so, too.

Space Jockey

JUST as they were leaving the telephone called his name. "Don't answer it," she pleaded. "We'll miss the curtain."

"Who is it?" he called out. The viewplate lighted; he recognized Olga Pierce, and behind her the Colorado Springs office of Trans-Lunar Transit.

"Calling Mr. Pemberton. Calling—Oh, it's you, Jake. You're on. Flight 27, Supra-New York to Space Terminal. I'll have a copter pick you up in twenty minutes."

"How come?" he protested. "I'm fourth down on the call board."

"You *were* fourth down. Now you are standby pilot to Hicks—and he just got a psycho downcheck."

"Hicks got psychoed? That's silly!"

"Happens to the best, chum. Be ready. 'Bye now."

His wife was twisting sixteen dollars worth of lace handkerchief to a shapeless mass. "Jake, this

21

is ridiculous. For three months I haven't seen enough of you to know what you look like."

"Sorry, kid. Take Helen to the show."

"Oh, Jake, I don't care about the show; I wanted to get you where they couldn't reach you for once."

"They would have called me at the theater."

"Oh, no! I wiped out the record you'd left."

"Phyllis! Are you trying to get me fired?"

"Don't look at me that way." She waited, hoping that he would speak, regretting the side issue, and wondering how to tell him that her own fretfulness was caused, not by disappointment, but by gnawing worry for his safety every time he went out into space.

She went on desperately, "You don't have to take this flight, darling; you've been on Earth less than the time limit. Please, Jake!"

He was peeling off his tux. "I've told you a thousand times: a pilot doesn't get a regular run by playing space-lawyer with the rule book. Wiping out my follow-up message—why did you do it, Phyllis? Trying to ground me?"

"No, darling, but I thought just this once—"

"When they offer me a flight I take it." He walked stiffly out of the room.

He came back ten minutes later, dressed for space and apparently in good humor; he was whistling: "—the caller called Casey at ha' past four; he kissed his—" He broke off when he saw her face, and set his mouth, "Where's my coverall?"

"I'll get it. Let me fix you something to eat."

"You know I can't take high acceleration on a full stomach. And why lose thirty bucks to lift another pound?"

Dressed as he was, in shorts, singlet, sandals,

and pocket belt, he was already good for about minus-fifty pounds in weight bonus; she started to tell him the weight penalty on a sandwich and a cup of coffee did not matter to them, but it was just one more possible cause for misunderstanding.

Neither of them said much until the taxicab clumped on the roof. He kissed her goodbye and told her not to come outside. She obeyed—until she heard the helicopter take off. Then she climbed to the roof and watched it out of sight.

The traveling-public gripes at the lack of direct Earth-to-Moon service, but it takes three types of rocket ships and two space-station changes to make a fiddling quarter-million-mile jump for a good reason: Money.

The Commerce Commission has set the charges for the present three-stage lift from here to the Moon at thirty dollars a pound. Would direct service be cheaper?—a ship designed to blast off from Earth, make an airless landing on the Moon, return and make an atmosphere landing, would be so cluttered up with heavy special equipment used only once in the trip that it could not show a profit at a thousand dollars a pound! Imagine combining a ferry boat, a subway train, and an express elevator—

So Trans-Lunar uses rockets braced for catapulting, and winged for landing on return to Earth to make the terrific lift from Earth to our satellite station Supra-New York. The long middle lap, from there to where Space Terminal circles the Moon, calls for comfort—but no landing gear. The *Flying Dutchman* and the *Philip Nolan* never land; they were even assembled in space, and they resemble winged rockets like the *Skysprite* and the *Firefly* as little as a Pullman train resembles a parachute.

The *Moonbat* and the *Gremlin* are good only for the jump from Space Terminal down to Luna . . . no wings, cocoonlike acceleration-and-crash hammocks, fractional controls on their enormous jets.

The change-over points would not have to be more than air-conditioned tanks. Of course Space Terminal is quite a city, what with the Mars and Venus traffic, but even today Supra-New York is still rather primitive, hardly more than a fueling point and a restaurant-waiting room. It has only been the past five years that it has even been equipped to offer the comfort of one-gravity centrifuge service to passengers with queasy stomachs.

Pemberton weighed in at the spaceport office, then hurried over to where the *Skysprite* stood cradled in the catapult. He shucked off his coverall, shivered as he handed it to the gateman, and ducked inside. He went to his acceleration hammock and went to sleep; the lift to Supra-New York was not his worry—his job was deep space.

He woke at the surge of the catapult and the nerve-tingling rush up the face of Pikes Peak. When the *Skysprite* went into free flight, flung straight up above the Peak, Pemberton held his breath; if the rocket jets failed to fire, the ground-to-space pilot must try to wrestle her into a glide and bring her down, on her wings.

The rockets roared on time; Jake went back to sleep.

When the *Skysprite* locked in with Supra-New York, Pemberton went to the station's stellar navigation room. He was pleased to find Shorty Weinstein, the computer, on duty. Jake trusted

Shorty's computations—a good thing when your ship, your passengers, and your own skin depend thereon. Pemberton had to be a better than average mathematician himself in order to be a pilot; his own limited talent made him appreciate the genius of those who computed the orbits.

"Hot Pilot Pemberton, the Scourge of the Spaceways—Hi!" Weinstein handed him a sheet of paper.

Jake looked at it, then looked amazed. "Hey, Shorty—you've made a mistake."

"Huh? Impossible. Mabel can't make mistakes." Weinstein gestured at the giant astrogation computer filling the far wall.

"*You* made a mistake. You gave me an easy fix—'Vega, Antares, Regulus.' You make things easy for the pilot and your guild'll chuck you out." Weinstein looked sheepish but pleased. "I see I don't blast off for seventeen hours. I could have taken the morning freight." Jake's thoughts went back to Phyllis.

"UN canceled the morning trip."

"Oh—" Jake shut up, for he knew Weinstein knew as little as he did. Perhaps the flight would have passed too close to an A-bomb rocket, circling the globe like a policeman. The General Staff of the Security Council did not give out information about the top secrets guarding the peace of the planet.

Pemberton shrugged. "Well, if I'm asleep, call me three hours minus."

"Right. Your tape will be ready."

While he slept, the *Flying Dutchman* nosed gently into her slip, sealed her airlocks to the Station, discharged passengers and freight from

Luna City. When he woke, her holds were filling, her fuel replenished, and passengers boarding. He stopped by the post office radio desk, looking for a letter from Phyllis. Finding none, he told himself that she would have sent it to Terminal. He went on into the restaurant, bought the facsimile *Herald-Tribune*, and settled down grimly to enjoy the comics and his breakfast.

A man sat down opposite him and proceeded to plague him with silly questions about rocketry, topping it by misinterpreting the insignia embroidered on Pemberton's singlet and miscalling him "Captain." Jake hurried through breakfast to escape him, then picked up the tape from his automatic pilot, and went aboard the *Flying Dutchman*.

After reporting to the Captain he went to the control room, floating and pulling himself along by the handgrips. He buckled himself into the pilot's chair and started his check off.

Captain Kelly drifted in and took the other chair as Pemberton was finishing his checking runs on the ballistic tracker. "Have a Camel, Jake."

"I'll take a rain check." He continued; Kelly watched him with a slight frown. Like captains and pilots on Mark Twain's Mississippi—and for the same reasons—a spaceship captain bosses his ship, his crew, his cargo, and his passengers, but the pilot is the final, legal, and unquestioned boss of how the ship is handled from blast-off to the end of the trip. A captain may turn down a given pilot—nothing more. Kelly fingered a slip of paper tucked in his pouch and turned over in his mind the words with which the Company psychiatrist on duty had handed it to him.

"I'm giving this pilot clearance, Captain, but you need not accept it."

"Pemberton's a good man. What's wrong?"

The psychiatrist thought over what he had observed while posing as a silly tourist bothering a stranger at breakfast. "He's a little more anti-social than his past record shows. Something on his mind. Whatever it is, he can tolerate it for the present. We'll keep an eye on him."

Kelly had answered, "Will you come along with him as pilot?"

"If you wish."

"Don't bother—I'll take him. No need to lift a deadhead."

Pemberton fed Weinstein's tape into the robot-pilot, then turned to Kelly. "Control ready, sir."

"Blast when ready, Pilot." Kelly felt relieved when he heard himself make the irrevocable decision.

Pemberton signaled the Station to cast loose. The great ship was nudged out by an expanding pneumatic ram until she swam in space a thousand feet away, secured by a single line. He then turned the ship to its blast-off direction by causing a fly-wheel, mounted on gymbals at the ship's center of gravity, to spin rapidly. The ship spun slowly in the opposite direction, by grace of Newton's Third Law of Motion.

Guided by the tape, the robot-pilot tilted prisms of the pilot's periscope so that Vega, Antares, and Regulus would shine as one image when the ship was headed right; Pemberton nursed the ship to that heading . . . fussily; a mistake of one minute of arc here meant two hundred miles at destination.

When the three images made a pinpoint, he

stopped the flywheels and locked in the gyros. He then checked the heading of his ship by direct observation of each of the stars, just as a salt-water skipper uses a sextant, but with incomparably more accurate instruments. This told him nothing about the correctness of the course Weinstein had ordered—he had to take that as Gospel—but it assured him that the robot and its tape were behaving as planned. Satisfied, he cast off the last line.

Seven minutes to go—Pemberton flipped the switch permitting the robot-pilot to blast away when its clock told it to. He waited, hands poised over the manual controls, ready to take over if the robot failed, and felt the old, inescapable sick excitement building up inside him.

Even as adrenalin poured into him, stretching his time sense, throbbing in his ears, his mind kept turning back to Phyllis.

He admitted she had a kick coming—spacemen shouldn't marry. Not that she'd starve if he messed up a landing, but a gal doesn't want insurance; she wants a husband—minus six minutes.

If he got a regular run she could live in Space Terminal.

No good—idle women at Space Terminal went bad. Oh, Phyllis wouldn't become a tramp or a rum bum; she'd just go bats.

Five minutes more—he didn't care much for Space Terminal himself. Nor for space! "The Romance of Interplanetary Travel"— it looked well in print, but he knew what it was: A job. Monotony. No scenery. Bursts of work, tedious waits. No home life.

Why didn't he get an honest job and stay home nights?

He knew! Because he was a space jockey and too old to change.

What chance has a thirty-year-old married man, used to important money, to change his racket? (Four minutes.) He'd look good trying to sell helicopters on commission, now, wouldn't he?

Maybe he could buy a piece of irrigated land and— Be your age, chum! You know as much about farming as a cow knows about cube root! No, he had made his bed when he picked rockets during his training hitch. If he had bucked for the electronics branch, or taken a GI scholarship—too late now. Straight from the service into Harriman's Lunar Exploitations, hopping ore on Luna. That had torn it.

"How's it going, Doc?" Kelly's voice was edgy.

"Minus two minutes some seconds." Damnation— Kelly knew better than to talk to the pilot on minus time.

He caught a last look through the periscope. Antares seemed to have drifted. He unclutched the gyro, tilted and spun the flywheel, braking it savagely to a stop a moment later. The image was again a pinpoint. He could not have explained what he did: it was virtuosity, exact juggling, beyond textbook and classroom.

Twenty seconds . . . across the chronometer's face beads of light trickled the seconds away while he tensed, ready to fire by hand, or even to disconnect and refuse the trip if his judgment told him to. A too-cautious decision might cause Lloyds' to cancel his bond; a reckless decision could cost his license or even his life—and others.

But he was not thinking of underwriters and licenses, nor even of lives. In truth he was not thinking at all; he was feeling, feeling his ship, as if his nerve ends extended into every part of her. Five seconds . . . the safety disconnects clicked out. Four seconds . . . three seconds . . . two seconds . . . . one——

He was stabbing at the hand-fire button when the roar hit him.

Kelly relaxed to the pseudo-gravity of the blast and watched. Pemberton was soberly busy, scanning dials, noting time, checking his progress by radar bounced off Supra-New York. Weinstein's figures, robot-pilot, the ship itself, all were clicking together.

Minutes later, the critical instant neared when the robot should cut the jets. Pemberton poised a finger over the hand cut-off, while splitting his attention among radarscope, accelerometer, periscope, and chronometer. One instant they were roaring along on the jets; the next split second the ship was in free orbit, plunging silently toward the Moon. So perfectly matched were human and robot that Pemberton himself did not know which had cut the power.

He glanced again at the board, then unbuckled. "How about that cigarette, Captain? And you can let your passengers unstrap."

No co-pilot is needed in space and most pilots would rather share a toothbrush than a control room. The pilot works about an hour at blast off, about the same before contact, and loafs during free flight, save for routine checks and corrections. Pemberton prepared to spend one hundred and four hours eating, reading, writing letters, and sleeping—especially sleeping.

When the alarm woke him, he checked the ship's position, then wrote to his wife. "Phyllis my dear," he began, "I don't blame you for being upset at missing your night out. I was disappointed, too. But bear with me, darling, I should be on a regular run before long. In less than ten years I'll be up for retirement and we'll have a chance to catch up on bridge and golf and things like that. I know it's pretty hard to—"

The voice circuit cut in. "Oh, Jake—put on your company face. I'm bringing a visitor to the control room."

"No visitors in the control room, Captain."

"Now, Jake. This lunkhead has a letter from Old Man Harriman himself. 'Every possible courtesy—' and so forth."

Pemberton thought quickly. He could refuse— but there was no sense in offending the big boss. "Okay, Captain. Make it short."

The visitor was a man, jovial, oversize—Jake figured him for an eighty pound weight penalty. Behind him a thirteen-year-old male counterpart came zipping through the door and lunged for the control console. Pemberton snagged him by the arm and forced himself to speak pleasantly. "Just hang on to that bracket, youngster. I don't want you to bump your head."

"Leggo me! Pop—make him let go."

Kelly cut in. "I think he had best hang on, Judge."

"Umm, uh—very well. Do as the Captain says, Junior."

"Aw, gee, Pop!"

"Judge Schacht, this is First Pilot Pemberton," Kelly said rapidly. "He'll show you around."

"Glad to know you, Pilot. Kind of you, and all that."

"What would you like to see, Judge?" Jake said carefully.

"Oh, this and that. It's for the boy—his first trip. I'm an old spacehound myself—probably more hours than half our crew." He laughed. Pemberton did not.

"There's not much to see in free flight."

"Quite all right. We'll just make ourselves at home—eh, Captain?"

"I wanna sit in the control seat," Schacht Junior announced.

Pemberton winced. Kelly said urgently, "Jake, would you mind outlining the control system for the boy? Then we'll go."

"He doesn't have to show me anything. I know all about it. I'm a Junior Rocketeer of America—see my button?" The boy shoved himself toward the control desk.

Pemberton grabbed him, steered him into the pilot's chair, and strapped him in. He then flipped the board's disconnect.

"Whatcha doing?"

"I cut off power to the controls so I could explain them."

"Aintcha gonna fire the jets?"

"No." Jake started a rapid description of the use and purpose of each button, dial, switch, meter, gimmick, and scope.

Junior squirmed. "How about meteors?" he demanded.

"Oh, that—maybe one collision in half a million Earth-Moon trips. Meteors are scarce."

"So what? Say you hit the jackpot? You're in the soup."

"Not at all. The anti-collision radar guards all directions five hundred miles out. If anything holds a steady bearing for three seconds, a direct hook-up starts the jets. First a warning gong so that everybody can grab something solid, then one second later—*Boom!*—We get out of there fast."

"Sounds corny to me. Lookee, I'll show you how Commodore Cartwright did it in *The Comet Busters*—"

"Don't touch those controls!"

"You don't own this ship. My pop says—"

"Oh, Jake!" Hearing his name, Pemberton twisted, fish-like, to face Kelly.

"Jake, Judge Schacht would like to know—" From the corner of his eye Jake saw the boy reach for the board. He turned, started to shout—acceleration caught him, while the jets roared in his ear.

An old spacehand can usually recover, catlike, in an unexpected change from weightlessness to acceleration. But Jake had been grabbing for the boy, instead of for anchorage. He fell back and down, twisted to try to avoid Schacht, banged his head on the frame of the open air-tight door below, and fetched up on the next deck, out cold.

Kelly was shaking him. "You all right, Jake?"

He sat up. "Yeah. Sure." He became aware of the thunder, the shivering deckplates. "The jets! Cut the power!"

He shoved Kelly aside and swarmed up into the control room, jabbed at the cut-off button. In sudden ringing silence, they were again weightless.

Jake turned, unstrapped Schacht Junior, and

hustled him to Kelly. "Captain, please remove this menace from my control room."

"Leggo! Pop—he's gonna hurt me!"

The elder Schacht bristled at once. "What's the meaning of this? Let go of my son!"

"Your precious son cut in the jets."

"Junior—did you do that?"

The boy shifted his eyes. "No, Pop. It . . . it was a meteor."

Schacht looked puzzled. Pemberton snorted. "I had just told him how the radar-guard can blast to miss a meteor. He's lying."

Schacht ran through the process he called "making up his mind," then answered, "Junior never lies. Shame on you, a grown man, to try to put the blame on a helpless boy. I shall report you, sir. Come, Junior."

Jake grabbed his arm. "Captain, I want those controls photographed for fingerprints before this man leaves the room. It was not a meteor; the controls were dead, until this boy switched them on. Furthermore, the anti-collision sounds an alarm."

Schacht looked wary. "This is ridiculous. I simply objected to the slur on my son's character. No harm has been done."

"No harm, eh? How about broken arms—or necks? And wasted fuel, with more to waste before we're back in the groove. Do you know, Mister 'Old Spacehound,' just how precious a little fuel will be when we try to match orbits with Space Terminal—if we haven't got it? We may have to dump cargo to save the ship, cargo at $60,000 a ton on freight charges alone. Finger prints will show the Commerce Commission whom to nick for it."

When they were alone again Kelly asked anxiously, "You won't really have to jettison? You've got a maneuvering reserve."

"Maybe we can't even get to Terminal. How long did she blast?"

Kelly scratched his head. "I was woozy myself."

"We'll open the accelerograph and take a look."

Kelly brightened. "Oh, sure! If the brat didn't waste too much, then we just swing ship and blast back the same length of time."

Jake shook his head. "You forgot the changed mass-ratio."

"Oh . . . oh, yes!" Kelly looked embarrassed. Mass-ratio . . . under power, the ship lost the weight of fuel burned. The thrust remained constant; the mass it pushed shrank. Getting back to proper position, course, and speed became a complicated problem in the calculus of ballistics. "But you can do it, can't you?"

"I'll have to. But I sure wish I had Weinstein here."

Kelly left to see about his passengers; Jake got to work. He checked his situation by astronomical observation and by radar. Radar gave him all three factors quickly but with limited accuracy. Sights taken of Sun, Moon, and Earth gave him position, but told nothing of course and speed, at that time—nor could he afford to wait to take a second group of sights for the purpose.

Dead reckoning gave him an estimated situation, by adding Weinstein's predictions to the calculated effect of young Schacht's meddling. This checked fairly well with the radar and visual observations, but still he had no notion of whether or not he could get back in the groove and reach his destination; it was now necessary to calculate what it would take and whether or not the remaining fuel would be enough to brake his speed and match orbits.

In space, it does no good to reach your journey's end if you flash on past at miles per second, or even crawling along at a few hundred miles per hour. To catch an egg on a plate—don't bump!

He started doggedly to work to compute how to do it using the least fuel, but his little Marchant electronic calculator was no match for the tons of IBM computer at Supra-New York, nor was he Weinstein. Three hours later he had an answer of sorts. He called Kelly. "Captain? You can start by jettisoning Schacht & Son."

"I'd like to. No way out, Jake?"

"I can't promise to get your ship in safely without dumping. Better dump now, before we blast. It's cheaper."

Kelly hesitated; he would as cheerfully lose a leg. "Give me time to pick out what to dump."

"Okay." Pemberton returned sadly to his figures, hoping to find a saving mistake, then thought better of it. He called the radio room. "Get me Weinstein at Supra-New York."

"Out of normal range."

"I know that. This is the Pilot. Safety priority—urgent. Get a tight beam on them and nurse it."

"Uh . . . aye aye, sir. I'll try."

Weinstein was doubtful. "Cripes, Jake, I can't pilot you."

"Dammit, you can work problems for me!"

"What good is seven-place accuracy with bum data?"

"Sure, sure. But you know what instruments I've got; you know about how well I can handle them. Get me a better answer."

"I'll try." Weinstein called back four hours later. "Jake? Here's the dope: You planned to blast back to match your predicted speed, then made side corrections for position. Orthodox but uneconomical. Instead I had Mabel solve for it as one maneuver."

"Good!"

"Not so fast. It saves fuel but not enough. You can't possibly get back in your old groove and then match Terminal without dumping."

Pemberton let it sink in, then said, "I'll tell Kelly."

"Wait a minute, Jake. Try this. Start from scratch."

"Huh?"

"Treat it as a brand-new problem. Forget about the orbit on your tape. With your present course, speed, and position, compute the cheapest orbit to match with Terminal's. Pick a new groove."

Pemberton felt foolish. "I never thought of that."

"Of course not. With the ship's little one-lung calculator it'd take you three weeks to solve it. You set to record?"

"Sure."

"Here's your data." Weinstein started calling it off.

When they had checked it, Jake said, "That'll get me there?"

"Maybe. If the data you gave me is up to your limit of accuracy; if you can follow instructions as exactly as a robot, *if* you can blast off and make contact so precisely that you don't need side corrections, then you might squeeze home. Maybe. Good luck, anyhow." The wavering reception muffled their goodbyes.

Jake signaled Kelly. "Don't jettison, Captain. Have your passengers strap down. Stand by to blast. Minus fourteen minutes."

"Very well, Pilot."

The new departure made and checked, he again had time to spare. He took out his unfinished letter, read it, then tore it up.

"Dearest Phyllis," he started again, "I've been doing some hard thinking this trip and have decided that I've just been stubborn. What am I doing way out here? I like my home. I like to see my wife.

"Why should I risk my neck and your peace of mind to herd junk through the sky? Why hang around a telephone waiting to chaperone fatheads to the Moon—numbskulls who couldn't pilot a rowboat and should have stayed at home in the first place?

"Money, of course. I've been afraid to risk a change. I won't find another job that will pay half as well, but, if you are game, I'll ground myself and we'll start over. All my love,

"Jake"

He put it away and went to sleep, to dream that an entire troop of Junior Rocketeers had been quartered in his control room.

The close-up view of the Moon is second only to the space-side view of the Earth as a tourist attraction; nevertheless Pemberton insisted that all passengers strap down during the swing around to Terminal. With precious little fuel for the matching maneuver, he refused to hobble his movements to please sightseers.

Around the bulge of the Moon, Terminal came into sight—by radar only, for the ship was tail foremost. After each short braking blast Pemberton caught a new radar fix, then compared his approach with a curve he had plotted from Weinstein's figures—with one eye on the time, another on the 'scope, a third on the plot, and a fourth on his fuel gauges.

"Well, Jake?" Kelly fretted. "Do we make it?"

"How should I know? You be ready to dump." They had agreed on liquid oxygen as the cargo to dump, since it could be let to boil out through the outer valves, without handling.

"Don't say it, Jake."

"Damn it—I won't if I don't have to." He was fingering his controls again; the blast chopped off his words. When it stopped, the radio maneuvering circuit was calling him.

"*Flying Dutchman*, Pilot speaking," Jake shouted back.

"Terminal Control—Supra reports you short on fuel."

"Right."

"Don't approach. Match speeds outside us. We'll send a transfer ship to refuel you and pick up passengers."

"I think I can make it."

"Don't try it. Wait for refueling."

"Quit telling me how to pilot my ship!" Pemberton switched off the circuit, then stared at the board, whistling morosely. Kelly filled in the words in his mind: *"Casey said to the fireman, 'Boy, you better jump, cause two locomotives are agoing to bump!'"*

"You going in the slip anyhow, Jake?"

"Mmm—no, blast it. I can't take a chance of caving in the side of Terminal, not with passengers aboard. But I'm not going to match speeds fifty miles outside and wait for a piggyback."

He aimed for a near miss just outside Terminal's orbit, conning by instinct, for Weinstein's figures meant nothing by now. His aim was good; he did not have to waste his hoarded fuel on last minute side corrections to keep from hitting Terminal. When at last he was sure of sliding safely on past if unchecked, he braked once more. Then, as he started to cut off the power, the jets coughed, sputtered, and quit.

The *Flying Dutchman* floated in space, five hundred yards outside Terminal, speeds matched.

Jake switched on the radio. "Terminal—stand by for my line. I'll warp her in."

He had filed his report, showered, and was headed for the post office to radiostat his letter, when the bullhorn summoned him to the Commodore-Pilot's office. Oh, oh, he told himself, Schacht has kicked to the Brass—I wonder just how much stock that bliffy owns? And there's that other matter—getting snotty with Control.

He reported stiffly. "First Pilot Pemberton, sir."

Commodore Soames looked up. "Pemberton—oh, yes. You hold two ratings, space-to-space and airless-landing."

Let's not stall around, Jake told himself. Aloud he said, "I have no excuses for anything this last trip. If the Commodore does not approve the way I run my control room, he may have my resignation."

"What are you talking about?"

"I, well—don't you have a passenger complaint on me?"

"Oh, that!" Soames brushed it aside. "Yes, he's been here. But I have Kelly's report, too—and your chief jetman's, and a special from Supra-New York. That was crack piloting, Pemberton."

"You mean there's no beef from the Company?"

"When have I failed to back up my pilots? You were perfectly right; I would have stuffed him out the air lock. Let's get down to business: You're on the space-to-space board, but I want to send a special to Luna City. Will you take it, as a favor to me?"

Pemberton hesitated: Soames went on, "That oxygen you saved is for the Cosmic Research Project. They blew the seals on the north tunnel and lost tons of the stuff. The work is stopped—about $130,000 a day in overhead, wages, and penalties. The *Gremlin* is here, but no pilot until the *Moonbat* gets in—except you. Well?"

"But I—look, Commodore, you can't risk people's necks on a jet landing of mine. I'm rusty; I need a refresher and a checkout."

"No passengers, no crew, no captain—your neck alone."

"I'll take her."

Twenty-eight minutes later, with the ugly, powerful hull of the *Gremlin* around him, he blasted away. One strong shove to kill her orbital speed and let her fall toward the Moon, then no more worries until it came time to "ride 'er down on her tail."

He felt good—until he hauled out two letters, the one he had failed to send, and one from Phyllis, delivered at Terminal.

The letter from Phyllis was affectionate—and superficial. She did not mention his sudden departure; she ignored his profession completely. The letter was a model of correctness, but it worried him.

He tore up both letters and started another. It said, in part: "—never said so outright, but you resent my job.

"I have to work to support us. You've got a job, too. It's an old, old job that women have been doing a long time—crossing the plains in covered wagons, waiting for ships to come back from China, or waiting around a mine head after an explosion—kiss him goodbye with a smile, take care of him at home.

"You married a spaceman, so part of your job is to accept my job cheerfully. I think you can do it, when you realize it. I hope so, for the way things have been going won't do for either of us.

> Believe me, I love you.
> Jake"

He brooded on it until time to bend the ship down for his approach. From twenty miles altitude down to one mile he let the robot brake her, then shifted to manual while still falling slowly. A perfect airless-landing would be the reverse of the take-off of a war rocket—free fall, then one long blast of the jets, ending with the ship stopped dead as she touched the ground. In practice a pilot must feel his way down, not too slowly; a ship could burn all the fuel this side of Venus fighting gravity too long.

Forty seconds later, falling a little more than 140 miles per hour, he picked up in his periscopes the thousand-foot static towers. At 300 feet he blasted five gravities for more than a second, cut it, and caught her with a one-sixth gravity, Moon-normal blast. Slowly he eased this off, feeling happy.

The *Gremlin* hovered, her bright jet splashing the soil of the Moon, then settled with dignity to land without a jar.

The ground crew took over; a sealed runabout jeeped Pemberton to the tunnel entrance. Inside Luna City, he found himself paged before he finished filing his report. When he took the call, Soames smiled at him from the viewplate. "I saw that landing from the field pick-up, Pemberton. You don't need a refresher course."

Jake blushed. "Thank you, sir."

"Unless you are dead set on space-to-space, I can use you on the regular Luna City run. Quarters here or Luna City? Want it?"

He heard himself saying, "Luna City. I'll take it."

He tore up his third letter as he walked into Luna City post office. At the telephone desk he spoke to a blonde in a blue moonsuit. "Get me Mrs. Jake Pemberton, Suburb six-four-oh-three, Dodge City, Kansas, please."

She looked him over. "You pilots sure spend money."

"Sometimes phone calls are cheap. Hurry it, will you?"

Phyllis was trying to phrase the letter she felt she should have written before. It was easier to say in writing that she was not complaining of loneliness nor lack of fun, but that she could not stand the strain of worrying about his safety. But then she found herself quite unable to state the logical conclusion. Was she prepared to face giving him up entirely if he would not give up space? She truly did not know . . . the phone call was a welcome interruption.

The viewplate stayed blank. "Long distance," came a thin voice. "Luna City calling."

Fear jerked at her heart. "Phyllis Pemberton speaking."

An interminable delay—she knew it took nearly three seconds for radio waves to make the Earth-Moon round trip, but she did not remember it and it would not have reassured her. All she could see was a broken home, herself a widow, and Jake, beloved Jake, dead in space.

"Mrs. Jake Pemberton?"

"Yes, yes! Go ahead." Another wait—had she sent him away in a bad temper, reckless, his judgment affected? Had he died out there, remembering only that she fussed at him for leaving her to go to work? Had she failed him when he needed her? She knew that her Jake could not be tied to apron strings; men—grown-up men, not mammas' boys—had to break away from mother's apron strings. Then why had she tried to tie him to hers?—she had known better; her own mother had warned her not to try it.

She prayed.

Then another voice, one that weakened her knees with relief: "That you, honey?"

"Yes, darling, yes! What are you doing on the Moon?"

"It's a long story. At a dollar a second it will keep. What I want to know is—are you willing to come to Luna City?"

It was Jake's turn to suffer from the inevitable lag in reply. He wondered if Phyllis were stalling, unable to make up her mind. At last he heard her say, "Of course, darling. When do I leave?"

"When—say, don't you even want to know *why*?"

She started to say that it did not matter, then said, "Yes, tell me." The lag was still present but neither of them cared. He told her the news, then added, "Run over to the Springs and get Olga Pierce to straighten out the red tape for you. Need my help to pack?"

She thought rapidly. Had he meant to come back anyhow, he would not have asked. "No. I can manage."

"Good girl. I'll radiostat you a long letter about what to bring and so forth. I love you. 'Bye now!"

"Oh, I love you, too. Goodbye, darling."

Pemberton came out of the booth whistling. Good girl, Phyllis. Staunch. He wondered why he had ever doubted her.

The Long Watch

"Nine ships blasted off from Moon Base. Once in space, eight of them formed a globe around the smallest. They held this formation all the way to Earth.

"The small ship displayed the insignia of an admiral—yet there was no living thing of any sort in her. She was not even a passenger ship, but a drone, a robot ship intended for radioactive cargo. This trip she carried nothing but a lead coffin— and a Geiger counter that was never quiet."

> —from the editorial *After Ten Years*, film 38, 17 June 2009, Archives of the·*N.Y. Times*

I

JOHNNY DAHLQUIST blew smoke at the Geiger counter. He grinned wryly and tried it again. His whole body was radioactive by now. Even his breath, the smoke from his cigarette, could make the Geiger counter scream.

How long had he been here? Time doesn't mean

much on the Moon. Two days? Three? A week? He let his mind run back: the last clearly marked time in his mind was when the Executive Officer had sent for him, right after breakfast—

"Lieutenant Dahlquist, reporting to the Executive Officer."

Colonel Towers looked up. "Ah, John Ezra. Sit down, Johnny. Cigarette?"

Johnny sat down, mystified but flattered. He admired Colonel Towers, for his brilliance, his ability to dominate, and for his battle record. Johnny had no battle record; he had been commissioned on completing his doctor's degree in nuclear physics and was now junior bomb officer of Moon Base.

The Colonel wanted to talk politics; Johnny was puzzled. Finally Towers had come to the point; it was not safe (so he said) to leave control of the world in political hands; power must be held by a scientifically selected group. In short—the Patrol.

Johnny was startled rather than shocked. As an abstract idea, Towers' notion sounded plausible. The League of Nations had folded up; what would keep the United Nations from breaking up, too, and thus lead to another World War. "And you know how bad such a war would be, Johnny."

Johnny agreed. Towers said he was glad that Johnny got the point. The senior bomb officer could handle the work, but it was better to have both specialists.

Johnny sat up with a jerk. "You are going to *do* something about it?" He had thought the Exec was just talking.

Towers smiled. "We're not politicians; we don't just talk. We act."

Johnny whistled. "When does this start?"

Towers flipped a switch. Johnny was startled to hear his own voice, then identified the recorded conversation as having taken place in the junior officers' messroom. A political argument he remembered, which he had walked out on . . . a good thing, too! But being spied on annoyed him.

Towers switched it off. "We *have* acted," he said. "We know who is safe and who isn't. Take Kelly—" He waved at the loudspeaker. "Kelly is politically unreliable. You noticed he wasn't at breakfast?"

"Huh? I thought he was on watch."

"Kelly's watch-standing days are over. Oh, relax; he isn't hurt."

Johnny thought this over. "Which list am I on?" he asked. "Safe or unsafe?"

"Your name has a question mark after it. But I have said all along that you could be depended on." He grinned engagingly. "You won't make a liar of me, Johnny?"

Dahlquist didn't answer; Towers said sharply, "Come now—what do you think of it? Speak up."

"Well, if you ask me, you've bitten off more than you can chew. While it's true that Moon Base controls the Earth, Moon Base itself is a sitting duck for a ship. One bomb—*blooie!*"

Towers picked up a message form and handed it over; it read: I HAVE YOUR CLEAN LAUNDRY— ZACK. "That means every bomb in the *Trygve Lie* has been put out of commission. I have reports from every ship we need worry about." He stood up. "Think it over and see me after lunch. Major Morgan needs your help right away to change control frequencies on the bombs."

"The control frequencies?"

"Naturally. We don't want the bombs jammed before they reach their targets."

"What? You said the idea was to *prevent* war."

Towers brushed it aside. "There won't be a war—just a psychological demonstration, an unimportant town or two. A little bloodletting to save an all-out war. Simple arithmetic."

He put a hand on Johnny's shoulder. "You aren't squeamish, or you wouldn't be a bomb officer. Think of it as a surgical operation. And think of your family."

Johnny Dahlquist had been thinking of his family. "Please, sir, I want to see the Commanding Officer."

Towers frowned. "The Commodore is not available. As you know, I speak for him. See me again—after lunch."

The Commodore was decidedly not available; the Commodore was dead. But Johnny did not know that.

Dahlquist walked back to the messroom, bought cigarettes, sat down and had a smoke. He got up, crushed out the butt, and headed for the Base's west airlock. There he got into his space suit and went to the lockmaster. "Open her up, Smitty."

The marine looked surprised. "Can't let anyone out on the surface without word from Colonel Towers, sir. Hadn't you heard?"

"Oh, yes! Give me your order book." Dahlquist took it, wrote a pass for himself, and signed it "by direction of Colonel Towers." He added, "Better call the Executive Officer and check it."

The lockmaster read it and stuck the book in his pocket. "Oh, no, Lieutenant. Your word's good."

"Hate to disturb the Executive Officer, eh? Don't blame you." He stepped in, closed the inner door, and waited for the air to be sucked out.

Out on the Moon's surface he blinked at the light and hurried to the track-rocket terminus; a car was waiting. He squeezed in, pulled down the hood, and punched the starting button. The rocket car flung itself at the hills, dived through and came out on a plain studded with projectile rockets, like candles on a cake. Quickly it dived into a second tunnel through more hills. There was a stomach-wrenching deceleration and the car stopped at the underground atom-bomb armory.

As Dahlquist climbed out he switched on his walkie-talkie. The space-suited guard at the entrance came to port-arms. Dahlquist said, "Morning, Lopez," and walked by him to the airlock. He pulled it open.

The guard motioned him back. "Hey! Nobody goes in without the Executive Officer's say-so." He shifted his gun, fumbled in his pouch and got out a paper. "Read it, Lieutenant."

Dahlquist waved it away. "I drafted that order myself. *You* read it; you've misinterpreted it."

"I don't see how, Lieutenant."

Dahlquist snatched the paper, glanced at it, then pointed to a line. "See? '—except persons specifically designated by the Executive Officer.' That's the bomb officers, Major Morgan and me."

The guard looked worried. Dahlquist said, "Damn it, look up 'specifically designated'—it's under '*Bomb Room, Security, Procedure for,*' in your standing orders. Don't tell me you left them in the barracks!"

"Oh, no, sir! I've got 'em." The guard reached into his pouch. Dahlquist gave him back the sheet; the guard took it, hesitated, then leaned his weapon against his hip, shifted the paper to his left hand, and dug into his pouch with his right.

Dahlquist grabbed the gun, shoved it between the guard's legs, and jerked. He threw the weapon away and ducked into the airlock. As he slammed the door he saw the guard struggling to his feet and reaching for his side arm. He dogged the outer door shut and felt a tingle in his fingers as a slug struck the door.

He flung himself at the inner door, jerked the spill lever, rushed back to the outer door and hung his weight on the handle. At once he could feel it stir. The guard was lifting up; the lieutenant was pulling down, with only his low Moon weight to anchor him. Slowly the handle raised before his eyes.

Air from the bomb room rushed into the lock through the spill valve. Dahlquist felt his space suit settle on his body as the pressure in the lock began to equal the pressure in the suit. He quit straining and let the guard raise the handle. It did not matter; thirteen tons of air pressure now held the door closed.

He latched open the inner door to the bomb room, so that it could not swing shut. As long as it was open, the airlock could not operate; no one could enter.

Before him in the room, one for each projectile rocket, were the atom bombs, spaced in rows far enough apart to defeat any faint possibility of spontaneous chain reaction. They were the deadliest things in the known universe, but they were his babies. He had placed himself between them and anyone who would misuse them.

But, now that he was here, he had no plan to use his temporary advantage.

The speaker on the wall sputtered into life. "Hey! Lieutenant! What goes on here? You gone crazy?" Dahlquist did not answer. Let Lopez stay confused—it would take him that much longer to make up his mind what to do. And Johnny Dahlquist needed as many minutes as he could squeeze. Lopez went on protesting. Finally he shut up.

Johnny had followed a blind urge not to let the bombs—*his* bombs!—be used for "demonstrations on unimportant towns." But what to do next? Well, Towers couldn't get through the lock. Johnny would sit tight until hell froze over.

Don't kid yourself, John Ezra! Towers could get in. Some high explosive against the outer door—then the air would whoosh out, our boy Johnny would drown in blood from his burst lungs—and the bombs would be sitting there, unhurt. They were built to stand the jump from Moon to Earth; vacuum would not hurt them at all.

He decided to stay in his space suit; explosive decompression didn't appeal to him. Come to think about it, death from old age was his choice.

Or they could drill a hole, let out the air, and open the door without wrecking the lock. Or Towers might even have a new airlock built outside the old. Not likely, Johnny thought; a *coup d'état* depended on speed. Towers was almost sure to take the quickest way—blasting. And Lopez was probably calling the Base right now. Fifteen minutes for Towers to suit up and get here, maybe a short dicker—then *whoosh!* the party is over.

Fifteen minutes—

In fifteen minutes the bombs might fall back into the hands of the conspirators; in fifteen minutes he must make the bombs unusable.

An atom bomb is just two or more pieces of fissionable metal, such as plutonium. Separated, they are no more explosive than a pound of butter; slapped together, they explode. The complications lie in the gadgets and circuits and gun used to slap them together in the exact way and at the exact time and place required.

These circuits, the bomb's "brain," are easily destroyed—but the bomb itself is hard to destroy because of its very simplicity. Johnny decided to smash the "brains"—and quickly!

The only tools at hand were simple ones used in handling the bombs. Aside from a Geiger counter, the speaker on the walkie-talkie circuit, a television rig to the base, and the bombs themselves, the room was bare. A bomb to be worked on was taken elsewhere—not through fear of explosion, but to reduce radiation exposure for personnel. The radioactive material in a bomb is buried in a "tamper"—in these bombs, gold. Gold stops alpha, beta, and much of the deadly gamma radiation—but not neutrons.

The slippery, poisonous neutrons which plutonium gives off had to escape, or a chain reaction—explosion!—would result. The room was bathed in an invisible, almost undetectable rain of neutrons. The place was unhealthy; regulations called for staying in it as short a time as possible.

The Geiger counter clicked off the "background" radiation, cosmic rays, the trace of radioactivity in the Moon's crust, and secondary radioactivity set up all through the room by neutrons. Free neutrons have the nasty trait of infecting what they strike, making it radioactive, whether it be concrete wall or human body. In time the room would have to be abandoned.

Dahlquist twisted a knob on the Geiger counter; the instrument stopped clicking. He had used a suppressor circuit to cut out noise of "background" radiation at the level then present. It reminded him uncomfortably of the danger of staying here. He took out the radiation exposure film all radiation personnel carry; it was a direct-response type and had been fresh when he arrived. The most sensitive end was faintly darkened already. Half way down the film a red line crossed it. Theoretically, if the wearer was exposed to enough radioactivity in a week to darken the film to that line, he was, as Johnny reminded himself, a "dead duck."

Off came the cumbersome space suit; what he needed was speed. Do the job and surrender—better to be a prisoner than to linger in a place as "hot" as this.

He grabbed a ball hammer from the tool rack and got busy, pausing only to switch off the television pick-up. The first bomb bothered him. He started to smash the cover plate of the "brain," then stopped, filled with reluctance. All his life he had prized fine apparatus.

He nerved himself and swung; glass tinkled, metal creaked. His mood changed; he began to feel a shameful pleasure in destruction. He pushed on with enthusiasm, swinging, smashing, destroying!

So intent was he that he did not at first hear his name called. "Dahlquist! Answer me! Are you there?"

He wiped sweat and looked at the TV screen. Towers' perturbed features stared out.

Johnny was shocked to find that he had wrecked only six bombs. Was he going to be caught before he could finish? Oh, no! He *had* to finish. Stall, son, stall! "Yes, Colonel? You called me?"

"I certainly did! What's the meaning of this?"

"I'm sorry, Colonel."

Towers' expression relaxed a little. "Turn on your pick-up, Johnny, I can't see you. What was that noise?"

"The pick-up is on," Johnny lied. "It must be out of order. That noise—uh, to tell the truth, Colonel, I was fixing things so that nobody could get in here."

Towers hesitated, then said firmly, "I'm going to assume that you are sick and send you to the Medical Officer. But I want you to come out of there, right away. That's an order, Johnny."

Johnny answered slowly. "I can't just yet, Colonel. I came here to make up my mind and I haven't quite made it up. You said to see you after lunch."

"I meant you to stay in your quarters."

"Yes, sir. But I thought I ought to stand watch on the bombs, in case I decided you were wrong."

"It's not for you to decide, Johnny. I'm your superior officer. You are sworn to obey me."

"Yes, sir." This was wasting time; the old fox might have a squad on the way now. "But I swore to keep the peace, too. Could you come out here and talk it over with me? I don't want to do the wrong thing."

Towers smiled. "A good idea, Johnny. You wait there. I'm sure you'll see the light." He switched off.

"There," said Johnny. "I hope you're convinced that I'm a half-wit—you slimy mistake!" He picked up the hammer, ready to use the minutes gained.

He stopped almost at once; it dawned on him that wrecking the "brains" was not enough. There were no spare "brains," but there was a well-stocked electronics shop. Morgan could jury-rig control circuits for bombs. Why, he could himself—not a neat job, but one that would work. Damnation! He would have to wreck the bombs themselves—and in the next ten minutes.

But a bomb was solid chunks of metal, encased in a heavy tamper, all tied in with a big steel gun. It couldn't be done—not in ten minutes.

Damn!

Of course, there was one way. He knew the control circuits; he also knew how to beat them. Take this bomb: if he took out the safety bar, unhooked the proximity circuit, shorted the delay circuit, and cut in the arming circuit by hand—then unscrewed *that* and reached in *there*, he could, with just a long stiff wire, set the bomb off.

Blowing the other bombs and the valley itself to Kingdom come.

Also Johnny Dahlquist. That was the rub.

All this time he was doing what he had thought out, up to the step of actually setting off the bomb.

Ready to go, the bomb seemed to threaten, as if crouching to spring. He stood up, sweating.

He wondered if he had the courage. He did not want to funk—and hoped that he would. He dug into his jacket and took out a picture of Edith and the baby. "Honeychile," he said, "if I get out of this, I'll never even try to beat a red light." He kissed the picture and put it back. There was nothing to do but wait.

What was keeping Towers? Johnny wanted to make sure that Towers was in blast range. What a joke on the jerk! Me—sitting here, ready to throw the switch on him. The idea tickled him; it led to a better: why blow himself up—alive?

There was another way to rig it—a "dead man" control. Jigger up some way so that the last step, the one that set off the bomb, would not happen as long as he kept his hand on a switch or a lever or something. Then, if they blew open the door, or shot him, or anything—up goes the balloon!

Better still, if he could hold them off with the threat of it, sooner or later help would come— Johnny was sure that most of the Patrol was not in this stinking conspiracy—and then: Johnny comes marching home! What a reunion! He'd resign and get a teaching job; he'd stood his watch.

All the while, he was working. Electrical? No, too little time. Make it a simple mechanical linkage. He had it doped out but had hardly begun to build it when the loudspeaker called him. "Johnny?"

"That you, Colonel?" His hands kept busy.

"Let me in."

"Well, now, Colonel, that wasn't in the agreement." Where in blue blazes was something to use as a long lever?

"I'll come in alone, Johnny, I give you my word. We'll talk face to face."

His word! "We can talk over the speaker, Colonel." Hey, that was it—a yardstick, hanging on the tool rack.

"Johnny, I'm warning you. Let me in, or I'll blow the door off."

A wire—he needed a wire, fairly long and stiff. He tore the antenna from his suit. "You wouldn't do that, Colonel. It would ruin the bombs."

"Vacuum won't hurt the bombs. Quit stalling."

"Better check with Major Morgan. Vacuum won't hurt them; explosive decompression would wreck every circuit." The Colonel was not a bomb specialist; he shut up for several minutes. Johnny went on working.

"Dahlquist," Towers resumed, "that was a clumsy lie. I checked with Morgan. You have sixty seconds to get into your suit, if you aren't already. I'm going to blast the door."

"No, you won't," said Johnny. "Ever hear of a 'dead man' switch?" Now for a counterweight—and a sling.

"Eh? What do you mean?"

"I've rigged number seventeen to set off by hand. But I put in a gimmick. It won't blow while I hang on to a strap I've got in my hand. But if anything happens to me—*up she goes!* You are about fifty feet from the blast center. Think it over."

There was a short silence. "I don't believe you."

"No? Ask Morgan. He'll believe me. He can inspect it, over the TV pick-up." Johnny lashed the belt of his space suit to the end of the yardstick.

"You said the pick-up was out of order."

"So I lied. This time I'll prove it. Have Morgan call me."

Presently Major Morgan's face appeared. "Lieutenant Dahlquist?"

"Hi, Stinky. Wait a sec." With great care Dahlquist made one last connection while holding down the end of the yardstick. Still careful, he shifted his grip to the belt, sat down on the floor, stretched an arm and switched on the TV pick-up. "Can you see me, Stinky?"

"I can see you," Morgan answered stiffly. "What is this nonsense?"

"A little surprise I whipped up." He explained it—what circuits he had cut out, what ones had been shorted, just how the jury-rigged mechanical sequence fitted in.

Morgan nodded. "But you're bluffing, Dahlquist. I feel sure that you haven't disconnected the 'K' circuit. You don't have the guts to blow yourself up."

Johnny chuckled. "I sure haven't. But that's the beauty of it. It can't go off, *so long as I am alive*. If your greasy boss, ex-Colonel Towers, blasts the door, then I'm dead and the bomb goes off. It won't matter to me, but it will to him. Better tell him." He switched off.

Towers came on over the speaker shortly. "Dahlquist?"

"I hear you."

"There's no need to throw away your life. Come out and you will be retired on full pay. You can go home to your family. That's a promise."

Johnny got mad. "You keep my family out of this!"

"Think of them, man."

"Shut up. Get back to your hole. I feel a need to scratch and this whole shebang might just explode in your lap."

II

Johnny sat up with a start. He had dozed, his hand hadn't let go the sling, but he had the shakes when he thought about it.

Maybe he should disarm the bomb and depend on their not daring to dig him out? But Towers' neck was already in hock for treason; Towers might risk it. If he did and the bomb were disarmed, Johnny would be dead and Towers would have the bombs. No, he had gone this far; he wouldn't let his baby girl grow up in a dictatorship just to catch some sleep.

He heard the Geiger counter clicking and remembered having used the suppressor circuit. The radioactivity in the room must be increasing, perhaps from scattering the "brain" circuits—the circuits were sure to be infected; they had lived too long too close to plutonium. He dug out his film.

The dark area was spreading toward the red line.

He put it back and said, "Pal, better break this deadlock or you are going to shine like a watch dial." It was a figure of speech; infected animal tissue does not glow—it simply dies, slowly.

The TV screen lit up; Towers' face appeared. "Dahlquist? I want to talk to you."

"Go fly a kite."

"Let's admit you have us inconvenienced."

"Inconvenienced, hell—I've got you stopped."

"For the moment. I'm arranging to get more bombs—"

"Liar."

"—but you are slowing us up. I have a proposition."

"Not interested."

"Wait. When this is over I will be chief of the world government. If you cooperate, even now, I will make you my administrative head."

Johnny told him what to do with it. Towers said, "Don't be stupid. What do you gain by dying?"

Johnny grunted. "Towers, what a prime stinker you are. You spoke of my family. I'd rather see them dead than living under a two-bit Napoleon like you. Now go away—I've got some thinking to do."

Towers switched off.

Johnny got out his film again. It seemed no darker but it reminded him forcibly that time was running out. He was hungry and thirsty—and he could not stay awake forever. It took four days to get a ship up from Earth; he could not expect rescue any sooner. And he wouldn't last four days— once the darkening spread past the red line he was a goner.

His only chance was to wreck the bombs beyond repair, and get out—before that film got much darker.

He thought about ways, then got busy. He hung a weight on the sling, tied a line to it. If Towers blasted the door, he hoped to jerk the rig loose before he died.

There was a simple, though arduous, way to wreck the bombs beyond any capacity of Moon Base to repair them. The heart of each was two hemispheres of plutonium, their flat surface polished smooth to permit perfect contact when slapped together. Anything less would prevent the chain reaction on which atomic explosion depended.

Johnny started taking apart one of the bombs.

He had to bash off four lugs, then break the glass envelope around the inner assembly. Aside from that the bomb came apart easily. At last he had in front of him two gleaming, mirror-perfect half globes.

A blow with the hammer—and one was no longer perfect. Another blow and the second cracked like glass; he had trapped its crystalline structure just right.

Hours later, dead tired, he went back to the armed bomb. Forcing himself to steady down, with extreme care he disarmed it. Shortly its silvery hemispheres too were useless. There was no longer a usable bomb in the room—but huge fortunes in the most valuable, most poisonous, and most deadly metal in the known world were spread around the floor.

Johnny looked at the deadly stuff. "Into your suit and out of here, son," he said aloud. "I wonder what Towers will say?"

He walked toward the rack, intending to hang up the hammer. As he passed, the Geiger counter chattered wildly.

Plutonium hardly affects a Geiger counter; secondary infection from plutonium does. Johnny looked at the hammer, then held it closer to the Geiger counter. The counter screamed.

Johnny tossed it hastily away and started back toward his suit.

As he passed the counter it chattered again. He stopped short.

He pushed one hand close to the counter. Its clicking picked up to a steady roar. Without moving he reached into his pocket and took out his exposure film.

It was dead black from end to end.

III

Plutonium taken into the body moves quickly to bone marrow. Nothing can be done; the victim is finished. Neutrons from it smash through the body, ionizing tissue, transmuting atoms into radioactive isotopes, destroying and killing. The fatal dose is unbelievably small; a mass a tenth the size of a grain of table salt is more than enough—a dose small enough to enter through the tiniest scratch. During the historic "Manhattan Project" immediate high amputation was considered the only possible first-aid measure.

Johnny knew all this but it no longer disturbed him. He sat on the floor, smoking a hoarded cigarette, and thinking. The events of his long watch were running through his mind.

He blew a puff of smoke at the Geiger counter and smiled without humor to hear it chatter more loudly. By now even his breath was "hot"—carbon-14, he supposed, exhaled from his blood stream as carbon dioxide. It did not matter.

There was no longer any point in surrendering, nor would he give Towers the satisfaction—he would finish out this watch right here. Besides, by keeping up the bluff that one bomb was ready to blow, he could stop them from capturing the raw material from which bombs were made. That might be important in the long run.

He accepted, without surprise, the fact that he was not unhappy. There was a sweetness about having no further worries of any sort. He did not hurt, he was not uncomfortable, he was no longer even hungry. Physically he still felt fine and his mind was at peace. He was dead—he knew that he was dead; yet for a time he was able to walk and breathe and see and feel.

He was not even lonesome. He was not alone; there were comrades with him—the boy with his finger in the dike, Colonel Bowie, too ill to move but insisting that he be carried across the line, the dying Captain of the *Chesapeake* still with death-less challenge on his lips, Rodger Young peering into the gloom. They gathered about him in the dusky bomb room.

And of course there was Edith. She was the only one he was aware of. Johnny wished that he could see her face more clearly. Was she angry? Or proud and happy?

Proud though unhappy—he could see her better now and even feel her hand. He held very still.

Presently his cigarette burned down to his fingers. He took a final puff, blew it at the Geiger counter, and put it out. It was his last. He gathered several butts and fashioned a roll-your-own with a bit of paper found in a pocket. He lit it carefully and settled back to wait for Edith to show up again. He was very happy.

He was still propped against the bomb case, the last of his salvaged cigarettes cold at his side, when

the speaker called out again. "Johnny? Hey, Johnny!
Can you hear me? This is Kelly. It's all over. The
Lafayette landed and Towers blew his brains out.
Johnny? *Answer me*."

When they opened the outer door, the first man
in carried a Geiger counter in front of him on the
end of a long pole. He stopped at the threshold
and backed out hastily. "Hey, chief!" he called.
"Better get some handling equipment—uh, and a
lead coffin, too."

*"Four days it took the little ship and her escort
to reach Earth. Four days while all of Earth's
people awaited her arrival. For ninety-eight hours
all commercial programs were off television; instead there was an endless dirge—the* Dead March
from Saul, *the* Valhalla *theme,* Going Home, *the
Patrol's own* Landing Orbit.

*"The nine ships landed at Chicago Port. A drone
tractor removed the casket from the small ship;
the ship was then refueled and blasted off in an
escape trajectory, thrown away into outer space,
never again to be used for a lesser purpose.*

*"The tractor progressed to the Illinois town where
Lieutenant Dahlquist had been born, while the
dirge continued. There it placed the casket on a
pedestal, inside a barrier marking the distance of
safe approach. Space marines, arms reversed and
heads bowed, stood guard around it; the crowds
stayed outside this circle. And still the dirge
continued.*

*"When enough time had passed, long, long after
the heaped flowers had withered, the lead casket
was enclosed in marble, just as you see it today."*

Gentlemen, Be Seated

IT TAKES both agoraphobes and claustrophobes to colonize the Moon. Or make it agoraphiles and claustrophiles, for the men who go out into space had better not have phobias. If anything on a planet, in a planet, or in the empty reaches around the planets can frighten a man, he should stick to Mother Earth. A man who would make his living away from *terra firma* must be willing to be shut up in a cramped spaceship, knowing that it may become his coffin, and yet he must be undismayed by the wide-open spaces of space itself. Spacemen—men who *work* in space, pilots and jetmen and astrogators and such—are men who like a few million miles of elbow room.

On the other hand the Moon colonists need to be the sort who feel cozy burrowing around underground like so many pesky moles.

On my second trip to Luna City I went over to Richardson Observatory both to see the Big Eye and to pick up a story to pay for my vacation. I flashed my Journalists' Guild card, sweet-talked a bit, and ended with the paymaster showing me around. We went out the north tunnel, which was then being bored to the site of the projected coronascope.

It was a dull trip—climb on a scooter, ride down a completely featureless tunnel, climb off and go through an airlock, get on another scooter and do it all over again. Mr. Knowles filled in with sales talk. "This is temporary," he explained. "When we get the second tunnel dug, we'll cross-connect, take out the airlocks, put a northbound slidewalk in this one, a southbound slidewalk in the other one, and you'll make the trip in less than three minutes. Just like Luna City—or Manhattan."

"Why not take out the airlocks now?" I asked, as we entered another airlock—about the seventh. "So far, the pressure is the same on each side of each lock."

Knowles looked at me quizzically. "You wouldn't take advantage of a peculiarity of this planet just to work up a sensational feature story?"

I was irked. "Look here," I told him. "I'm as reliable as the next word-mechanic, but if something is not kosher about this project let's go back right now and forget it. I won't hold still for censorship."

"Take it easy, Jack," he said mildly—it was the first time he had used my first name; I noted it and discounted it. "Nobody's going to censor you. We're glad to cooperate with you fellows, but the Moon's had too much bad publicity now—publicity it didn't deserve."

I didn't say anything.

"Every engineering job has its own hazards," he insisted, "and its advantages, too. Our men don't get malaria and they don't have to watch out for rattlesnakes. I can show you figures that prove it's safer to be a sandhog in the Moon than it is to be a file clerk in Des Moines—all things considered. For example, we rarely have any broken bones in the Moon; the gravity is so low—while that Des Moines file clerk takes his life in his hands every time he steps in or out of his bathtub."

"Okay, okay," I interrupted, "so the place is safe. What's the catch?"

"It *is* safe. Not company figures, mind you, nor Luna City Chamber of Commerce, but Lloyd's of London."

"So you keep unnecessary airlocks. Why?"

He hesitated before he answered, "Quakes."

Quakes. Earthquakes—moonquakes, I mean. I glanced at the curving walls sliding past and I wished I were in Des Moines. Nobody wants to be buried alive, but to have it happen in the Moon— why, you wouldn't stand a chance. No matter how quick they got to you, your lungs would be ruptured. No air.

"They don't happen very often," Knowles went on, "but we have to be prepared. Remember, the Earth is eighty times the mass of the Moon, so the tidal stresses here are eighty times as great as the Moon's effect on Earth tides."

"Come again," I said. "There isn't any water on the Moon. How can there be tides?"

"You don't have to have water to have tidal stresses. Don't worry about it; just accept it. What you get is unbalanced stresses. They can cause quakes."

I nodded. "I see. Since everything in the Moon has to be sealed airtight, you've got to watch out for quakes. These airlocks are to confine your losses." I started visualizing myself as one of the losses.

"Yes and no. The airlocks would limit an accident all right, if there was one—which there won't be—this place is *safe*. Primarily they let us work on a section of the tunnel at no pressure without disturbing the rest of it. But they are more than that; each one is a temporary expansion joint. You can tie a compact structure together and let it ride out a quake, but a thing as long as this tunnel has to give, or it will spring a leak. A flexible seal is hard to accomplish in the Moon."

"What's wrong with rubber?" I demanded. I was feeling jumpy enough to be argumentative. "I've got a ground-car back home with two hundred thousand miles on it, yet I've never touched the tires since they were sealed up in Detroit."

Knowles sighed. "I should have brought one of the engineers along, Jack. The volatiles that keep rubbers soft tend to boil away in vacuum and the stuff gets stiff. Same for the flexible plastics. When you expose them to low temperature as well they get brittle as eggshells."

The scooter stopped as Knowles was speaking and we got off just in time to meet half a dozen men coming out of the next airlock. They were wearing spacesuits, or, more properly, pressure suits, for they had hose connections instead of oxygen bottles, and no sun visors. Their helmets were thrown back and each man had his head pushed through the opened zipper in the front of his suit, giving him a curiously two-headed look. Knowles called out, "Hey, Konski!"

One of the men turned around. He must have been six feet two and fat for his size. I guessed him at three hundred pounds, earthside. "It's Mr. Knowles," he said happily. "Don't tell me I've gotten a raise."

"You're making too much money now, Fatso. Shake hands with Jack Arnold. Jack, this is Fatso Konski—the best sandhog in four planets."

"Only four?" inquired Konski. He slid his right arm out of his suit and stuck his bare hand into mine. I said I was glad to meet him and tried to get my hand back before he mangled it.

"Jack Arnold wants to see how you seal these tunnels," Knowles went on. "Come along with us."

Konski stared at the overhead. "Well, now that you mention it, Mr. Knowles, I've just finished my shift."

Knowles said, "Fatso, you're a money grubber and inhospitable as well. Okay—time-and-a-half." Konski turned and started unsealing the airlock.

The tunnel beyond looked much the same as the section we had left except that there were no scooter tracks and the lights were temporary, rigged on extensions. A couple of hundred feet away the tunnel was blocked by a bulkhead with a circular door in it. The fat man followed my glance. "That's the movable lock," he explained. "No air beyond it. We excavate just ahead of it."

"Can I see where you've been digging?"

"Not without we go back and get you a suit."

I shook my head. There were perhaps a dozen bladder-like objects in the tunnel, the size and shape of toy balloons. They seemed to displace exactly their own weight of air; they floated without displaying much tendency to rise or settle. Konski batted one out of his way and answered me before I could ask. "This piece of tunnel was pressurized today," he told me. "These tag-alongs search out stray leaks. They're sticky inside. They get sucked up against a leak, break, and the goo gets sucked in, freezes and seals the leak."

"Is that a permanent repair?" I wanted to know.

"Are you kidding? It just shows the follow-up man where to weld."

"Show him a flexible joint," Knowles directed.

"Coming up." We paused half-way down the tunnel and Konski pointed to a ring segment that ran completely around the tubular tunnel. "We put in a flex joint every hundred feet. It's glass cloth, gasketed onto the two steel sections it joins. Gives the tunnel a certain amount of springiness."

"Glass cloth? To make an airtight seal?" I objected.

"The cloth doesn't seal; it's for strength. You got ten layers of cloth, with a silicone grease spread between the layers. It gradually goes bad, from the outside in, but it'll hold five years or more before you have to put on another coat."

I asked Konski how he liked his job, thinking I might get some story. He shrugged. "It's all right. Nothing to it. Only one atmosphere of pressure. Now you take when I was working under the Hudson—"

"And getting paid a tenth of what you get here," put in Knowles.

"Mr. Knowles, you grieve me," Konski protested. "It ain't the money; it's the art of the matter. Take Venus. They pay as well on Venus and a man has to be on his toes. The muck is so loose you have to freeze it. It takes real caisson men to work there. Half of these punks here are just miners; a case of the bends would scare 'em silly."

"Tell him why you left Venus, Fatso."

Konski expressed dignity. "Shall we examine the movable shield, gentlemen?" he asked.

We puttered around a while longer and I was ready to go back. There wasn't much to see, and the more I saw of the place the less I liked it. Konski was undogging the door of the airlock leading back when something happened.

I was down on my hands and knees and the place was pitch dark. Maybe I screamed—I don't know. There was a ringing in my ears. I tried to get up and then stayed where I was. It was the darkest dark I ever saw, complete blackness. I thought I was blind.

A torchlight beam cut through it, picked me out, and then moved on. "What was it?" I shouted. "What happened? Was it a quake?"

"Stop yelling," Konski's voice answered me casually. "That was no quake, it was some sort of explosion. Mr. Knowles—you all right?"

"I guess so." He gasped for breath. "What happened?"

"Dunno. Let's look around a bit." Konski stood up and poked his beam around the tunnel, whistling softly. His light was the sort that has to be pumped; it flickered.

"Looks tight, but I hear— Oh, oh! sister!" His beam was focused on a part of the flexible joint, near the floor.

The "tag-along" balloons were gathering at this

spot. Three were already there; others were drifting in slowly. As we watched, one of them burst and collapsed in a sticky mass that marked the leak.

The hole sucked up the burst balloon and began to hiss. Another rolled onto the spot, joggled about a bit, then it, too, burst. It took a little longer this time for the leak to absorb and swallow the gummy mass.

Konski passed me the light. "Keep pumping it, kid." He shrugged his right arm out of the suit and placed his bare hand over the spot where, at that moment, a third bladder burst.

"How about it, Fats?" Mr. Knowles demanded.

"Couldn't say. Feels like a hole as big as my thumb. Sucks like the devil."

"How could you get a hole like that?"

"Search me. Poked through from the outside, maybe."

"You got the leak checked?"

"I think so. Go back and check the gauge. Jack, give him the light."

Knowles trotted back to the airlock. Presently he sang out, "Pressure steady!"

"Can you read the vernier?" Konski called to him.

"Sure. Steady by the vernier."

"How much we lose?"

"Not more than a pound or two. What was the pressure before?"

"Earth-normal."

"Lost a pound four tenths, then."

"Not bad. Keep on going, Mr. Knowles. There's a tool kit just beyond the lock in the next section. Bring me back a number three patch, or bigger."

"Right." We heard the door open and clang shut, and we were again in total darkness. I must have made some sound for Konski told me to keep my chin up.

Presently we heard the door, and the blessed light shone out again. "Got it?" said Konski.

"No, Fatso. No . . ." Knowles' voice was shaking. "There's no air on the other side. The other door wouldn't open."

"Jammed, maybe?"

"No. I checked the manometer. There's no pressure in the next section."

Konski whistled again. "Looks like we'll wait till they come for us. In that case— Keep the light on me, Mr. Knowles. Jack, help me out of this suit."

"What are you planning to do?"

"If I can't get a patch, I got to make one, Mr. Knowles. This suit is the only thing around." I started to help him—a clumsy job since he had to keep his hand on the leak.

"You can stuff my shirt in the hole," Knowles suggested.

"I'd as soon bail water with a fork. It's got to be the suit; there's nothing else around that will hold the pressure." When he was free of the suit, he had me smooth out a portion of the back, then, as he snatched his hand away, I slapped the suit down over the leak. Konski promptly sat on it. "There," he said happily, "we've got it corked. Nothing to do but wait."

I started to ask him why he hadn't just sat down on the leak while wearing the suit; then I realized that the seat of the suit was corrugated with insulation—he needed a smooth piece to seal on to the sticky stuff left by the balloons.

"Let me see your hand," Knowles demanded.

"It's nothing much." But Knowles examined it anyway. I looked at it and got a little sick. He had a mark like a stigma on the palm, a bloody, oozing wound. Knowles made a compress of his handkerchief and then used mine to tie it in place.

"Thank you, gentlemen," Konski told us, then added, "We've got time to kill. How about a little pinochle?"

"With your cards?" asked Knowles.

"Why, Mr. Knowles! Well—never mind. It isn't right for paymasters to gamble anyhow. Speaking of paymasters, you realize this is pressure work now, Mr. Knowles?"

"For a pound and four tenths differential?"

"I'm sure the union would take that view—in the circumstances."

"Suppose *I* sit on the leak?"

"But the rate applies to helpers, too."

"Okay, miser—triple-time it is."

"That's more like your own sweet nature, Mr. Knowles. I hope it's a nice long wait."

"How long a wait do you think it will be, Fatso?"

"Well, it shouldn't take them more than an hour, even if they have to come all the way from Richardson."

"Hmm . . . what makes you think they will be looking for us?"

"Huh? Doesn't your office know where you are?"

"I'm afraid not. I told them I wouldn't be back today."

Konski thought about it. "I didn't drop my time card. They'll know I'm still inside."

"Sure they will—tomorrow, when your card doesn't show up at my office."

"There's that lunkhead on the gate. He'll know he's got three extra inside."

"Provided he remembers to tell his relief. And provided he wasn't caught in it, too."

"Yes, I guess so," Konski said thoughtfully. "Jack—better quit pumping that light. You just use up more oxygen."

We sat there in the darkness for quite a long time, speculating about what had happened. Konski was sure it was an explosion; Knowles said that it put him in mind of a time when he had seen a freight rocket crash on take off. When the talk started to die out, Konski told some stories. I tried to tell one, but I was so nervous—so *afraid*, I should say—that I couldn't remember the snapper. I wanted to scream.

After a long silence Konski said, "Jack, give us the light again. I got something figured out."

"What is it?" Knowles asked.

"If we had a patch, you could put on my suit and go for help."

"There's no oxygen for the suit."

"That's why I mentioned you. You're the smallest—there'll be enough air in the suit itself to take you through the next section."

"Well—okay. What are you going to use for a patch?"

"I'm sitting on it."

"Huh?"

"This big broad, round thing I'm sitting on. I'll take my pants off. If I push one of my hams against that hole, I'll guarantee you it'll be sealed tight."

"But—No, Fats, it won't do. Look what happened to your hand. You'd hemorrhage through your skin and bleed to death before I could get back."

"I'll give you two to one I wouldn't—for fifty, say."

"If I win, how do I collect?"

"You're a cute one, Mr. Knowles. But look— I've got two or three inches of fat padding me. I won't bleed much—a strawberry mark, no more."

Knowles shook his head. "It's not necessary. If we keep quiet, there's air enough here for several days."

"It's not the air, Mr. Knowles. Noticed it's getting chilly?"

I had noticed, but hadn't thought about it. In my misery and funk being cold didn't seem anything more than appropriate. Now I thought about it. When we lost the power line, we lost the heaters, too. It would keep getting colder and colder . . . and colder.

Mr. Knowles saw it, too. "Okay, Fats. Let's get on with it."

I sat on the suit while Konski got ready. After he got his pants off he snagged one of the tag-alongs, burst it, and smeared the sticky insides on his right buttock. Then he turned to me. "Okay, kid—up off the nest." We made the swap-over fast, without losing much air, though the leak hissed angrily. "Comfortable as an easy chair, folks." He grinned.

Knowles hurried into the suit and left, taking the light with him. We were in darkness again.

After a while, I heard Konski's voice. "There a game we can play in the dark, Jack. You play chess?"

"Why, yes—play at it, that is."

"A good game. Used to play it in the decompression chamber when I was working under the Hudson. What do you say to twenty on a side, just to make it fun?"

"Uh? Well, all right." He could have made it a thousand; I didn't care.

"Fine. King's pawn to king three."

"Uh—king's pawn to king's four."

"Conventional, aren't you? Puts me in mind of a girl I knew in Hoboken—" What he told about her had nothing to do with chess, although it did prove she was conventional, in a manner of speaking. "King's bishop to queen's bishop four. Remind me to tell you about her sister, too. Seems she hadn't always been a redhead, but she wanted people to think so. So she—sorry. Go ahead with your move."

I tried to think but my head was spinning. "Queen's pawn to queen three."

"Queen to king's bishop three. Anyhow, she—" He went on in great detail. It wasn't new and I doubt if it ever happened to him, but it cheered me up. I actually smiled, there in the dark. "It's your move," he added.

"Oh." I couldn't remember the board. I decided to get ready to castle, always fairly safe in the early game. "Queen's knight to queen's bishop three."

"Queen advances to capture your king's bishop's pawn—checkmate. You owe me twenty, Jack."

"Huh? Why that can't be!"

"Want to run over the moves?" He checked them off.

I managed to visualize them, then said, "Why,

I'll be a dirty name! You hooked me with a fool's mate!"

He chuckled. "You should have kept your eye on my queen instead of on the redhead."

I laughed out loud. "Know any more stories?"

"Sure." He told another. But when I urged him to go on, he said, "I think I'll just rest a little while, Jack."

I got up. "You all right, Fats?" He didn't answer; I felt my way over to him in the dark. His face was cold and he didn't speak when I touched him. I could hear his heart faintly when I pressed an ear to his chest, but his hands and feet were like ice.

I had to pull him loose; he was frozen to the spot. I could feel the ice, though I knew it must be blood. I started to try to revive him by rubbing him, but the hissing of the leak brought me up short. I tore off my own trousers, had a panicky time before I found the exact spot in the dark, and sat down on it, with my right buttock pressed firmly against the opening.

It grabbed me like a suction cup, icy cold. Then it was fire spreading through my flesh. After a time I couldn't feel anything at all, except a dull ache and coldness.

There was a light someplace. It flickered on, then went out again. I heard a door clang. I started to shout.

"Knowles!" I screamed. "Mr. Knowles!"

The light flickered on again. "Coming, Jack—"

I started to blubber. "Oh, you made it! You made it."

"I didn't make it, Jack. I couldn't reach the next section. When I got back to the lock I passed out."

He stopped to wheeze. "There's a crater—" The light flickered off and fell clanging to the floor. "Help me, Jack," he said querulously. "Can't you see I need help? I tried to—"

I heard him stumble and fall. I called to him, but he didn't answer.

I tried to get up, but I was stuck fast, a cork in a bottle . . .

I came to, lying face down—with a clean sheet under me. "Feeling better?" someone asked. It was Knowles, standing by my bed, dressed in a bathrobe.

"You're dead," I told him.

"Not a bit." He grinned. "They got to us in time."

"What happened?" I stared at him, still not believing my eyes.

"Just like we thought—a crashed rocket. An unmanned mail rocket got out of control and hit the tunnel."

"Where's Fats?"

"Hi!"

I twisted my head around; it was Konski, face down like myself.

"You owe me twenty," he said cheerfully.

"I owe you—" I found I was dripping tears for no good reason. "Okay, I owe you twenty. But you'll have to come to Des Moines to collect it."

The Black Pits of Luna

THE morning after we got to the Moon we went over to Rutherford. Dad and Mr. Latham—Mr. Latham is the man from the Harriman Trust that Dad came to Luna City to see—Dad and Mr. Latham had to go anyhow, on business. I got Dad to promise I could go along because it looked like just about my only chance to get out on the surface of the Moon. Luna City is all right, I guess, but I defy you to tell a corridor in Luna City from the sublevels in New York—except that you're light on your feet, of course.

When Dad came into our hotel suite to say we were ready to leave, I was down on the floor, playing mumblety-peg with my kid brother. Mother was lying down and had asked me to keep the runt quiet. She had been dropsick all the way out from Earth and I guess she didn't feel very good. The runt had been fiddling with the lights, switching them from "dusk" to "desert suntan" and back again. I collared him and sat him down on the floor.

Of course, I don't play mumblety-peg any more,

but, on the Moon, it's a right good game. The knife practically floats and you can do all kinds of things with it. We made up a lot of new rules.

Dad said, "Switch in plans, my dear. We're leaving for Rutherford right away. Let's pull ourselves together."

Mother said, "Oh, mercy me—I don't think I'm up to it. You and Dickie run along. Baby Darling and I will just spend a quiet day right here."

Baby Darling is the runt.

I could have told her it was the wrong approach. He nearly put my eye out with the knife and said, "Who? What? I'm going too. Let's go!"

Mother said, "Oh, now, Baby Darling—don't cause Mother Dear any trouble. We'll go to the movies, just you and I."

The runt is seven years younger than I am, but don't call him "Baby Darling" if you want to get anything out of him. He started to bawl. "You said I could go!" he yelled.

"No, Baby Darling. I haven't mentioned it to you. I—"

"Daddy said I could go!"

"Richard, did you tell Baby he could go?"

"Why, no, my dear, not that I recall. Perhaps I—"

The kid cut in fast. "You said I could go anywhere Dickie went. You promised me you promised me you promised me." Sometimes you have to hand it to the runt; he had them jawing about who told him what in nothing flat. Anyhow, this is how, twenty mintues later, the four of us were up at the rocket port with Mr. Latham and climbing into the shuttle for Rutherford.

*　　*　　*

The trip only takes about ten minutes and you don't see much, just a glimpse of the Earth while the rocket is still near Luna City and then not even that, since the atom plants where we were going are all on the back side of the Moon, of course. There were maybe a dozen tourists along and most of them were dropsick as soon as we went into free flight. So was Mother. Some people never will get used to rockets.

But Mother was all right as soon as we grounded and were inside again. Rutherford isn't like Luna City; instead of extending a tube out to the ship, they send a pressurized car out to latch on to the airlock of the rocket, then you jeep back about a mile to the entrance to underground. I liked that and so did the runt. Dad had to go off on business with Mr. Latham, leaving Mother and me and the runt to join up with the party of tourists for the trip through the laboratories.

It was all right but nothing to get excited about. So far as I can see, one atomics plant looks about like another; Rutherford could just as well have been the main plant outside Chicago. I mean to say everything that is anything is out of sight, covered up, shielded. All you get to see are some dials and instrument boards and people watching them. Remote control stuff, like Oak Ridge. The guide tells you about the experiments going on and they show you some movies—that's all.

I liked our guide. He looked like Tom Jeremy in *The Space Troopers*. I asked him if he was a spaceman and he looked at me kind of funny and said, no, that he was just a Colonial Services ranger. Then he asked me where I went to school and if I belonged to the Scouts. He said he was scoutmaster of Troop One, Rutherford City, Moonbat Patrol.

I found out there was just the one patrol—not many scouts on the Moon, I suppose.

Dad and Mr. Latham joned us just as we finished the tour while Mr. Perrin—that's our guide—was announcing the trip outside. "The conducted tour of Rutherford," he said, talking as if it were a transcription, "includes a trip by spacesuit out on the surface of the Moon, without extra charge, to see the Devil's Graveyard and the site of the Great Disaster of 1984. The trip is optional. There is nothing particularly dangerous about it and we've never had anyone hurt, but the Commission requires that you sign a separate release for your own safety if you choose to make this trip. The trip takes about one hour. Those preferring to remain behind will find movies and refreshments in the coffee shop."

Dad was rubbing his hands together. "This is for me," he announced. "Mr. Latham, I'm glad we got back in time. I wouldn't have missed this for the world."

"You'll enjoy it," Mr. Latham agreed, "and so will you, Mrs. Logan. I'm tempted to come along myself."

"Why don't you?" Dad asked.

"No, I want to have the papers ready for you and the Director to sign when you get back and before you leave for Luna City."

"Why knock yourself out?" Dad urged him. "If a man's word is no good, his signed contract is no better. You can mail the stuff to me at New York."

Mr. Latham shook his head. "No, really—I've

been out on the surface dozens of times. But I'll come along and help you into your spacesuits."

Mother said, "Oh dear," she didn't think she'd better go; she wasn't sure she could stand the thought of being shut up in a spacesuit and besides glaring sunlight always gave her a headache.

Dad said, "Don't be silly, my dear; it's the chance of a lifetime," and Mr. Latham told her that the filters on the helmets kept the light from being glaring. Mother always objects and then gives in. I suppose women just don't have any force of character. Like the night before—earthnight, I mean, Luna City time—she had bought a fancy moonsuit to wear to dinner in the Earth-View room at the hotel, then she got cold feet. She complained to Dad that she was too plump to dare to dress like that.

Well, she did show an awful lot of skin. Dad said, "Nonsense, my dear. You look ravishing." So she wore it and had a swell time, especially when a pilot tried to pick her up.

It was like that this time. She came along. We went into the outfitting room and I looked around while Mr. Perrin was getting them all herded in and having the releases signed. There was the door to the airlock to the surface at the far end, with a bull's-eye window in it and another one like it in the door beyond. You could peek through and see the surface of the Moon beyond, looking hot and bright and sort of improbable, in spite of the amber glass in the windows. And there was a double row of spacesuits hanging up, looking like empty men. I snooped around until Mr. Perrin got around to our party.

"We can arrange to leave the youngster in the

care of the hostess in the coffee shop," he was telling Mother. He reached down and tousled the runt's hair. The runt tried to bite him and he snatched his hand away in a hurry.

"Thank you, Mr. Perkins," Mother said, "I suppose that's best—though perhaps I had better stay behind with him."

" 'Perrin' is the name," Mr. Perrin said mildly. "It won't be necessary. The hostess will take good care of him."

Why do adults talk in front of kids as if they couldn't understand English? They should have just shoved him into the coffee shop. By now the runt knew he was being railroaded. He looked around belligerently. "I go, too," he said loudly. "You promised me."

"Now Baby Darling," Mother tried to stop him. "Mother Dear didn't tell you—" But she was just whistling to herself; the runt turned on the sound effects.

"You said I could go where Dickie went; you promised me when I was sick. You promised me you promised me—" and on and on, his voice getting higher and louder all the time.

Mr. Perrin looked embarrassed. Mother said, "Richard, you'll just have to deal with your child. After all, you were the one who promised him."

"Me, dear?" Dad looked surprised. "Anyway, I don't see anything so complicated about it. Suppose we did promise him that he could do what Dickie does—we'll simply take him along; that's all."

Mr. Perrin cleared his throat. "I'm afraid not. I can outfit your older son with a woman's suit; he's tall for his age. But we just don't make any provision for small children."

Well, we were all tangled up in a mess in no time at all. The runt can always get Mother to running in circles. Mother has the same effect on Dad. He gets red in the face and starts laying down the law to me. It's sort of a chain reaction, with me on the end and nobody to pass it along to. They came out with a very simple solution—I was to stay behind and take care of Baby Darling brat!

"But, Dad, you said—" I started in.

"Never mind!" he cut in. "I won't have this family disrupted in a public squabble. You heard what your mother said."

I was desperate. "Look, Dad," I said, keeping my voice low, "if I go back to Earth without once having put on a spacesuit and set foot on the surface, you'll just have to find another school to send me to. I won't go back to Lawrenceville; I'd be the joke of the whole place."

"We'll settle that when we get home."

"But, Dad, you promised me specifically—"

"That'll be enough out of you, young man. The matter is closed."

Mr. Latham had been standing near by, taking it in but keeping his mouth shut. At this point he cocked an eyebrow at Dad and said very quietly, "Well, R.J.—I thought your word was your bond?"

I wasn't supposed to hear it and nobody else did—a good thing, too, for it doesn't do to let Dad know that you know that he's wrong; it just makes him worse. I changed the subject in a hurry. "Look, Dad, maybe we all can go out. How about that suit over there?" I pointed at a rack that was inside a railing with a locked gate on it. The rack had a couple of dozen suits on it and at the far end, almost out of sight, was a small suit—the boots on it hardly came down to the waist of the suit next to it.

"Huh?" Dad brightened up. "Why, just the thing! Mr. Perrin! Oh, Mr. Perrin—here a minute! I thought you didn't have any small suits, but here's one that I think will fit."

Dad was fiddling at the latch of the railing gate. Mr. Perrin stopped him. "We can't use that suit, sir."

"Uh? Why not?"

"All the suits inside the railing are private property, not for rent."

"What? Nonsense—Rutherford is a public enterprise. I want that suit for my child."

"Well, you can't have it."

"I'll speak to the Director."

"I'm afraid you'll have to. That suit was specially built for his daughter."

And that's just what they did. Mr. Latham got the Director on the line, Dad talked to him, then the Director talked to Mr. Perrin, then he talked to Dad again. The Director didn't mind lending the suit, not to Dad, anyway, but he wouldn't order Mr. Perrin to take a below-age child outside.

Mr. Perrin was feeling stubborn and I don't blame him, but Dad soothed his feathers down and presently we were all climbing into our suits and getting pressure checks and checking our oxygen supply and switching on our walkie-talkies. Mr. Perrin was calling the roll by radio and reminding us that we were all on the same circuit, so we had better let him do most of the talking and not to make casual remarks or none of us would be able to hear. Then we were in the airlock and he was warning us to stick close together and not try to see how fast we could run or how high we could jump. My heart was knocking around in my chest.

The outer door of the lock opened and we filed out on the face of the Moon. It was just as wonderful as I dreamed it would be, I guess, but I was so excited that I hardly knew it at the time. The glare of the sun was the brightest thing I ever saw and the shadows so inky black you could hardly see into them. You couldn't hear anything but voices over your radio and you could reach down and switch off that.

The pumice was soft and kicked up around our feet like smoke, settling slowly, falling in slow motion. Nothing else moved. It was the *deadest* place you can imagine.

We stayed on a path, keeping close together for company, except twice when I had to take out after the runt when he found out he could jump twenty feet. I wanted to smack him, but did you ever try to smack anybody wearing a spacesuit? It's no use.

Mr. Perrin told us to halt presently and started his talk. "You are now in the Devil's Graveyard. The twin spires behind you are five thousand feet above the floor of the plain and have never been scaled. The spires, or monuments, have been named for apocryphal or mythological characters because of the fancied resemblance of this fantastic scene to a giant cemetery. Beelzebub, Thor, Siva, Cain, Set—" He pointed around us. "Lunologists are not agreed as to the origin of the strange shapes. Some claim to see indications of the action of air and water as well as volcanic action. If so, these spires must have been standing for an unthinkably long period, for today, as you see, the Moon—" It was the same sort of stuff you can read any month in *Spaceways Magazine*, only we were seeing it and that makes a difference, let me tell you.

The spires reminded me a bit of the rocks below the lodge in the Garden of the Gods in Colorado Springs when we went there last summer, only these spires were lots bigger and, instead of blue sky, there was just blackness and hard, sharp stars overhead. Spooky.

Another ranger had come with us, with a camera. Mr. Perrin tried to say something else, but the runt had started yapping away and I had to switch off his radio before anybody could hear anything. I kept it switched off until Mr. Perrin finished talking.

He wanted us to line up for a picture with the spires and the black sky behind us for a background. "Push your faces forward in your helmets so that your features will show. Everybody look pretty. There!" he added as the other guy snapped the shot. "Prints will be ready when you return, at ten dollars a copy."

I thought it over. I certainly needed one for my room at school and I wanted one to give to— anyhow, I needed another one. I had eighteen bucks left from my birthday money; I could sweet-talk Mother for the balance. So I ordered two of them.

We climbed a long rise and suddenly we were staring out across the crater, the disaster crater, all that was left of the first laboratory. It stretched away from us, twenty miles across, with the floor covered with shiny, bubbly green glass instead of pumice. There was a monument. I read it:

HERE ABOUT YOU
ARE THE MORTAL REMAINS
OF
Kurt Schaeffer
Maurice Feinstein
Thomas Dooley
Hazel Hayakawa
G. Washington Slappey
Sam Houston Adams
WHO DIED FOR THE TRUTH
THAT MAKES MEN FREE
On the Eleventh Day of August 1984

I felt sort of funny and backed away and went to listen to Mr. Perrin. Dad and some of the other men were asking him questions. "They don't know exactly," he was saying. "Nothing was left. Now we telemeter all the data back to Luna City, as it comes off the instruments, but that was before the line-of-sight relays were set up."

"What would have happened," some man asked, "if this blast had gone off on Earth?"

"I'd hate to try to tell you—but that's why they put the lab here, back of the Moon." He glanced at his watch. "Time to leave, everybody." They were milling around, heading back down toward the path, when Mother screamed.

"Baby! Where's Baby Darling?"

I was startled but I wasn't scared, not yet. The runt is always running around, first here and then there, but he doesn't go far away, because he always wants to have somebody to yap to.

My father had one arm around Mother; he signalled to me with the other. "Dick," he snapped, his voice sharp in my earphones, "what have you done with your brother?"

"Me?" I said. "Don't look at me—the last I saw Mother had him by the hand, walking up the hill here."

"Don't stall around, Dick. Mother sat down to rest when we got here and sent him to you."

"Well, if she did, he never showed up." At that, Mother started to scream in earnest. Everybody had been listening, of course—they had to; there was just the one radio circuit. Mr. Perrin stepped up and switched off Mother's talkie, making a sudden silence.

"Take care of your wife, Mr. Logan," he ordered, then added, "When did you see your child last?"

Dad couldn't help him any; when they tried switching Mother back into the hook-up, they switched her right off again. She couldn't help and she deafened us. Mr. Perrin addressed the rest of us. "Has anyone seen the small child we had with us? Don't answer unless you have something to contribute. Did anyone see him wander away?"

Nobody had. I figured he probably ducked out when everybody was looking at the crater and had their backs to him. I told Mr. Perrin so. "Seems likely," he agreed. "Attention, everybody! I'm going to search for the child. Stay right where you are. Don't move away from this spot. I won't be gone more than ten minutes."

"Why don't we all go?" somebody wanted to know.

"Because," said Mr. Perrin, "right now I've only got one lost. I don't want to make it a dozen." Then he left, taking big easy lopes that covered fifty feet at a step.

Dad started to take out after him, then thought better of it, for Mother suddenly keeled over, collapsing at the knees and floating gently to the ground. Everybody started talking at once. Some idiot wanted to take her helmet off, but Dad isn't crazy. I switched off my radio so I could hear myself think and started looking around, not leaving the crowd but standing up on the lip of the crater and trying to see as much as I could.

I was looking back the way we had come; there was no sense in looking at the crater—if he had been in there he would have shown up like a fly on a plate.

Outside the crater was different; you could have hidden a regiment within a block of us, rocks standing up every which way, boulders big as houses with blow holes all through them, spires, gulleys—it was a mess. I could see Mr. Perrin every now and then, casting around like a dog after a rabbit, and making plenty of time. He was practically flying. When he came to a big boulder he would jump right over it, leveling off face down at the top of his jump, so he could see better.

Then he was heading back toward us and I switched my radio back on. There was still a lot of talk. Somebody was saying, "We've got to find him before sundown," and somebody else answered, "Don't be silly; the sun won't be down for a week. It's his air supply, I tell you. These suits are only good for four hours." The first voice said, "Oh!"

then added softly, "like a fish out of water—" It was then I got scared.

A woman's voice, sounding kind of choked, said, "The poor, poor darling! We've got to find him before he suffocates," and my father's voice cut in sharply, "Shut up talking that way!" I could hear somebody sobbing. It might have been Mother.

Mr. Perrin was almost up to us and he cut in, "Silence, everybody! I've got to call the base," and he added urgently,

"Perrin, calling airlock control; Perrin, calling airlock control!"

A woman's voice answered, "Come in, Perrin." He told her what was wrong and added, "Send out Smythe to take this party back in; I'm staying. I want every ranger who's around and get me volunteers from among any of the experienced Moon hands. Send out a radio direction-finder by the first ones to leave."

We didn't wait long, for they came swarming toward us like grasshoppers. They must have been running forty or fifty miles an hour. It would have been something to see, if I hadn't been so sick at my stomach.

Dad put up an argument about going back, but Mr. Perrin shut him up. "If you hadn't been so confounded set on having your own way, we wouldn't be in a mess. If you had kept track of your kid, he wouldn't be lost. I've got kids of my own; I don't let 'em go out on the face of the Moon when they're too young to take care of themselves. You go on back—I can't be burdened by taking care of you, too."

I think Dad might even have gotten in a fight

with him if Mother hadn't gotten faint again. We went on back with the party.

The next couple of hours were pretty awful. They let us sit just outside the control room where we could hear Mr. Perrin directing the search, over the loudspeaker. I thought at first that they would snag the runt as soon as they started using the radio direction-finder—pick up his power hum, maybe, even if he didn't say anything—but no such luck; they didn't get anything with it. And the searchers didn't find anything either.

A thing that made it worse was that Mother and Dad didn't even try to blame me. Mother was crying quietly and Dad was consoling her, when he looked over at me with an odd expression. I guess he didn't really see me at all, but I thought he was thinking that if I hadn't insisted on going out on the surface this wouldn't have happened. I said, "Don't go looking at me, Dad. Nobody told me to keep an eye on him. I thought he was with Mother."

Dad just shook his head without answering. He was looking tired and sort of shrunk up. But Mother, instead of laying in to me and yelling, stopped her crying and managed to smile. "Come here, Dickie," she said, and put her other arm around me. "Nobody blames you, Dickie. Whatever happens, you weren't at fault. Remember that, Dickie."

So I let her kiss me and then sat with them for a while, but I felt worse than before. I kept thinking about the runt, somewhere out there, and his oxygen running out. Maybe it wasn't my fault, but I could have prevented it and I knew it. I shouldn't have depended on Mother to look out for him;

she's no good at that sort of thing. She's the kind of person that would mislay her head if it wasn't knotted on tight—the ornamental sort. Mother's *good*, you understand, but she's not practical.

She would take it pretty hard if the runt didn't come back. And so would Dad—and so would I. The runt is an awful nuisance, but it was going to seem strange not to have him around underfoot. I got to thinking about that remark, "Like a fish out of water." I accidentally busted an aquarium once; I remember yet how they looked. Not pretty. If the runt was going to die like that—

I shut myself up and decided I just had to figure out some way to help find him.

After a while I had myself convinced that I *could* find him if they would just let me help look. But they wouldn't of course.

Dr. Evans the Director showed up again—he'd met us when we first came in—and asked if there was anything he could do for us and how was Mrs. Logan feeling? "You know I wouldn't have had this happen for the world," he added. "We're doing all we can. I'm having some ore-detectors shot over from Luna City. We might be able to spot the child by the metal in his suit."

Mother asked how about bloodhounds and Dr. Evans didn't even laugh at her. Dad suggested helicopters, then corrected himself and made it rockets. Dr.Evans pointed out that it was impossible to examine the ground closely from a rocket.

I got him aside presently and braced him to let me join the hunt. He was polite but unimpressed, so I insisted. "What makes you think you can find him?" he asked me. "We've got the most experienced Moon men available out there now. I'm afraid, son, that you would get yourself lost or hurt if you tried to keep up with them. In this country, if you once lose sight of landmarks, you can get hopelessly lost."

"But look, Doctor," I told him, "I know the runt—I mean my kid brother, better than anyone else in the world. I won't get lost—I mean I will get lost but just the way he did. You can send somebody to follow me."

He thought about it. "It's worth trying," he said suddenly. "I'll go with you. Let's suit up."

We made a fast trip out, taking thirty-foot strides—the best I could manage even with Dr. Evans hanging on to my belt to keep me from stumbling. Mr. Perrin was expecting us. He seemed dubious about my scheme. "Maybe the old 'lost mule' dodge will work," he admitted, "but I'll keep the regular search going just the same. Here, Shorty, take this flashlight. You'll need it in the shadows."

I stood on the edge of the crater and tried to imagine I was the runt, feeling bored and maybe a little bit griped at the lack of attention. What would I do next?

I went skipping down the slope, not going anywhere in particular, the way the runt would have done. Then I stopped and looked back, to see if Mother and Daddy and Dickie had noticed me. I was being followed all right; Dr. Evans and Mr. Perrin were close behind me. I pretended that no one was looking and went on. I was pretty close to the first rock outcroppings by now and I ducked behind the first one I came to. It wasn't high enough to hide me but it would have covered the runt. It felt like what he would do; he loved to play hide-and-go-seek—it made him the center of attention.

I thought about it. When the runt played that game, his notion of hiding was always to crawl *under* something, a bed, or a sofa, or an automobile, or even under the sink. I looked around. There were a lot of good places; the rocks were filled with blowholes and overhangs. I started working them over. It seemed hopeless; there must have been a hundred such places right around close.

Mr. Perrin came up to me as I was crawling out of the fourth tight spot. "The men have shined flashlights around in every one of these places," he told me. "I don't think it's much use, Shorty."

"Okay," I said, but I kept at it. I knew I could get at spots a grown man couldn't reach; I just hoped the runt hadn't picked a spot I couldn't reach.

It went on and on and I was getting cold and stiff and terribly tired. The direct sunlight is hot on the Moon, but the second you get in the shade, it's cold. Down inside those rocks it never got warm at all. The suits they gave us tourists are well enough insulated, but the extra insulation is in the gloves and the boots and the seats of the pants—and I had been spending most of my time down on my stomach, wiggling into tight places.

I was so numb I could hardly move and my whole front felt icy. Besides, it gave me one more thing to worry about—how about the runt? Was he cold, too?

If it hadn't been for thinking how those fish looked and how, maybe, the runt would be frozen stiff before I could get to him, I would have quit. I was about beat. Besides, it's rather scarey down inside those holes—you don't know what you'll come to next.

Dr. Evans took me by the arm as I came out of one of them, and touched his helmet to mine, so that I got his voice directly. "Might as well give up, son. You're knocking yourself out and you haven't covered an acre." I pulled away from him.

The next place was a little overhang, not a foot off the ground. I flashed a light into it. It was empty and didn't seem to go anywhere. Then I saw there was a turn in it. I got down flat and wiggled in. The turn opened out a little and dropped off. I didn't think it was worthwhile to go any deeper as the runt wouldn't have crawled very far in the dark, but I scrunched ahead a little farther and flashed the light down.

I saw a boot sticking out.

That's about all there is to it. I nearly bashed in my helmet getting out of there, but I was dragging the runt after me. He was limp as a cat and his face was funny. Mr. Perrin and Dr. Evans were all over me as I came out, pounding me on the back and shouting. "Is he *dead*, Mr. Perrin?" I asked, when I could get my breath. "He looks awful bad."

Mr. Perrin looked him over. "No . . . I can see a pulse in his throat. Shock and exposure, but this suit was specially built—we'll get him back fast." He picked the runt up in his arms and I took out after him.

Ten minutes later the runt was wrapped in blankets and drinking hot cocoa. I had some, too. Everybody was talking at once and Mother was crying again, but she looked normal and Dad had filled out.

He tried to write out a check for Mr. Perrin, but he brushed it off. "I don't need any reward; your boy found him. You can do me just one favor—"

"Yes?" Dad was all honey.

"Stay off the Moon. You don't belong here; you're not the pioneer type."

Dad took it. "I've already promised my wife that," he said without batting an eye. "You needn't worry."

I followed Mr. Perrin as he left and said to him privately, "Mr. Perrin—I just wanted to tell you that I'll be back, if you don't mind."

He shook hands with me and said, "I know you will, Shorty."

"It's Great to Be Back!"

"HURRY up, Allan!" Home—back to Earth again! Her heart was pounding.

"Just a second." She fidgeted while her husband checked over a bare apartment. Earth-Moon freight rates made it silly to ship their belongings; except for the bag he carried, they had converted everything to cash. Satisfied, he joined her at the lift; they went on up to the administration level and there to a door marked: LUNA CITY COMMUNITY ASSOCIATION—*Anna Stone, Service Manager*.

Miss Stone accepted their apartment keys grimly. "Mr. and Mrs. MacRae. So you're actually leaving us?"

Josephine bristled. "Think we'd change our minds?"

The manager shrugged. "No. I knew nearly three years ago that you would go back—from your complaints."

"From my comp—Miss Stone, I've been as patient about the incredible inconveniences of this, this pressurized rabbit warren as anyone. I don't blame you personally, but—"

103

"Take it easy, Jo!" her husband cautioned her.

Josephine flushed. "Sorry, Miss Stone."

"Never mind. We just see things differently. I was here when Luna City was three air-sealed Quonset huts connected by tunnels you crawled through, on your knees." She stuck out a square hand. "I hope you enjoy being groundhogs again, I honestly do. Hot jets, good luck, and a safe landing."

Back in the lift, Josephine sputtered. " 'Groundhogs' indeed! Just because we prefer our native planet, where a person can draw a breath of fresh air—"

"You use the term," Allan pointed out.

"But I use it about people who've never been off Terra."

"We've both said more than once that we wished we had had sense enough never to have left Earth. We're groundhogs at heart, Jo."

"Yes, but—Oh, Allan, you're being obnoxious. This is the happiest day of my life. Aren't you glad to be going home? Aren't you?"

"Of course I am. It'll be great to be back. Horseback riding. Skiing."

"And opera. Real, live grand opera. Allan, we've simply got to have a week or two in Manhattan before we go to the country."

"I thought you wanted to feel rain on your face."

"I want that, too. I want it all at once and I can't wait. Oh, darling, it's like getting out of jail." She clung to him.

He unwound her as the lift stopped. "Don't blubber."

"Allan, you're a beast," she said dreamily. "I'm so happy."

They stopped again, in bankers' row. The clerk in the National City Bank office had their transfer of account ready. "Going home, eh? Just sign there, and your print. I envy you. Hunting, fishing."

"Surf bathing is more my style. And sailing."

"I," said Jo, "simply want to see green trees and blue sky."

The clerk nodded. "I know what you mean. It's long ago and far away. Well, have fun. Are you taking three months or six?"

"We're not coming back," Allan stated flatly. "Three years of living like a fish in an aquarium is enough."

"So?" The clerk shoved the papers toward him and added without expression, "Well—hot jets."

"Thanks." They went on up to the subsurface level and took the crosstown slidewalk out to the rocket port. The slidewalk tunnel broke the surface at one point, becoming a pressurized shed; a view window on the west looked out on the surface of the Moon—and, beyond the hills, the Earth.

The sight of it, great and green and bountiful, against the black lunar sky and harsh, unwinking stars, brought quick tears to Jo's eyes. Home— that lovely planet was hers! Allan looked at it more casually, noting the Greenwich. The sunrise line had just touched South America—must be about eight-twenty; better hurry.

They stepped off the slidewalk into the arms of some of their friends, waiting to see them off. "Hey—where have you lugs been? The *Gremlin* blasts off in seven minutes."

"But we aren't going in it," MacRae answered. "No, siree."

"What? Not going? Did you change your minds?"

Josephine laughed. "Pay no attention to him, Jack. We're going in the express instead; we swapped reservations. So we've got twenty minutes yet."

"Well! A couple of rich tourists, eh?"

"Oh, the extra fare isn't so much and I didn't want to make two changes and spend a week in space when we could be home in two days." She rubbed her bare middle significantly.

"She can't take free flight, Jack," her husband explained.

"Well, neither can I—I was sick the whole trip out. Still, I don't think you'll be sick, Jo; you're used to Moon weight now."

"Maybe," she agreed, "but there is a lot of difference between one-sixth gravity and no gravity."

Jack Crail's wife cut in. "Josephine MacRae, are you going to risk your life in an atomic-powered ship?"

"Why not, darling? You work in an atomics laboratory."

"Hummph! In the laboratory we take precautions. The Commerce Commission should never have licensed the expresses. I may be old-fashioned, but I'll go back the way I came, via Terminal and Supra-New York, in good old reliable fuel-rockets."

"Don't try to scare her, Emma," Crail objected. "They've worked the bugs out of those ships."

"Not to my satisfaction. I—"

"Never mind," Allan interrupted her. "The matter is settled, and we've still got to get over to the express launching site. Good-by, everybody! Thanks for the send-off. It's been grand knowing you. If you come back to God's country, look us up."

"Good-by, kids!" "Good-by, Jo—good-by, Allan," "Give my regards to Broadway!" "So long—be sure to write." "Good-by." "Aloha—hot jets!" They showed their tickets, entered the air lock, and climbed into the pressurized shuttle between Leyport proper and the express launching site. "Hang on, folks," the shuttle operator called back over his shoulder; Jo and Allan hurriedly settled into the cushions. The lock opened; the tunnel ahead was airless. Five minutes later they were climbing out twenty miles away, beyond the hills that shielded the lid of Luna City from the radioactive splash of the express ships.

In the *Sparrowhawk* they shared a compartment with a missionary family. The Reverend Doctor Simmons felt obliged to explain why he was traveling in luxury. "It's for the child," he told them, as his wife strapped the baby girl into a small acceleration couch rigged stretcher-fashion between her parents' couches. "Since she's never been in space, we daren't take a chance of her being sick for days on end." They all strapped down at the warning siren. Jo felt her heart begin to pound. At last . . . at long last!

The jets took hold, mashing them into the cushions. Jo had not known she could feel so heavy. This was worse, much worse, than the trip out. The baby cried as long as acceleration lasted, in wordless terror and discomfort.

After an interminable time they were suddenly weightless, as the ship went into free flight. When the terrible binding weight was free of her chest, Jo's heart felt as light as her body. Allan threw off his upper strap and sat up. "How do you feel, kid?"

"Oh, I feel fine!" Jo unstrapped and faced him. Then she hiccoughed. "That is, I think I do."

Five minutes later she was not in doubt; she merely wished to die. Allan swam out of the compartment and located the ship's surgeon, who gave her an injection. Allan waited until she had succumbed to the drug, then left for the lounge to try his own cure for spacesickness—Mothersill's Seasick Remedy washed down with champagne. Presently he had to admit that these two sovereign remedies did not work for him—or perhaps he should not have mixed them.

Little Gloria Simmons was not spacesick. She thought being weightless was fun, and went bouncing off floorplate, overhead, and bulkhead like a dimpled balloon. Jo feebly considered strangling the child, if she floated within reach—but it was too much effort.

Deceleration, logy as it made them feel, was welcome relief after nausea—except to little Gloria. She cried again, in fear and hurt, while her mother tried to explain. Her father prayed.

After a long, long time came a slight jar and the sound of the siren. Jo managed to raise her head. "What's the matter? Is there an accident?"

"I don't think so. I think we've landed."

"We can't have! We're still braking—I'm heavy as lead."

Allan grinned feebly. "So am I. Earth gravity—remember?"

The baby continued to cry.

They said good-by to the missionary family, as Mrs. Simmons decided to wait for a stewardess from the skyport. The MacRaes staggered out of the ship, supporting each other. "It can't be just the gravity," Jo protested, her feet caught in invisible quicksand. "I've taken Earth-normal acceleration in the centrifuge at the 'Y' back home—I mean back in Luna City. We're weak from space-sickness."

Allan steadied himself. "That's it. We haven't eaten anything for two days."

"Allan—didn't you eat anything either?"

"No. Not *permanently*, so to speak. Are you hungry?"

"Starving."

"How about dinner at Kean's Chophouse?"

"Wonderful. Oh, Allan, we're back!" Her tears started again.

They glimpsed the Simmons' once more, after chuting down the Hudson Valley and into Grand Central Station. While they were waiting at the tube dock for their bag, Jo saw the Reverend Doctor climb heavily out of the next tube capsule, carrying his daughter and followed by his wife. He set the child down carefully. Gloria stood for a moment, trembling on her pudgy legs, then collapsed to the dock. She lay there, crying thinly.

A spaceman—pilot, by his uniform—stopped and looked pityingly at the child. "Born in the Moon?" he asked.

"Why yes, she was, sir." Simmons' courtesy transcended his troubles.

"Pick her up and carry her. She'll have to learn to walk all over again." The spaceman shook his head sadly and glided away. Simmons looked still more troubled, then sat down on the dock beside his child, careless of the dirt.

Jo felt too weak to help. She looked around for Allan, but he was busy; their bag had arrived. It was placed at his feet and he started to pick it up, and then felt suddenly silly. It seemed nailed to the dock. He knew what was in it, rolls of micro-film and colorfilm, a few souvenirs, toilet articles, various irreplaceables—fifty pounds of mass. It *couldn't* weigh what it seemed to.

But it did. He had forgotten what fifty pounds weigh on Earth.

"Porter, mister?" The speaker was grey-haired and thin, but he scooped up the bag quite casually. Allan called out, "Come along, Jo," and fol-lowed him, feeling foolish. The porter slowed to match Allan's labored steps.

"Just down from the Moon?" he asked.

"Why, yes."

"Got a reservation?"

"No."

"You stick with me. I've got a friend on the desk at the Commodore." He led them to the Con-course slidewalk and thence to the hotel.

They were too weary to dine out; Allan had dinner sent to their room. Afterward, Jo fell asleep in a hot tub and he had trouble getting her out—she liked the support the water gave her. But he persuaded her that a rubber-foam mattress was nearly as good. They got to sleep very early.

She woke up, struggling, about four in the morn-ing. "Allan. Allan!"

"Huh? What's the matter?" His hand fumbled at the light switch.

"Uh . . . nothing I guess. I dreamed I was back in the ship. The jets had run away with her. Allan, what makes it so stuffy in here? I've got a splitting headache."

"Huh? It can't be stuffy. This joint is air-conditioned." He sniffed the air. "I've got a headache, too," he admitted.

"Well, do something. Open a window."

He stumbled out of bed, shivered when the outer air hit him, and hurried back under the covers. He was wondering whether he could get to sleep with the roar of the city pouring in through the window when his wife spoke again. "Allan?"

"Yes. What is it?"

"Honey, I'm *cold*. May I crawl in with you?"

"Sure."

The sunlight streamed in the window, warm and mellow. When it touched his eyes, he woke and found his wife awake beside him. She sighed and snuggled. "Oh, darling, look! Blue sky—we're *home*. I'd forgotten how lovely it is."

"It's great to be back, all right. How do you feel?"

"Much better. How are you?"

"Okay, I guess." He pushed off the covers.

Jo squealed and jerked them back. "Don't do that!"

"Huh?"

"Mamma's great big boy is going to climb out and close that window while mamma stays here under the covers."

"Well—all right." He could walk more easily than the night before—but it was good to get back into bed. Once there, he faced the telephone and shouted at it, "Service!"

"Order, please," it answered in a sweet contralto.

"Orange juice and coffee for two—extra coffee—six eggs, scrambled medium, and whole-wheat toast. And send up a *Times*, and the *Saturday Evening Post*."

"Ten minutes."

"Thank you." The delivery cupboard buzzed while he was shaving. He answered it and served Jo breakfast in bed. Breakfast over, he laid down his newspaper and said, "Can you pull your nose out of that magazine?"

"Glad to. The darn thing is too big and heavy to hold."

"Why don't you have the stat edition mailed to you from Luna City? Wouldn't cost more than eight or nine times as much."

"Don't be silly. What's on your mind?"

"How about climbing out of that frowsty little nest and going with me to shop for clothes?"

"Unh-uh. No, I am not going outdoors in a moonsuit."

"'Fraid of being stared at? Getting prudish in your old age?"

"No, me lord, I simply refuse to expose myself to the outer air in six ounces of nylon and a pair of sandals. I want some warm clothes first." She squirmed further down under the covers.

"The Perfect Pioneer Woman. Going to have fitters sent up?"

"We can't afford that. Look—you're going anyway. Buy me just any old rag so long as it's warm."

MacRae looked stubborn. "I've tried shopping for you before."

"Just this once—please. Run over to Saks and pick out a street dress in a blue wool jersey, size ten. And a pair of nylons."

"Well—all right."

"That's a lamb. I won't be loafing. I've a list as long as your arm of people I've promised to call up, look up, have lunch with."

He attended to his own shopping first; his sensible shorts and singlet seemed as warm as a straw hat in a snow storm. It was not really cold and was quite balmy in the sun, but it seemed cold to a man used to a never-failing seventy-two degrees. He tried to stay underground, or stuck to the roofed-over section of Fifth Avenue.

He suspected that the salesman had outfitted him in clothes that made him look like a yokel. But they were warm. They were also heavy; they added to the pain across his chest and made him walk even more unsteadily. He wondered how long it would be before he got his ground-legs.

A motherly saleswoman took care of Jo's order and sold him a warm cape for her as well. He headed back, stumbling under his packages, and trying futilely to flag a ground-taxi. Everyone seemed in such a hurry! Once he was nearly knocked down by a teen-aged boy who said, "Watch it, Gramps!" and rushed off, before he could answer.

He got back, aching all over and thinking about a hot bath. He did not get it; Jo had a visitor. "Mrs. Appleby, my husband— Allan, this is Emma Crail's mother."

"Oh, how do you do, Doctor—or should it be 'Professor'?"

"Mister—"

"—when I heard you were in town I just couldn't wait to hear all about my poor darling. How is she? Is she thin? Does she look well? These modern girls—I've told her time and again that she must get out of doors—I walk in the Park every day—and look at me. She sent me a picture—I have it here somewhere; at least I think I have— and she doesn't look a bit well, undernourished. Those synthetic foods—"

"She doesn't eat synthetic foods, Mrs. Appleby."

"—must be quite impossible, I'm sure, not to mention the taste. What were you saying?"

"Your daughter doesn't live on synthetic foods," Allan repeated. "Fresh fruits and vegetables are one thing we have almost too much of in Luna City. The air-conditioning plant, you know."

"That's just what I was saying. I confess I don't see just how you get food out of air-conditioning machinery on the Moon—"

"*In* the Moon, Mrs. Appleby."

"—but it can't be healthy. Our air-conditioner at home is always breaking down and making the most horrible smells—simply unbearable, my dears—you'd think they could build a simple little thing like an air-conditioner so that—though of course if you expect them to manufacture synthetic foods as well—"

"Mrs. Appleby—"

"Yes, Doctor? What were you saying? Don't let me—"

"Mrs. Appleby," MacRae said desperately, "the air-conditioning plant in Luna City is a hydroponic farm, tanks of growing plants, green things. The plants take the carbon dioxide out of the air and put oxygen back in."

"But— Are you quite sure, Doctor? I'm sure Emma said—"

"Quite sure."

"Well . . . I don't pretend to understand these

things, I'm the artistic type. Poor Herbert often said—Herbert was Emma's father; simply wrapped up in his engineering though I always saw to it that he heard good music and saw the reviews of the best books. Emma takes after her father, I'm afraid—I do wish she would give up that silly work she is in. Hardly the sort of work for a woman, do you think, Mrs. MacRae? All those atoms and neuters and things floating around in the air. I read all about it in the *Science Made Simple* column in the—"

"She's quite good at it and she seems to like it."

"Well, yes, I suppose. That's the important thing, to be happy at what you are doing no matter how silly it is. But I worry about the child—buried away from civilization, no one of her own sort to talk to, no theaters, no cultural life, no society—"

"Luna City has stereo transcriptions of every successful Broadway play." Jo's voice had a slight edge.

"Oh! Really? But it's not just going to the theater, my dear; it's the society of gentlefolk. Now when I was a girl, my parents—"

Allan butted in, loudly. "One o'clock. Have you had lunch, my dear?"

Mrs. Appleby sat up with a jerk. "Oh, heavenly days! I simply must fly. My dress designer—such a tyrant, but a genius; I must give you her address. It's been charming, my dears, and I can't thank you too much for telling me all about my poor darling. I do wish she would be sensible like you two; she knows I'm always ready to make a home for her—and her husband, for that matter. Now do come and see me, often. I love to talk to people who've been on the Moon—"

"In the Moon."

"It makes me feel closer to my darling. Good-by, then."

With the door locked behind her, Jo said, "Allan, I need a drink."

"I'll join you."

Jo cut her shopping short; it was too tiring. By four o'clock they were driving in Central Park, enjoying fall scenery to the lazy clop-clop of horse's hoofs. The helicopters, the pigeons, the streak in the sky where the Antipodes rocket had passed, made a scene idyllic in beauty and serenity. Jo swallowed a lump in her throat and whispered, "Allan, isn't it beautiful?"

"Sure is. It's great to be back. Say, did you notice they've torn up 42nd Street again?"

Back in their room, Jo collapsed on her bed, while Allan took off his shoes. He sat, rubbing his feet, and remarked, "I'm going barefooted all evening. Golly, how my feet hurt!"

"So do mine. But we're going to your father's, my sweet."

"Huh? Oh, damn, I forgot. Jo, whatever possessed you? Call him up and postpone it. We're still half dead from the trip."

"But, Allan, he's invited a lot of your friends."

"Balls of fire and cold mush! I haven't any real friends in New York. Make it next week."

" 'Next week' . . . h'm'm . . . look, Allan, let's go out to the country right away." Jo's parents had left her a tiny place in Connecticut, a worn-out farm.

"I thought you wanted a couple of weeks of plays and music first. Why the sudden change?"

"I'll show you." She went to the window, open since noon. "Look at that window sill." She drew their initials in the grime. "Allan, this city is *filthy*."

"You can't expect ten million people not to kick up dust."

"But we're breathing that stuff into our lungs. What's happened to the smog-control laws?"

"That's not smog; that's normal city dirt."

"Luna City was never like this. I could wear a white outfit there till I got tired of it. One wouldn't last a day here."

"Manhattan doesn't have a roof—and precipitrons in every air duct."

"Well, it should have. I either freeze or suffocate."

"I thought you were anxious to feel rain on your face?"

"Don't be tiresome. I want it out in the clean, green country."

"Okay. I want to start my book anyhow. I'll call your real estate agent."

"I called him this morning. We can move in anytime; he started fixing up the place when he got my letter."

It was a stand-up supper at his father's home, though Jo sat down at once and let food be fetched. Allan wanted to sit down, but his status as guest of honor forced him to stay on his aching feet. His father buttonholed him at the buffet. "Here, son, try this goose liver. It ought to go well after a diet of green cheese."

Allan agreed that it was good.

"See here, son, you really ought to tell these folks about your trip."

"No speeches, Dad. Let 'em read the *National Geographic*."

"Nonsense!" He turned around. "Quiet, everybody! Allan is going to tell us how the Lunatics live."

Allan bit his lip. To be sure, the citizens of Luna City used the term to each other, but it did not sound the same here. "Well, really, I haven't anything to say. Go on and eat."

"You talk and we'll eat." "Tell us about Looney City." "Did you see the Man-in-the-Moon?" "Go on, Allan, what's it like to live on the Moon?"

"Not 'on the Moon'—*in* the Moon."

"What's the difference?"

"Why, none, I guess." He hesitated; there was really no way to explain why the Moon colonists emphasized that they lived under the surface of the satellite planet—but it irritated him the way "Frisco" irritates a San Franciscan. " 'In the Moon' is the way we say it. We don't spend much time on the surface, except for the staff at Richardson Observatory, and the prospectors, and so forth. The living quarters are underground, naturally."

"Why 'naturally'? Afraid of meteors?"

"No more than you are afraid of lightning. We go underground for insulation against heat and cold and as support for pressure sealing. Both are cheaper and easier underground. The soil is easy to work and the interstices act like vacuum in a thermos bottle. It is vacuum."

"But Mr. MacRae," a serious-looking lady inquired, "doesn't it hurt your ears to live under pressure?"

Allan fanned the air. "It's the same pressure here—fifteen pounds."

She looked puzzled, then said, "Yes, I suppose so, but it is a little hard to imagine. I think it would terrify me to be sealed up in a cave. Suppose you had a blow-out?"

"Holding fifteen pounds pressure is no problem; engineers work in thousands of pounds per square inch. Anyhow, Luna City is compartmented like a ship. It's safe enough. The Dutch live behind dikes; down in Mississippi they have levees. Subways, ocean liners, aircraft—they're all artificial ways of living. Luna City seems strange just because it's far away."

She shivered. "It scares me."

A pretentious little man pushed his way forward. "Mr. MacRae—granted that it is nice for science and all that, why should taxpayers' money be wasted on a colony on the Moon?"

"You seem to have answered yourself," Allan told him slowly.

"Then how do you justify it? Tell me that, sir."

"It isn't necessary to justify it; the Lunar corporations are all paying propositions. Artemis Mines, Spaceways, Spaceways Provisioning Corporation, Diana Recreations, Electronics Research Company, Lunar biological Labs, not to mention all of Rutherford—look 'em up. I'll admit the Cosmic Research Project nicks the taxpayer a little, since it's a joint enterprise of the Harriman Foundation and the government."

"Then you admit it. It's the principle of the thing."

Allan's feet were hurting him very badly indeed. "What principle? Historically, research has always paid off." He turned his back and looked for some more goose liver.

A man touched him on the arm; Allan recognized an old schoolmate. "Allan, old boy, congratulations on the way you ticked off old Beetle. He's been needing it—I think he's some sort of a radical."

Allan grinned. "I shouldn't have lost my temper."

"A good job you did. Say, Allan, I'm going to take a couple of out-of-town buyers around to the hot spots tomorrow night. Come along."

"Thanks a lot, but we're going out in the country."

"Oh, you can't afford to miss this party. After all, you've been buried on the Moon; you owe yourself some relaxation after that deadly monotony."

Allan felt his cheeks getting warm. "Thanks just the same, but—ever seen the Earth View Room in Hotel Moon Haven?"

"No. Plan to take the trip when I've made my pile, of course."

"Well, there's a night club for you. Ever see a dancer leap thirty feet into the air and do slow rolls on the way down? Ever try a lunacy cocktail? Ever see a juggler work in low gravity?" Jo caught his eye across the room. "Er . . . excuse me, old man. My wife wants me." He turned away, then flung back over his shoulder, "Moon Haven itself isn't just a spaceman's dive, by the way—it's recommended by the Duncan Hines Association."

Jo was very pale. "Darling, you've got to get me out of here. I'm suffocating. I'm really ill."

"Suits." They made their excuses.

Jo woke up with a stuffy cold, so they took a cab directly to her country place. There were low-lying clouds under them, but the weather was fine above. The sunshine and the drowsy beat of the rotors regained for them the joy of homecoming.

Allan broke the lazy reverie. "Here's a funny thing. Jo. You couldn't hire me to go back to the Moon—but last night I found myself defending the Loonies every time I opened my mouth."

She nodded. "I know. Honest to Heaven, Allan, some people act as if the Earth were flat. Some of them don't really believe in anything, and some of them are so matter-of-fact that you know they don't really understand—and I don't know which sort annoys me the more."

It was foggy when they landed, but the house was clean, the agent had laid a fire and had stocked the refrigerator. They were sipping hot punch and baking the weariness out of their bones within ten minutes after the copter grounded. "This," said Allan, stretching, "is all right. It really is great to be back."

"Uh-huh. All except the highway." A new express-and-freight superhighway now ran not fifty yards from the house. They could hear the big diesels growling as they struck the grade.

"Forget the highway. Turn your back and you stare straight into the woods."

They regained their ground-legs well enough to enjoy short walks in the woods; they were favored with a long, warm Indian summer; the cleaning woman was efficient and taciturn. Allan worked on the results of three years research preparatory to starting his book. Jo helped him with the statistical work, got reacquainted with the delights of cooking, dreamed, and rested.

It was the day of the first frost that the toilet stopped up.

The village plumber was persuaded to show up the next day. Meanwhile they resorted to a homely little building, left over from another era and still standing out beyond the wood pile. It was spider-infested and entirely too well ventilated.

The plumber was not encouraging. "New septic tank. New sile pipe. Pay you to get new fixtures at the same time. Fifteen, sixteen hundred dollars. Have to do some calculating."

"That's all right," Allan told him. "Can you start today?"

The man laughed. "I can see plainly, Mister, that you don't know what it is to get materials and labor these days. Next spring—soon as the frost is out of the ground."

"That's impossible, man. Never mind the cost. Get it done."

The native shrugged. "Sorry not to oblige you. Good day."

When he left, Jo exploded. "Allan, he doesn't want to help us."

"Well—maybe. I'll try to get someone from Norwalk, or even from the city. You can't trudge through the snow out to that Iron Maiden all winter."

"I hope not."

"You must not. You've already had one cold." He stared morosely at the fire. "I suppose I brought it on by my misplaced sense of humor."

"How?"

"Well, you know how we've been subjected to steady kidding ever since it got noised around that we were colonials. I haven't minded much, but some of it rankled. You remember I went into the village by myself last Saturday?"

"Yes. What happened?"

"They started in on me in the barbershop. I let it ride at first, then the worm turned. I started talking about the Moon, sheer double-talk—corny old stuff like the vacuum worms and the petrified air. It was some time before they realized I was ribbing them—and when they did, nobody laughed. Our friend the rustic sanitary engineer was one of the group. I'm sorry."

"Don't be." She kissed him. "If I have to tramp through the snow, it will cheer me that you gave them back some of their sass."

The plumber from Norwalk was more helpful, but rain, and then sleet, slowed down the work. They both caught colds. On the ninth miserable day Allan was working at his desk when he heard Jo come in the back door, returning from a shopping trip. He turned back to his work, then presently became aware that she had not come in to say "hello." He went to investigate.

He found her collapsed on a kitchen chair, crying quietly. "Darling," he said urgently, "honey baby, whatever is the matter?"

She looked up. "I didn't bead to led you doe."

"Blow your nose. Then wipe your eyes. What do you mean, 'you didn't mean to let me know.' What happened?"

She let it out, punctuated with her handkerchief. First, the grocer had said he had no cleansing tissues; then, when she pointed to them, had stated that they were "sold." Finally, he had mentioned "bringing outside labor into town and taking the bread out of the mouths of honest folk."

Jo had blown up and had rehashed the incident of Allan and the barbershop wits. The grocer had simply grown more stiff. " 'Lady,' he said to me, 'I don't know whether you and your husband have been to the Moon or not, and I don't care. I don't take much stock in such things. In any case, I don't need your trade.' Oh, Allan, I'm so unhappy."

"Not as unhappy as he's going to be! Where's my hat?"

"Allan! You're not leaving this house. I won't have you fighting."

"I won't have him bullying you."

"He won't again. Oh my dear, I've tried so hard, but I can't stay here any longer. It's not just the villagers; it's the cold and the cockroaches and always having a runny nose. I'm tired out and my feet hurt all the time." She started to cry again.

"There, there! We'll leave, honey. We'll go to Florida. I'll finish my book while you lie in the sun."

"Oh, I don't want to go to Florida. *I want to go home!*"

"Huh? You mean—back to Luna City?"

"Yes. Oh, dearest, I know you don't want to, but I can't stand it any longer. It's not just the dirt and the cold and the comic-strip plumbing—it's not being understood. It wasn't any better in New York. These groundhogs don't know *anything*."

He grinned at her. "Keep sending, kid; I'm on your frequency."

"Allan!"

He nodded. "I found out I was a Loony at heart quite a while ago—but I was afraid to tell you. My feet hurt, too—and I'm damn sick of being treated like a freak. I've tried to be tolerant, but I can't stand groundhogs. I miss the folks in dear old Luna. They're civilized."

She nodded. "I guess it's prejudice, but I feel the same way."

"It's *not* prejudice. Let's be honest. What does it take to get to Luna City?"

"A ticket."

"Smarty pants. I don't mean as a tourist; I mean to get a job there. You know the answer: Intelligence. It costs a lot to send a man to the Moon and more to keep him there. To pay off, he has to be worth a lot. High I.Q., good compatibility index, superior education—everything that makes a person pleasant and easy and interesting to have around. We've been spoiled; the ordinary human cussedness that groundhogs take for granted, we now find intolerable, because Loonies *are* different. The fact that Luna City is the most comfortable environment man ever built for himself is beside the point—it's the people who count. Let's go home."

He went to the telephone—an old-fashioned, speech-only rig—and called the Foundation's New York office. While he was waiting, truncheon-like "receiver" to his ear, she said, "Suppose they won't have us?"

"That's what worries me." They knew that the Lunar companies rarely rehired personnel who had once quit; the physical examination was reputed to be much harder the second time.

"Hello . . . hello. Foundation? May I speak to the recruiting office? . . . hello—I *can't* turn on my view plate; this instrument is a hangover from the dark ages. this is Allan MacRae, physical chemist, contract number 1340729. And my wife, Jose-

phine MacRae, 1340730. We want to sign up again.
I said we wanted to sign up again . . . okay, I'll
wait."

"Pray, darling, pray!"

"I'm praying—How's that! My appointment's still
vacant? Fine, fine! How about my wife?" He listened with a worried look; Jo held her breath.
Then he cupped the speaker. "Hey, Jo—your job's
filled. They want to know if you'll take an interim
job as a junior accountant?"

"Tell 'em 'yes!' "

"That'll be fine. When can we take our exams?
That's fine, thanks. Good-by." He hung up and
turned to his wife. "Physical and psycho as soon as
we like; professional exams waived."

"What are we waiting for?"

"Nothing." He dialed the Norwalk Copter Service. "Can you run us into Manhattan? Well, good
grief, don't you have radar? All right, all right,
g'-by!" He snorted. "Cabs all grounded by the
weather. I'll call New York and try to get a modern cab."

Ninety minutes later they landed on top of Harriman Tower.

The psychologist was very cordial. "Might as
well get this over before you have your chests
thumped. Sit down. Tell me about yourselves."
He drew them out, nodding from time to time. "I
see. Did you ever get the plumbing repaired?"

"Well, it was being fixed."

"I can sympathize with your foot trouble, Mrs.
MacRae; my arches always bother me here. That's
your real reason, isn't it?"

"Oh, no!"

"Now, Mrs. MacRae——"

"Really it's not—truly. I want people to talk to who know what I mean. All that's really wrong with me is that I'm homesick for my own sort. I want to go home—and I've got to have this job to get there. I'll steady down, I know I will."

The doctor looked grave. "How about you, Mr. MacRae?"

"Well—it's about the same story. I've been trying to write a book, but I can't work. I'm homesick. I want to go back."

Feldman suddenly smiled. "It won't be too difficult."

"You mean we're in? If we pass the physical?"

"Never mind the physical—your discharge examinations are recent enough. Of course you'll have to go out to Arizona for reconditioning and quarantine. You're probably wondering why it seems so easy when it is supposed to be so hard. It's really simple: We don't want people lured back by the high pay. We do want people who will be happy and as permanent as possible—in short, we want people who think of Luna City as 'home.' Now that you're 'Moonstruck,' we want you back." He stood up and shoved out his hand.

Back in the Commodore that night, Jo was struck by a thought. "Allan—do you suppose we could get our own apartment back?"

"Why, I don't know. We could send old lady Stone a radio."

"Call her up instead, Allan. We can afford it."

"All right! I will!"

It took about ten minutes to get the circuit

through. Miss Stone's face looked a trifle less grim when she recognized them.

"Miss Stone, we're coming home!"

There was the usual three-second lag, then—"Yes, I know. It came over the tape about twenty minutes ago."

"Oh. Say, Miss Stone, is our old apartment vacant?" They waited.

"I've held it; I knew you'd come back—after a bit. Welcome home, Loonies."

When the screen cleared, Jo said, "What did she mean, Allan?"

"Looks like we're in, kid. Members of the Lodge."

"I guess so—oh, Allan, look!" She had stepped to the window; scudding clouds had just uncovered the Moon. It was three days old and *Mare Fecunditatis*—the roll of hair at the back of the Lady-in-the-Moon's head—was cleared by the Sunrise line. Near the righthand edge of that great, dark "sea" was a tiny spot, visible only to their inner eyes—Luna City.

The crescent hung, serene and silvery, over the tall buildings. "Darling, isn't it beautiful?"

"Certainly is. It'll be great to be back. Don't get your nose all runny."

"—We Also Walk Dogs"

"GENERAL Services—Miss Cormet speaking!" She addressed the view screen with just the right balance between warm hospitable friendliness and impersonal efficiency. The screen flickered momentarily, then built up a stereo-picture of a dowager, fat and fretful, overdressed and underexercised.

"Oh, my dear," said the image, "I'm *so* upset. I wonder if you *can* help me."

"I'm sure we can," Miss Cormet purred as she quickly estimated the cost of the woman's gown and jewels (if real—she made a mental reservation) and decided that here was a client that could be profitable. "Now tell me your trouble. Your name first, if you please." She touched a button on the horseshoe desk which enclosed her, a button marked CREDIT DEPARTMENT.

"But it's all so *involved*," the image insisted. "Peter *would* go and break his hip." Miss Cormet immediately pressed the button marked MEDI-

CAL. "I've *told* him that polo is dangerous. You've no idea, my dear, how a mother suffers. And just at this time, too. It's *so* inconvenient—"

"You wish us to attend him? Where is he now?"

"Attend him? Why, how silly! The Memorial Hospital will do that. We've endowed them enough, I'm sure. It's my dinner party I'm worried about. The Principessa will be so annoyed."

The answer light from the Credit Department was blinking angrily. Miss Cormet headed her off. "Oh, I see. We'll arrange it for you. Now, your name, please, and your address and present location."

"But don't you *know* my name?"

"One might guess," Miss Cormet diplomatically evaded, "but General Services always respects the privacy of its clients."

"Oh, yes, of course. How considerate. I am Mrs. Peter van Hogbein Johnson." Miss Cormet controlled her reaction. No need to consult the Credit Department for this one. But its transparency flashed at once, rating AAA—unlimited. "But I don't see what you can *do*," Mrs. Johnson continued. "I can't be two places at once."

"General Services likes difficult assignments," Miss Cormet assured her. "Now—if you will let me have the details . . ."

She wheedled and nudged the woman into giving a fairly coherent story. Her son, Peter III, a slightly shopworn Peter Pan, whose features were familiar to Grace Cormet through years of stereogravure, dressed in every conceivable costume affected by the richly idle in their pastimes, had been so thoughtless as to pick the afternoon before his mother's most important social function to bung himself up—seriously. Furthermore, he had been so thoughtless as to do so half a continent away from his mater.

Miss Cormet gathered that Mrs. Johnson's technique for keeping her son safely under thumb required that she rush to his bedside at once, and, incidentally, to select his nurses. But her dinner party that evening represented the culmination of months of careful maneuvering. What was she to *do*?

Miss Cormet reflected to herself that the prosperity of General Services and her own very substantial income was based largely on the stupidity, lack of resourcefulness, and laziness of persons like this silly parasite, as she explained that General Services would see that her party was a smooth, social success while arranging for a portable full-length stereo screen to be installed in her drawing room in order that she might greet her guests and make her explanations while hurrying to her son's side. Miss Cormet would see that a most adept social manager was placed in charge, one whose own position in society was irreproachable and whose connection with General Services was known to no one. With proper handling the disaster could be turned into a social triumph, enhancing Mrs. Johnson's reputation as a clever hostess and as a devoted mother.

"A sky car will be at your door in twenty minutes," she added, as she cut in the circuit marked TRANSPORTATION, "to take you to the rocket port. One of our young men will be with it to get additional details from you on the way to the port. A compartment for yourself and a berth for your maid will be reserved on the 16:45 rocket for

Newark. You may rest easy now. General Services will do your worrying."

"Oh, thank you, my dear. You've been such a help. You've no idea of the *responsibilities* a person in my position has."

Miss Cormet cluck-clucked in professional sympathy while deciding that this particular old girl was good for still more fees. "You *do* look exhausted, madame," she said anxiously. "Should I not have a masseuse accompany you on the trip? Is your health at all delicate? Perhaps a physician would be still better."

"How thoughtful you are!"

"I'll send both," Miss Cormet decided, and switched off, with a faint regret that she had not suggested a specially chartered rocket. Special service, not listed in the master price schedule, was supplied on a cost-plus basis. In cases like this "plus" meant all the traffic would bear.

She switched to EXECUTIVE; an alert-eyed young man filled the screen. "Stand by for transcript, Steve," she said. "Special service, triple-A. I've started the immediate service."

His eyebrows lifted. "Triple-A—bonuses?"

"Undoubtedly. Give this old battleaxe the works—smoothly. And look—the client's son is laid up in a hospital. Check on his nurses. If any one of them has even a shred of sex-appeal, fire her out and put a zombie in."

"Gotcha, kid. Start the transcript."

She cleared her screen again; the "available-for-service" light in her booth turned automatically to green, then almost at once turned red again and a new figure built up in her screen.

No stupid waster, this. Grace Cormet saw a well-kempt man in his middle forties, flat-waisted, shrewd-eyed, hard but urbane. The cape of his formal morning clothes was thrown back with careful casualness. "General Services," she said. "Miss Cormet speaking."

"Ah, Miss Cormet," he began, "I wish to see your chief."

"Chief of switchboard?"

"No, I wish to see the President of General Services."

"Will you tell me what it is you wish? Perhaps I can help you."

"Sorry, but I can't make explanations. I must see him, at once."

"And General Services is sorry. Mr. Clare is a very busy man; it is impossible to see him without appointment and without explanation."

"Are you recording?"

"Certainly."

"Then please cease doing so."

Above the console, in sight of the client, she switched off the recorder. Underneath the desk she switched it back on again. General Services was sometimes asked to perform illegal acts; its confidential employees took no chances. He fished something out from the folds of his chemise and held it out to her. The stereo effect made it appear as if he were reaching right out through the screen.

Trained features masked her surprise—it was the sigil of a planetary official, and the color of the badge was green.

"I will arrange it," she said.

"Very good. Can you meet me and conduct me in from the waiting room? In ten minutes?"

"I will be there, Mister . . . Mister—" But he had cut off.

Grace Cormet switched to the switchboard chief and called for relief. Then, with her board cut out of service, she removed the spool bearing the clandestine record of the interview, stared at it as if undecided, and after a moment, dipped it into an opening in the top of the desk where a strong magnetic field wiped the unfixed patterns from the soft metal.

A girl entered the booth from the rear. She was blonde, decorative, and looked slow and a little dull. She was neither. "Okay, Grace," she said. "Anything to turn over?"

"No. Clear board."

"'S matter? Sick?"

"No." With no further explanation Grace left the booth, went on out past the other booths housing operators who handled unlisted services and into the large hall where the hundreds of catalogue operators worked. These had no such complex equipment as the booth which Grace had quitted. One enormous volume, a copy of the current price list of all of General Services' regular price-marked functions, and an ordinary look-and-listen enabled a catalogue operator to provide for the public almost anything the ordinary customer could wish for. If a call was beyond the scope of the catalogue it was transferred to the aristocrats of resourcefulness, such as Grace.

She took a short cut through the master files room, walked down an alleyway between dozens of chattering punched-card machines, and entered the foyer of that level. A pneumatic lift bounced her up to the level of the President's office. The

President's receptionist did not stop her, nor, apparently, announce her. But Grace noted that the girl's hands were busy at the keys of her voder.

Switchboard operators do not walk into the office of the president of a billion-credit corporation. But General Services was not organized like any other business on the planet. It was a *sui generis* business in which special training was a commodity to be listed, bought, and sold, but general resourcefulness and a ready wit were all important. In its hierarchy Jay Clare, the president, came first, his handyman, Saunders Francis, stood second, and the couple of dozen operators, of which Grace was one, who took calls on the unlimited switchboard came immediately after. They, and the field operators who handled the most difficult unclassified commissions—one group in fact, for the unlimited switchboard operators and the unlimited field operators swapped places indiscriminately.

After them came the tens of thousands of other employees spread over the planet, from the chief accountant, the head of the legal department, the chief clerk of the master files on down through the local managers, the catalogue operators to the last classified part time employee—stenographers prepared to take dictation when and where ordered, gigolos ready to fill an empty place at a dinner, the man who rented both armadillos and trained fleas.

Grace Cormet walked into Mr. Clare's office. It was the only room in the building not cluttered up with electro-mechanical recording and communicating equipment. It contained nothing but his desk (bare), a couple of chairs, and a stereo screen, which, when not in use, seemed to be Krantz' famous painting "The Weeping Buddha." The original was in fact in the sub-basement, a thousand feet below.

"Hello, Grace," he greeted her, and shoved a piece of paper at her. "Tell me what you think of that. Sance says it's lousy." Saunders Francis turned his mild pop eyes from his chief to Grace Cormet, but neither confirmed nor denied the statement.

Miss Cormet read:

CAN YOU AFFORD IT?

Can You Afford GENERAL SERVICES?

Can You Afford NOT to have General Services?????

In this jet-speed age can you afford to go on wasting time doing your own shopping, paying bills yourself, taking care of your living compartment?

We'll spank the baby and feed the cat.

We'll rent you a house and buy your shoes.

We'll write to your mother-in-law and add up your check stubs.

No job too large; No job too small—

and all amazingly Cheap!

GENERAL SERVICES

Dial H-U-R-R-Y—U-P

P.S. *WE ALSO WALK DOGS*

"Well?" said Clare.

"Sance is right. It smells."

"Why?"

"Too logical. Too verbose. No drive."

"What's your idea of an ad to catch the marginal market?"

She thought a moment, then borrowed his stylus and wrote:

DO YOU WANT SOMEBODY MURDERED?
(Then *don't* call GENERAL SERVICES)
But for *any* other job dial HURRY-UP—*It pays!*
P.S. We also walk dogs.

"Mmmm . . . well, maybe," Mr. Clare said cautiously. "We'll try it. Sance, give this a type B coverage, two weeks, North America, and let me know how it takes." Francis put it away in his kit, still with no change in his mild expression. "Now as I was saying—"

"Chief," broke in Grace Cormet. "I made an appointment for you in—" She glanced at her watchfinger. "—exactly two minutes and forty seconds. Government man."

"Make him happy and send him away. I'm busy."

"Green Badge."

He looked up sharply. Even Francis looked interested. "So?" Clare remarked. "Got the interview transcript with you?"

"I wiped it."

"You did? Well, perhaps you know best. I like your hunches. Bring him in."

She nodded thoughtfully and left.

She found her man just entering the public reception room and escorted him past half a dozen gates whose guardians would otherwise have demanded his identity and the nature of his business. When he was seated in Clare's office, he looked around. "May I speak with you in private, Mr. Clare?"

"Mr. Francis is my right leg. You've already spoken to Miss Cormet."

"Very well." He produced the green sigil again

and held it out. "No names are necessary just yet. I am sure of your discretion."

The President of General Services sat up impatiently. "Let's get down to business. You are Pierre Beaumont, Chief of Protocol. Does the administration want a job done?"

Beaumont was unperturbed by the change in pace. "You know me. Very well. We'll get down to business. The government may want a job done. In any case our discussion must not be permitted to leak out—"

"All of General Services relations are confidential."

"This is not confidential; this is secret." He paused.

"I understand you," agreed Clare. "Go on."

"You have an interesting organization here, Mr. Clare. I believe it is your boast that you will undertake any commission whatsoever—for a price."

"If it is legal."

"Ah, yes, of course. But legal is a word capable of interpretation. I admired the way your company handled the outfitting of the Second Plutonian Expedition. Some of your methods were, ah, ingenious."

"If you have any criticism of our actions in that case they are best made to our legal department through the usual channels."

Beaumont pushed a palm in his direction. "Oh, no, Mr. Clare—please! You misunderstand me. I was not criticizing; I was admiring. Such resource! What a diplomat you would have made!"

"Let's quit fencing. What do you want?"

Mr. Beaumont pursed his lips. "Let us suppose that you had to entertain a dozen representatives of each intelligent race in this planetary system and you wanted to make each one of them completely comfortable and happy. Could you do it?"

Clare thought aloud. "Air pressure, humidity, radiation densities, atmosphere, chemistry, temperature, cultural conditions—those things are all simple. But how about acceleration? We could use a centrifuge for the Jovians, but Martians and Titans—that's another matter. There is no way to reduce earth-normal gravity. No, you would have to entertain them out in space, or on Luna. That makes it not our pigeon; we never give service beyond the stratosphere."

Beaumount shook his head. "It won't be beyond the stratosphere. You may take it as an absolute condition that you are to accomplish your results on the surface of the Earth."

"Why?"

"Is it the custom of General Services to inquire why a client wants a particular type of service?"

"No. Sorry."

"Quite all right. But you do need more information in order to understand what must be accomplished and why it must be secret. There will be a conference, held on this planet, in the near future—ninety days at the outside. Until the conference is called no suspicion that it is to be held must be allowed to leak out. If the plans for it were to be anticipated in certain quarters, it would be useless to hold the conference at all. I suggest that you think of this conference as a round-table of leading, ah, scientists of the system, about the same size and makeup as the session of the Academy held on Mars last spring. You are to make all preparations for the entertainments of the delegates, but you are to conceal these preparations in the ramifications of your organization until needed. As for the details—"

But Clare interrupted him. "You appear to have assumed that we will take on this commission. As you have explained it, it would involve us in a ridiculous failure. General Services does not like failures. You know and I know that low-gravity people cannot spend more than a few hours in high gravity without seriously endangering their health. Interplanetary get-togethers are always held on a low-gravity planet and always will be."

"Yes," answered Beaumont patiently, "they always have been. Do you realize the tremendous diplomatic handicap which Earth and Venus labor under in consequence?"

"I don't get it."

"It isn't necessary that you should. Political psychology is not your concern. Take it for granted that it does and that the Administration is determined that *this* conference shall take place on Earth."

"Why not Luna?"

Beaumont shook his head. "Not the same thing at all. Even though we administer it, Luna City is a treaty port. Not the same thing, psychologically."

Clare shook his head. "Mr. Beaumont, I don't believe that you understand the nature of General Services, even as I fail to appreciate the subtle requirements of diplomacy. We don't work miracles and we don't promise to. We are just the handyman of the last century, gone speed-lined and corporate. We are the latter day equivalent of the old servant class, but we are not Aladdin's genie. We don't even maintain research laboratories in the scientific sense. We simply make the best possible use of modern advances in communication and organization to do what already *can* be done." He waved a hand at the far wall, on which there was cut in intaglio the time-honored trademark of the business—a Scottie dog, pulling against a leash and sniffing at a post. "*There* is the spirit of the sort of work we do. We walk dogs for people who are too busy to walk 'em themselves. My grandfather worked his way through college walking dogs. I'm still walking them. I don't promise miracles, nor monkey with politics."

Beaumont fitted his fingertips carefully together. "You walk dogs for a fee. But of course you do— you walk my pair. Five minim-credits seems rather cheap."

"It is. But a hundred thousand dogs, twice a day, soon runs up the gross take."

"The 'take' for walking this 'dog' would be considerable."

"How much?" asked Francis. It was his first sign of interest.

Beaumont turned his eyes on him. "My dear sir, the outcome of this, ah, roundtable should make a difference of literally hundreds of billions of credits to this planet. We will not bind the mouth of the kine that tread the corn, if you pardon the figure of speech."

"How much?"

"Would thirty percent over cost be reasonable?"

Francis shook his head. "Might not come to much."

"Well, I certainly won't haggle. Suppose we leave it up to you gentlemen—your pardon, Miss Cormet—to decide what the service is worth. I think I can rely on your planetary and racial patriotism to make it reasonable and proper."

Francis sat back, said nothing, but looked pleased.

"Wait a minute," protested Clare. "We haven't taken this job."

"We have discussed the fee," observed Beaumont.

Clare looked from Francis to Grace Cormet, then examined his fingernails. "Give me twenty-four hours to find out whether or not it is possible," he said finally, "and I'll tell you whether or not we will walk your dog."

"I feel sure," answered Beaumont, "that you will." He gathered his cape about him.

"Okay, masterminds," said Clare bitterly, "you've bought it."

"I've been wanting to get back to field work," said Grace.

"Put a crew on everything but the gravity problem," suggested Francis. "It's the only catch. The rest is routine."

"Certainly," agreed Clare, "but you had better deliver on that. If you can't, we are out some mighty expensive preparations that we will never be paid for. Who do you want? Grace?"

"I suppose so," answered Francis. "She can count up to ten."

Grace Cormet looked at him coldly. "There are times, Sance Francis, when I regret having married you."

"Keep your domestic affairs out of the office," warned Clare. "Where do you start?"

"Let's find out who knows most about gravitation," decided Francis. "Grace, better get Doctor Krathwohl on the screen."

"Right," she acknowledged, as she stepped to the stereo controls. "That's the beauty about this business. You don't have to know anything; you just have to know where to find out."

Dr. Krathwohl was a part of the permanent staff of General Services. He had no assigned duties. The company found it worthwhile to support him in comfort while providing him with an unlimited drawing account for scientific journals and for attendance at the meetings which the learned hold from time to time. Dr. Krathwohl lacked the single-minded drive of the research scientist; he was a dilettante by nature.

Occasionally they asked him a question. It paid.

"Oh, hello, my dear!" Doctor Krathwohl's gentle face smiled out at her from the screen. "Look—I've just come across the most amusing fact in the latest issue of *Nature*. It throws a most interesting sidelight on Brownlee's theory of—"

"Just a second, Doc," she interrupted. "I'm kinda in a hurry."

"Yes, my dear?"

"Who knows the most about gravitation?"

"In what way do you mean that? Do you want an astrophysicist, or do you want to deal with the subject from a standpoint of theoretical mechanics? Farquarson would be the man in the first instance, I suppose."

"I want to know what makes it tick."

"Field theory, eh? In that case you don't want Farquarson. He is a descriptive ballistician, primarily. Dr. Julian's work in that subject is authoritative, possibly definitive."

"Where can we get hold of him?"

"Oh, but you can't. He died last year, poor fellow. A great loss."

Grace refrained from telling him how great a loss and asked, "Who stepped into his shoes?"

"Who what? Oh, you were jesting! I see. You want the name of the present top man in field theory. I would say O'Neil."

"Where is he?"

"I'll have to find out. I know him slightly—a difficult man."

"Do, please. In the meantime who could coach us a bit on what it's all about?"

"Why don't you try young Carson, in our engineering department? He was interested in such things before he took a job with us. Intelligent chap—I've had many an interesting talk with him."

"I'll do that. Thanks, Doc. Call the Chief's office as soon as you have located O'Neil. Speed." She cut off.

Carson agreed with Krathwohl's opinion, but looked dubious. "O'Neil is arrogant and non-cooperative. I've worked under him. But he undoubtedly knows more about field theory and space structure than any other living man."

Carson had been taken into the inner circle, the problem explained to him. He had admitted that he saw no solution. "Maybe we are making something hard out of this," Clare suggested. "I've got some ideas. Check me if I'm wrong, Carson."

"Go ahead, Chief."

"Well, the acceleration of gravity is produced by the proximity of a mass—right? Earth-normal gravity being produced by the proximity of the Earth. Well, what would be the effect of placing a large mass just over a particular point on the earth's surface. Would not that serve to counteract the pull of the Earth?"

"Theoretically, yes. But it would have to be a damn big mass."

"No matter."

"You don't understand, Chief. To offset fully the pull of the Earth at a given point would require another planet the size of the Earth in contact with the Earth at that point. Of course since you don't want to cancel the pull completely, but simply to reduce it, you gain a certain advantage through using a smaller mass which would have its center of gravity closer to the point in question than would be the center of gravity of the Earth. Not enough, though. While the attraction builds up inversely as the square of the distance—in this case the half-diameter—the mass and the consequent attraction drops off directly as the *cube* of the diameter."

"What does that give us?"

Carson produced a sliderule and figured for a few moments. He looked up. "I'm almost afraid to answer. You would need a good-sized asteroid, of lead, to get anywhere at all."

"Asteroids have been moved before this."

"Yes, but what is to *hold it up?* No, Chief, there is no conceivable source of power, or means of applying it, that would enable you to hang a big planetoid over a particular spot on the Earth's surface and keep it there."

"Well, it was a good idea while it lasted," Clare said pensively.

Grace's smooth brow had been wrinkled as she followed the discussion. Now she put in, "I gathered that you could use an extremely heavy small mass more effectively. I seem to have read somewhere about some stuff that weighs *tons* per cubic inch."

"The core of dwarf stars," agreed Carson. "All we would need for that would be a ship capable of going light-years in a few days, some way to mine the interior of a star, and a new space-time theory."

"Oh, well, skip it."

"Wait a minute," Francis observed. "Magnetism is a lot like gravity, isn't it?"

"Well—yes."

"Could there be some way to *magnetize* these gazebos from the little planets? Maybe something odd about their body chemistry?"

"Nice idea," agreed Carson, "but while their internal economy is odd, it's not that odd. They are still organic."

"I suppose not. If pigs had wings they'd be pigeons."

The stereo annunciator blinked. Doctor Krathwohl announced that O'Neil could be found at his summer home in Portage, Wisconsin. He had not screened him and would prefer not to do so, unless the Chief insisted.

Clare thanked him and turned back to the others. "We are wasting time," he announced. "After years in this business we should know better than to try to decide technical questions. I'm not a physicist and I don't give a damn how gravitation works. That's O'Neil's business. And Carson's. Carson, shoot up to Wisconsin and get O'Neil on the job."

"Me?"

"You. You're an operator for this job—with pay

to match. Bounce over to the port—there will be a rocket and a credit facsimile waiting for you. You ought to be able to raise ground in seven or eight minutes."

Carson blinked. "How about my job here?"

"The engineering department will be told, likewise the accounting. Get going."

Without replying Carson headed for the door. By the time he reached it he was hurrying.

Carson's department left them with nothing to do until he reported back—nothing to do, that is, but to start action on the manifold details of reproducing the physical and cultural details of three other planets and four major satellites, exclusive of their characteristic surface-normal gravitational accelerations. The assignment, although new, presented no real difficulties—to General Services. Somewhere there were persons who knew all the answers to these matters. The vast loose organization called General Services was geared to find them, hire them, put them to work. Any of the unlimited operators and a considerable percent of the catalogue operators could take such an assignment and handle it without excitement or hurry.

Francis called in one unlimited operator. He did not even bother to select him, but took the first available on the ready panel—they were all "Can do!" people. He explained in detail the assignment, then promptly forgot about it. It would be done, and on time. The punched-card machines would chatter a bit louder, stereo screens would flash, and bright young people in all parts of the Earth would drop what they were doing and dig out the specialists who would do the actual work.

He turned back to Clare, who said, "I wish I knew what Beaumont is up to. Conference of scientists—phooey!"

"I thought you weren't interested in politics, Jay."

"I'm not. I don't give a hoot in hell about politics, interplanetary or otherwise, except as it affects this business. But if I knew what was being planned, we might be able to squeeze a bigger cut out of it."

"Well," put in Grace, "I think you can take it for granted that the real heavyweights from all the planets are about to meet and divide Gaul into three parts."

"Yes, but who gets cut out?"

"Mars, I suppose."

"Seems likely. With a bone tossed to the Venerians. In that case we might speculate a little in Pan-Jovian Trading Corp."

"Easy, son, easy," Francis warned. "Do that, and you might get people interested. This is a hush-hush job."

"I guess you're right. Still, keep your eyes open. There ought to be some way to cut a slice of pie before this is over."

Grace Cormet's telephone buzzed. She took it out of her pocket and said, "Yes?"

"A Mrs. Hogbein Johnson wants to speak to you."

"You handle her. I'm off the board."

"She won't talk to anyone but you."

"All right. Put her on the Chief's stereo, but stay

in parallel yourself. You'll handle it after I've talked to her."

The screen came to life, showing Mrs. Johnson's fleshy face alone, framed in the middle of the screen in flat picture. "Oh, Miss Cormet," she moaned, "some dreadful mistake has been made. There is no stereo on this ship."

"It will be installed in Cincinnati. That will be in about twenty minutes."

"You are *sure*?"

"Quite sure."

"Oh, thank you! It's such a relief to talk with you. Do you know, I'm *thinking* of making you my social secretary."

"Thank you," Grace replied evenly, "but I am under contract."

"But how stupidly tiresome! You can break it."

"No, I'm sorry Mrs. Johnson. Good-by." She switched off the screen and spoke again into her telephone. "Tell Accounting to double her fee. And I *won't* speak with her again." She cut off and shoved the little instrument savagely back into her pocket. "Social secretary!"

It was after dinner and Clare had retired to his living apartment before Carson called back. Francis took the call in his own office.

"Any luck?" he asked, when Carson's image had built up.

"Quite a bit. I've seen O'Neil."

"Well? Will he do it?"

"You mean can he do it, don't you?"

"Well—can he?"

"Now that is a funny thing—I didn't think it was theoretically possible. But after talking with him,

I'm convinced that it is. O'Neil has a new outlook on field theory—stuff he's never published. The man is a genius."

"I don't care," said Francis, "whether he's a genius or a Mongolian idiot—can he build some sort of a gravity thinner-outer?"

"I believe he can. I really do believe he can."

"Fine. You hired him?"

"No. That's the hitch. That's why I called back. It's like this: I happened to catch him in a mellow mood, and because we had worked together once before and because I had not aroused his ire quite as frequently as his other assistants he invited me to stay for dinner. We talked about a lot of things (you can't hurry him) and I broached the proposition. It interested him mildly—the idea, I mean; not the proposition—and he discussed the theory with me, or, rather, at me. But he won't work on it."

"Why not? You didn't offer him enough money. I guess I'd better tackle him."

"No, Mr. Francis, no. You don't understand. He's not interested in money. He's independently wealthy and has more than he needs for his research, or anything else he wants. But just at present he is busy on wave mechanics theory and he just won't be bothered with anything else."

"Did you make him realize it was important?"

"Yes and no. Mostly no. I tried to, but there isn't anything important to him but what *he* wants. It's a sort of intellectual snobbishness. Other people simply don't count."

"All right," said Francis. "You've done well so far. Here's what you do: After I switch off, you call EXECUTIVE and make a transcript of everything you can remember of what he said about gravitational theory. We'll hire the next best men, feed it to them, and see if it gives them any ideas to work on. In the meantime I'll put a crew to work on the details of Dr. O'Neil's background. He'll have a weak point somewhere; it's just a matter of finding it. Maybe he's keeping a woman somewhere—"

"He's long past that."

"—or maybe he has a by-blow stashed away somewhere. We'll see. I want you to stay there in Portage. Since you can't hire him, maybe you can persuade him to hire you. You're our pipeline, I want it kept open. We've got to find something he wants, or something he is afraid of."

"He's not afraid of *anything*. I'm positive of that."

"Then he wants something. If it's not money, or women, it's something else. It's a law of nature."

"I doubt it," Carson replied slowly. "Say! Did I tell you about his hobby?"

"No. What is it?"

"It's china. In particular, Ming china. He has the best collection in the world, I'd guess. But I know what he wants!"

"Well, spill it, man, spill it. Don't be dramatic."

"It's a little china dish, or bowl, about four inches across and two inches high. It's got a Chinese name that means 'Flower of Forgetfulness.' "

"Hmmm—doesn't seem significant. You think he wants it pretty bad?"

"I *know* he does. He has a solid colorgraph of it in his study, where he can look at it. But it hurts him to talk about it."

"Find out who owns it and where it is."

"I know. British Museum. That's why he can't buy it."

"So?" mused Francis. "Well, you can forget it. Carry on."

Clare came down to Francis' office and the three talked it over. "I guess we'll need Beaumont on this," was his comment when he had heard the report. "It will take the Government to get anything loose from the British Museum." Francis looked morose. "Well—what's eating you? What's wrong with that?"

"I know," offered Grace. "You remember the treaty under which Great Britain entered the planetary confederation?"

"I was never much good at history."

"It comes to this: I doubt if the planetary government can touch anything that belongs to the Museum without asking the British Parliament."

"Why not? Treaty or no treaty, the planetary government is sovereign. That was established in the Brazilian Incident."

"Yeah, sure. But it could cause questions to be asked in the House of Commons and that would lead to the one thing Beaumont wants to avoid at all costs—publicity."

"Okay. What do you propose?"

"I'd say that Sance and I had better slide over to England and find out just how tight they have the 'Flower of Forgetfulness' nailed down—and who does the nailing and what his weaknesses are."

Clare's eyes travelled past her to Francis, who was looking blank in the fashion that indicated assent to his intimates. "Okay," agreed Clare, "it's your baby. Taking a special?"

"No, we've got time to get the midnight out of New York. By-by."

"By. Call me tomorrow."

When Grace screened the Chief the next day he took one look at her and exclaimed, "Good Grief, kid! What have you done to your hair?"

"We located the guy," she explained succinctly. "His weakness is blondes."

"You've had your skin bleached, too."

"Of course. How do you like it?"

"It's stupendous—though I preferred you the way you were. But what does Sance think of it?"

"He doesn't mind—it's business. But to get down to cases, Chief, there isn't much to report. This will have to be a left-handed job. In the ordinary way, it would take an earthquake to get anything out of that tomb."

"Don't do anything that can't be fixed!"

"You know me, Chief, I won't get you in trouble. But it will be expensive."

"Of course."

"That's all for now. I'll screen tomorrow."

She was a brunette again the next day. "What is this?" asked Clare. "A masquerade?"

"I wasn't the blonde he was weak for," she explained, "but I found the one he was interested in."

"Did it work out?"

"I think it will. Sance is having a fascimile integrated now. With luck, we'll see you tomorrow."

They showed up on the next day, apparently empty handed. "Well?" said Clare, "well?"

"Seal the place up, Jay," suggested Francis. "Then we'll talk."

Clare flipped a switch controlling an interference shield which rendered his office somewhat more private than a coffin. "How about it?" he demanded. "Did you get it?"

"Show it to him, Grace."

Grace turned her back, fumbled at her clothing for a moment, then turned around and placed it gently on the Chief's desk.

It was not that it was beautiful—it *was* beauty. Its subtle simple curve had no ornamentation, decoration would have sullied it. One spoke softly in its presence, for fear a sudden noise would shatter it.

Clare reached out to touch, then thought better of it and drew his hand back. But he bent his head over it and stared down into it. It was strangely hard to focus—to allocate—the bottom of the bowl. It seemed as if his sight sank deeper and ever deeper into it, as if he were drowning in a pool of light.

He jerked up his head and blinked. "God," he whispered, "God—I didn't know such things existed."

He looked at Grace and looked away to Francis. Francis had tears in his eyes, or perhaps his own were blurred.

"Look, Chief," said Francis. "Look—couldn't we just keep it and call the whole thing off?"

"There's no use talking about it any longer," said Francis wearily. "We can't keep it, Chief. I shouldn't have suggested it and you shouldn't have listened to me. Let's screen O'Neil."

"We might just wait another day before we do anything about it," Clare ventured. His eyes returned yet again to the "Flower of Forgetfulness."

Grace shook her head. "No good. It will just be harder tomorrow. I *know*." She walked decisively over to the stereo and manipulated the controls.

O'Neil was annoyed at being disturbed and twice annoyed that they had used the emergency signal to call him to his disconnected screen.

"What is this?" he demanded. "What do you mean by disturbing a private citizen when he has disconnected? Speak up—and it had better be good, or, so help me, I'll sue you!"

"We want you to do a little job of work for us, Doctor," Clare began evenly.

"What!" O'Neil seemed almost too surprised to be angry. "Do you mean to stand there, sir, and tell me that you have invaded the privacy of my home to ask *me* to work for *you?*"

"The pay will be satisfactory to you."

O'Neil seemed to be counting up to ten before answering. "Sir," he said carefully, "there are men in the world who seem to think they can buy anything, or anybody. I grant you that they have much to go on in that belief. But I am not for sale. Since you seem to be one of those persons, I will do my best to make this interview expensive for you. You will hear from my attorneys. Good night!"

"Wait a moment," Clare said urgently. "I believe that you are interested in China—"

"What if I am?"

"Show it to him, Grace." Grace brought the "Flower of Forgetfulness" up near the screen, handling it carefully, reverently.

O'Neil said nothing. He leaned forward and

stared. He seemed to be about to climb through the screen. "Where did you get it?" he said at last.

"That doesn't matter."

"I'll buy it from you—at your own price."

"It's not for sale. But you may have it—if we can reach an agreement."

O'Neil eyed him. "It's stolen property."

"You're mistaken. Nor will you find anyone to take an interest in such a charge. Now about this job—"

O'Neil pulled his eyes away from the bowl. "What is it you wish me to do?"

Clare explained the problem to him. When he had concluded O'Neil shook his head. "That's ridiculous," he said.

"We have reason to feel that it is theoretically possible."

"Oh, certainly! It's theoretically possible to live forever, too. But no one has ever managed it."

"We think you can do it."

"Thank you for nothing. Say!" O'Neil stabbed a finger at him out of the screen. "You set that young pup Carson on me!"

"He was acting under my orders."

"Then, sir, I do not like your manners."

"How about the job? And this?" Clare indicated the bowl.

O'Neil gazed at it and chewed his whiskers. "Suppose," he said, at last, "I make an honest attempt to the full extent of my ability, to supply what you want—and I fail."

Clare shook his head. "We pay only for results. Oh, your salary, of course, but not *this*. This is a bonus in addition to your salary, *if* you are successful."

O'Neil seemed about to agree, then said suddenly, "You may be fooling me with a colorgraph. I can't tell through this damned screen."

Clare shrugged. "Come see for yourself."

"I shall. I will. Stay where you are. Where are you? Damn it, sir, what's your *name?*"

He came storming in two hours later. "You've tricked me! The 'Flower' is still in England. I've investigated. I'll . . . I'll *punish* you, sir, with my own two hands."

"See for yourself," answered Clare. He stepped aside, so that his body no longer obscured O'Neil's view of Clare's desk top.

They let him look. They respected his need for quiet and let him look. After a long time he turned to them, but did not speak.

"Well?" asked Clare.

"I'll build your damned gadget," he said huskily. "I figured out an approach on the way here."

Beaumont came in person to call the day before the first session of the conference. "Just a social call, Mr. Clare," he stated. "I simply wanted to express to you my personal appreciation for the work you have done. And to deliver this." "This" turned out to be a draft on the Bank Central for the agreed fee. Clare accepted it, glanced at it, nodded, and placed it on his desk.

"I take it, then," he remarked, "that the Government is satisfied with the service rendered."

"That is putting it conservatively," Beaumont assured him. "To be perfectly truthful, I did not think you could do so much. You seem to have thought of everything. The Callistan delegation is out now, riding around and seeing the sights in one of the little tanks you had prepared. They are delighted. Confidentially, I think we can depend on their vote in the coming sessions."

"Gravity shields working all right, eh?"

"Perfectly. I stepped into their sightseeing tank before we turned it over to them. I was as light as the proverbial feather. Too light—I was very nearly spacesick." He smiled in wry amusement. "I entered the Jovian apartments, too. That was quite another matter."

"Yes, it would be," Clare agreed. "Two and a half times normal weight is oppressive to say the least."

"It's a happy ending to a difficult task. I must be going. Oh, yes, one other little matter—I've discussed with Doctor O'Neil the possibility that the Administration may be interested in other uses for his new development. In order to simplify the matter it seems desirable that you provide me with a quitclaim to the O'Neil effect from General Services."

Clare gazed thoughtfully at the "Weeping Buddha" and chewed his thumb. "No," he said slowly, "No. I'm afraid that would be difficult."

"Why not?" asked Beaumont. "It avoids the necessity of adjudication and attendant waste of time. We are prepared to recognize your service and recompense you."

"Hmmm. I don't believe you fully understand the situation, Mr. Beaumont. There is a certain amount of open territory between our contract with Doctor O'Neil and your contract with us. You asked of us certain services and certain chattels with which to achieve that service. We provide them—for a fee. All done. But our contract with

Doctor O'Neil made him a full-time employee for the period of his employment. His research results and the patents embodying them are the property of General Services."

"Really?" said Beaumont. "Doctor O'Neil has a different impression."

"Doctor O'Neil is mistaken. Seriously, Mr. Beaumont—you asked us to develop a siege gun, figuratively speaking, to shoot a gnat. Did you expect us, as businessmen, to throw away the siege gun after one shot?"

"No, I suppose not. What do you propose to do?"

"We expect to exploit the gravity modulator commercially. I fancy we could get quite a good price for certain adaptations of it on Mars."

"Yes. Yes, I suppose you could. But to be brutally frank, Mr. Clare, I am afraid that is impossible. It is a matter of imperative public policy that this development be limited to terrestrials. In fact, the administration would find it necessary to intervene and make it government monopoly."

"Have you considered how to keep O'Neil quiet?"

"In view of the change in circumstances, no. What is your thought?"

"A corporation, in which he would hold a block of stock and be president. One of our bright young men would be chairman of the board." Clare thought of Carson. "There would be stock enough to go around," he added, and watched Beaumont's face.

Beaumont ignored the bait. "I suppose that this corporation would be under contract to the Government—its sole customer?"

"That is the idea."

"Mmmm . . . yes, it seems feasible. Perhaps I had better speak with Doctor O'Neil."

"Help yourself."

Beaumont got O'Neil on the screen and talked with him in low tones. Or, more properly, Beaumont's tones, were low. O'Neil displayed a tendency to blast the microphone. Clare sent for Francis and Grace and explained to them what had taken place.

Beaumont turned away from the screen. "The Doctor wishes to speak with you, Mr. Clare."

O'Neil looked at him frigidly. "What is this claptrap I've had to listen to, sir? What's this about the O'Neil effect being your property?"

"It was in your contract, Doctor. Don't you recall?"

"Contract! I never read the damned things. But I can tell you this: I'll take you to court. I'll tie you in knots before I'll let you make a fool of me that way."

"Just a moment, Doctor, please!" Clare soothed. "We have no desire to take advantage of a mere legal technicality, and no one disputes your interest. Let me outline what I had in mind—" He ran rapidly over the plan. O'Neil listened, but his expression was still unmollified at the conclusion.

"I'm not interested," he said gruffly. "So far as I am concerned the Government can have the whole thing. And I'll see to it."

"I had not mentioned one other condition," added Clare.

"Don't bother."

"I must. This will be just a matter of agreement

between gentlemen, but it is essential. You have custody of the 'Flower of Forgetfulness.' "

O'Neil was at once on guard. "What do you mean, 'custody.' I own it. Understand me—*own* it."

" 'Own it,' " repeated Clare. "Nevertheless, in return for the concessions we are making you with respect to your contract, we want something in return."

"What?" asked O'Neil. The mention of the bowl had upset his confidence.

"You own it and you retain possession of it. But I want your word that I, or Mr. Francis, or Miss Cormet, may come look at it from time to time—frequently."

O'Neil looked unbelieving. "You mean that you simply want to come to *look* at it?"

"That's all."

"Simply to *enjoy* it?"

"That's right."

O'Neil looked at him with new respect. "I did not understand you before, Mr. Clare. I apologize. As for the corporation nonsense—do as you like. I don't care. You and Mr. Francis and Miss Cormet may come to see the 'Flower' whenever you like. You have my word."

"Thank you, Doctor O'Neil—for all of us." He switched off as quickly as could be managed gracefully.

Beaumont was looking at Clare with added respect, too. "I think," he said, "that the next time I shall not interfere with your handling of the details. I'll take my leave. Adieu, gentlemen—and Miss Cormet."

When the door had rolled down behind him Grace remarked, "That seems to polish it off."

"Yes," said Clare. "We've 'walked his dog' for him; O'Neil has what he wants; Beaumont got what he wanted, and more besides."

"Just what is he after?"

"I don't know, but I suspect that he would like to be first president of the Solar System Federation, if and when there is such a thing. With the aces we have dumped in his lap, he might make it. Do you realize the potentialities of the O'Neil effect?"

"Vaguely," said Francis.

"Have you thought about what it will do to space navigation? Or the possibilities it adds in the way of colonization? Or its recreational uses? There's a fortune in that alone."

"What do we get out of it?"

"What do we get out of it? Money, old son. Gobs and gobs of money. There's always money in giving people what they want." He glanced up at the Scottie dog trademark.

"Money," repeated Francis. "Yeah, I suppose so."

"Anyhow," added Grace, "we can always go look at the 'Flower.'"

Ordeal in Space

Maybe we should never have ventured out into space. Our race has but two basic, innate fears; noise and the fear of falling. Those terrible heights— Why should any man in his right mind let himself be placed where he could fall . . . and fall . . . and fall—But all Spacemen are crazy. Everybody knows that.

The medicos had been very kind, he supposed. "You're lucky. You want to remember that, old fellow. You're still young and your retired pay relieves you of all worry about your future. You've got both arms and legs and are in fine shape."

"Fine shape!" His voice was unintentionally contemptuous.

"No, I mean it," the chief psychiatrist had persisted gently. "The little quirk you have does you no harm at all—except that you can't go out into space again. I can't honestly call acrophobia a neurosis; fear of falling is normal and sane. You've just got it a little more strongly than most—but that is not abnormal, in view of what you have been through."

163

The reminder set him to shaking again. He closed his eyes and saw the stars wheeling below him again. He was falling . . . falling endlessly. The psychiatrist's voice came through to him and pulled him back. "Steady, old man! Look around you."

"Sorry."

"Not at all. Now tell me, what do you plan to do?"

"I don't know. Get a job, I suppose."

"The Company will give you a job, you know."

He shook his head. "I don't want to hang around a spaceport." Wear a little button in his shirt to show that he was once a man, be addressed by a courtesy title of captain, claim the privileges of the pilots' lounge on the basis of what he used to be, hear the shop talk die down whenever he approached a group, wonder what they were saying behind his back—no, thank you!

"I think you're wise. Best to make a clean break, for a while at least, until you are feeling better."

"You think I'll get over it?"

The psychiatrist pursed his lips. "Possible. It's functional, you know. No trauma."

"But you don't think so?"

"I didn't say that. I honestly don't know. We still know very little about what makes a man tick."

"I see. Well, I might as well be leaving."

The psychiatrist stood up and shoved out his hand. "Holler if you want anything. And come back to see us in any case."

"Thanks."

"You're going to be all right. I know it."

But the psychiatrist shook his head as his patient walked out. The man did not walk like a spaceman; the easy, animal self-confidence was gone.

Only a small part of Great New York was roofed over in those days; he stayed underground until he was in that section, then sought out a passageway lined with bachelor rooms. He stuck a coin in the slot of the first one which displayed a lighted "vacant" sign, chucked his jump bag inside, and left. The monitor at the intersection gave him the address of the nearest placement office. He went there, seated himself at an interview desk, stamped in his finger prints, and started filling out forms. It gave him a curious back-to-the-beginning feeling; he had not looked for a job since pre-cadet days.

He left filling in his name to the last and hesitated even then. He had had more than his bellyful of publicity; he did not want to be recognized; he certainly did not want to be throbbed over—and most of all he did not want anyone telling him he was a hero. Presently he printed in the name "William Saunders" and dropped the forms in the slot.

He was well into his third cigarette and getting ready to strike another when the screen in front of him at last lighted up. He found himself staring at a nice-looking brunette. "Mr. Saunders," the image said, "will you come inside, please? Door seventeen."

The brunette in person was there to offer him a seat and a cigarette. "Make yourself comfortable, Mr. Saunders. I'm Miss Joyce. I'd like to talk with you about your application."

He settled himself and waited, without speaking.

When she saw that he did not intend to speak, she added, "Now take this name 'William Saunders' which you have given us—we know who you are, of course, from your prints."

"I suppose so."

"Of course I know what everybody knows about you, but your action in calling yourself 'William Saunders,' Mr.—"

"Saunders."

"—Mr. Saunders, caused me to query the files." She held up a microfilm spool, turned so that he might read his own name on it. "I know quite a lot about you now—more than the public knows and more than you saw fit to put into your application. It's a good record, Mr. Saunders."

"Thank you."

"But I can't use it in placing you in a job. I can't even refer to it if you insist on designating yourself as 'Saunders.' "

"The name is Saunders." His voice was flat, rather than emphatic.

"Don't be hasty, Mr. Saunders. There are many positions in which the factor of prestige can be used quite legitimately to obtain for a client a much higher beginning rate of pay than—"

"I'm not interested."

She looked at him and decided not to insist. "As you wish. If you will go to reception room B, you can start your classification and skill tests."

"Thank you."

"*If* you should change your mind later, Mr. Saunders, we will be glad to reopen the case. Through that door, please."

Three days later found him at work for a small firm specializing in custom-built communication systems. His job was calibrating electronic equipment. It was soothing work, demanding enough to occupy his mind, yet easy for a man of his training and experience. At the end of his three months probation he was promoted out of the helper category.

He was building himself a well-insulated rut, working, sleeping, eating, spending an occasional evening at the public library or working out at the YMCA—and never, under any circumstances, going out under the open sky nor up to any height, not even a theater balcony.

He tried to keep his past life shut out of his mind, but his memory of it was still fresh; he would find himself day-dreaming—the star-sharp, frozen sky of Mars, or the roaring night life of Venusburg. He would see again the swollen, ruddy bulk of Jupiter hanging over the port on Ganymede, its oblate bloated shape impossibly huge and crowding the sky.

Or he might, for a time, feel again the sweet quiet of the long watches on the lonely reaches between the planets. But such reveries were dangerous; they cut close to the edge of his new peace of mind. It was easy to slide over and find himself clinging for life to his last handhold on the steel sides of the *Valkyrie*, fingers numb and failing, and nothing below him but the bottomless well of space.

Then he would come back to Earth, shaking uncontrollably and gripping his chair or the workbench.

The first time it had happened at work he had found one of his benchmates, Joe Tully, staring at him curiously. "What's the trouble, Bill?" he had asked. "Hangover?"

"Nothing," he had managed to say. "Just a chill."

"You had better take a pill. Come on—let's go to lunch."

Tully led the way to the elevator; they crowded in. Most of the employees—even the women—preferred to go down via the drop chute, but Tully always used the elevator. "Saunders," of course, never used the drop chute; this had eased them into the habit of lunching together. He knew that the chute was safe, that, even if the power should fail, safety nets would snap across at each floor level—but he could not force himself to step off the edge.

Tully said publicly that a drop-chute landing hurt his arches, but he confided privately to Saunders that he did not trust automatic machinery. Saunders nodded understandingly but said nothing. It warmed him toward Tully. He began feeling friendly and not on the defensive with another human being for the first time since the start of his new life. He began to want to tell Tully the truth about himself. If he could be sure that Joe would not insist on treating him as a hero—not that he really objected to the role of hero. As a kid, hanging around spaceports, trying to wangle chances to go inside the ships, cutting classes to watch take-offs, he had dreamed of being a "hero" someday, a hero of the spaceways, returning in triumph from some incredible and dangerous piece of exploration. But he was troubled by the fact that he still had the same picture of what a hero should look like and how he should behave; it did not include shying away from open windows, being fearful of walking across an open square, and growing too upset to speak at the mere thought of boundless depths of space.

Tully invited him home for dinner. He wanted to go, but fended off the invitation while he inquired where Tully lived. The Shelton Homes, Tully told him, naming one of those great, boxlike warrens that used to disfigure the Jersey flats. "It's a long way to come back," Saunders said doubtfully, while turning over in his mind ways to get there without exposing himself to the things he feared.

"You won't have to come back," Tully assured him. "We've got a spare room. Come on. My old lady does her own cooking—that's why I keep her."

"Well, all right," he conceded. "Thanks, Joe." The La Guardia Tube would take him within a quarter of a mile; if he could not find a covered way he would take a ground cab and close the shades.

Tully met him in the hall and apologized in a whisper. "Meant to have a young lady for you, Bill. Instead we've got my brother-in-law. He's a louse. Sorry."

"Forget it, Joe. I'm glad to be here." He was indeed. The discovery that Bill's flat was on the thirty-fifth floor had dismayed him at first, but he was delighted to find that he had no feeling of height. The lights were on, the windows occulted, the floor under him was rock solid; he felt warm and safe. Mrs. Tully turned out in fact to be a good cook, to his surprise—he had the bachelor's usual distrust of amateur cooking. He let himself go to the pleasure of feeling at home and safe and

wanted; he managed not even to hear most of the
aggressive and opinionated remarks of Joe's-in-law.

After dinner he relaxed in an easy chair, glass of
beer in hand, and watched the video screen. It
was a musical comedy; he laughed more heartily
than he had in months. Presently the comedy gave
way to a religious program, the National Cathedral
Choir; he let it be, listening with one ear and
giving some attention to the conversation with
the other.

The choir was more than halfway through *Prayer
for Travelers* before he became fully aware of
what they were singing:

> *"—hear us when we pray to Thee
> For those in peril on the sea.*
>
> *"Almighty Ruler of the all
> Whose power extends to great and small,
> Who guides the stars with steadfast law,
> Whose least creation fills with awe;
> Oh, grant Thy mercy and Thy grace
> To those who venture into space."*

He wanted to switch it off, but he had to hear it
out, he could not stop listening to it, though it
hurt him in his heart with the unbearable home-
sickness of the hopelessly exiled. Even as a cadet
this one hymn could fill his eyes with tears; now
he kept his face turned away from the others to try
to hide from them the drops wetting his cheeks.

When the choir's "amen" let him do so he
switched quickly to some other—any other—program and remained bent over the instrument, pre-
tending to fiddle with it, while he composed his

features. Then he turned back to the company, outwardly serene, though it seemed to him that anyone could see the hard, aching knot in his middle.

The brother-in-law was still sounding off.

"We ought to annex 'em," he was saying. "That's what we ought to do. Three-Planets Treaty—what a lot of ruddy rot! What right have they got to tell us what we can and can't do on Mars?"

"Well, Ed," Tully said mildly, "it's their planet, isn't it? They were there first."

Ed brushed it aside. "Did we ask the Indians whether or not they wanted us in North America? Nobody has any right to hang on to something he doesn't know how to use. With proper exploitation—"

"You been speculating, Ed?"

"Huh? It wouldn't be speculation if the government wasn't made up of a bunch of weak-spined old women. 'Rights of Natives,' indeed. What rights do a bunch of degenerates have?"

Saunders found himself contrasting Ed Schultz with Knath Sooth, the only Martian he himself had ever known well. Gentle Knath, who had been old before Ed was born, and yet was rated as young among his own kind. Knath. . . . why, Knath could sit for hours with a friend or trusted acquaintance, saying nothing, needing to say nothing. "Growing together" they called it—his entire race had so grown together that they had needed no government, until the Earthman came.

Saunders had once asked his friend why he exerted himself so little, was satisfied with so little. More than an hour passed and Saunders was beginning to regret his inquisitiveness when

Knath replied, "My fathers have labored and I am weary."

Saunders sat up and faced the brother-in-law. "They are not degenerate."

"Huh? I suppose *you* are an expert!"

"The Martians aren't degenerate, they're just tired," Saunders persisted.

Tully grinned. His brother-in-law saw it and became surly. "What gives you the right to an opinion? Have you ever been to Mars?"

Saunders realized suddenly that he had let his censors down. "Have you?" he answered cautiously.

"That's beside the point. The best minds all agree—" Bill let him go on and did not contradict him again. It was a relief when Tully suggested that, since they all had to be up early, maybe it was about time to think about beginning to get ready to go to bed.

He said goodnight to Mrs. Tully and thanked her for a wonderful dinner, then followed Tully into the guest room. "Only way to get rid of that family curse we're saddled with, Bill," he apologized. "Stay up as long as you like." Tully stepped to the window and opened it. "You'll sleep well here. We're up high enough to get honest-to-goodness fresh air." He stuck his head out and took a couple of big breaths. "Nothing like the real article," he continued as he withdrew from the window. "I'm a country boy at heart. What's the matter, Bill?"

"Nothing. Nothing at all."

"I thought you looked a little pale. Well, sleep tight. I've already set your bed for seven; that'll give us plenty of time."

"Thanks, Joe. Goodnight." As soon as Tully was

out of the room he braced himself, then went over and closed the window. Sweating, he turned away and switched the ventilation back on. That done, he sank down on the edge of the bed.

He sat there for a long time, striking one cigarette after another. He knew too well that the peace of mind he thought he had regained was unreal. There was nothing left to him but shame and a long, long hurt. To have reached the point where he had to knuckle under to a tenth-rate knothead like Ed Schultz—it would have been better if he had never come out of the *Valkyrie* business.

Presently he took five grains of "Fly-Rite" from his pouch, swallowed it, and went to bed. He got up almost at once, forced himself to open the window a trifle, then compromised by changing the setting of the bed so that it would not turn out the lights after he got to sleep.

He had been asleep and dreaming for an indefinitely long time. He was back in space again—indeed, he had never been away from it. He was happy, with the full happiness of a man who has awakened to find it was only a bad dream.

The crying disturbed his serenity. At first it made him only vaguely uneasy, then he began to feel in some way responsible—he must do something about it. The transition to falling had only dream logic behind it, but it was real to him. He was grasping, his hands were slipping, had slipped—and there was nothing under him but the black emptiness of space—

He was awake and gasping, on Joe Tully's guestroom bed; the lights burned bright around him.

But the crying persisted.

He shook his head, then listened. It was real all right. Now he had it identified—a cat, a kitten by the sound of it.

He sat up. Even if he had not had the spaceman's traditional fondness for cats, he would have investigated. However, he liked cats for themselves, quite aside from their neat shipboard habits, their ready adaptability to changing accelerations, and their usefulness in keeping the ship free of those other creatures that go wherever man goes. So he got up at once and looked for this one.

A quick look showed him that the kitten was not in the room, and his ear led him to the correct spot; the sound came in through the slightly opened window. He shied off, stopped, and tried to collect his thoughts.

He told himself that it was unnecessary to do anything more; if the sound came in through his window, then it must be because it came out of some nearby window. But he knew that he was lying to himself; the sound was close by. In some impossible way the cat was just outside his window, thirty-five stories above the street.

He sat down and tried to strike a cigarette, but the tube broke in his fingers. He let the fragments fall to the floor, got up and took six nervous steps toward the window, as if he were being jerked along. He sank down to his knees, grasped the window and threw it wide open, then clung to the windowsill, his eyes shut tight.

After a time the sill seemed to steady a bit. He opened his eyes, gasped, and shut them again. Finally he opened them again, being very careful not to look out at the stars, not to look down at the street. He had half expected to find the cat on a balcony outside his room—it seemed the only reasonable explanation. But there was no balcony, no place at all where a cat could reasonably be.

However, the mewing was louder than ever. It seemed to come from directly under him. Slowly he forced his head out, still clinging to the sill, and made himself look down. Under him, about four feet lower than the edge of the window, a narrow ledge ran around the side of the building. Seated on it was a woebegone ratty-looking kitten. It stared up at him and meowed again.

It was barely possible that, by clinging to the sill with one hand and making a long arm with the other, he could reach it without actually going out the window, he thought—if he could bring himself to do it. He considered calling Tully, then thought better of it. Tully was shorter than he was, had less reach. And the kitten had to be rescued now, before the fluff-brained idiot jumped or fell.

He tried for it. He shoved his shoulders out, clung with his left arm and reached down with his right. Then he opened his eyes and saw that he was a foot or ten inches away from the kitten still. It sniffed curiously in the direction of his hand.

He stretched till his bones cracked. The kitten promptly skittered away from his clutching fingers, stopping a good six feet down the ledge. There it settled down and commenced washing its face.

He inched back inside and collapsed, sobbing, on the floor underneath the window. "I can't do it," he whispered. "I can't do it. Not again—"

The Rocket Ship *Valkyrie* was two hundred and forty-nine days out from Earth-Luna Space Terminal and approaching Mars Terminal on Deimos, outer Martian satellite. William Cole, Chief Communications Officer and relief pilot, was sleeping sweetly when his assistant shook him. "Hey! Bill! Wake up—we're in a jam."

"Huh? Wazzat?" But he was already reaching for his socks. "What's the trouble, Tom?"

Fifteen minutes later he knew that his junior officer had not exaggerated; he was reporting the facts to the Old Man—the primary piloting radar was out of whack. Tom Sandburg had discovered it during a routine check, made as soon as Mars was inside the maximum range of the radar pilot. The captain had shrugged. "Fix it, Mister—and be quick about it. We need it."

Bill Cole shook his head. "There's nothing wrong with it, Captain—inside. She acts as if the antenna were gone completely."

"That's impossible. We haven't even had a meteor alarm."

"Might be anything, Captain. Might be metal fatigue and it just fell off. But we've got to replace that antenna. Stop the spin on the ship and I'll go out and fix it. I can jury-rig a replacement while she loses her spin."

The *Valkyrie* was a luxury ship, of her day. She was assembled long before anyone had any idea of how to produce an artificial gravity field. Nevertheless she had pseudogravity for the comfort of her passengers. She spun endlessly around her main axis, like a shell from a rifled gun; the resulting angular acceleration—miscalled "centrifugal force"—kept her passengers firm in their beds, or steady on their feet. The spin was started as soon as her rockets stopped blasting at the beginning of a trip and was stopped only when it was necessary to maneuver into a landing. It was accomplished, not by magic, but by reaction against the contrary spin of a flywheel located on her centerline.

The captain looked annoyed. "I've started to take the spin off, but I can't wait that long. Jury-rig the astrogational radar for piloting."

Cole started to explain why the astrogational radar could not be adapted to short-range work, then decided not to try. "It can't be done, sir. It's a technical impossibility."

"When I was your age I could jury-rig anything! Well, find me an answer, Mister. I can't take this ship down blind. Not even for the Harriman Medal."

Bill Cole hesitated for a moment before replying, "I'll have to go out while she's still got spin on her, Captain, and make the replacement. There isn't any other way to do it."

The captain looked away from him, his jaw muscles flexed. "Get the replacement ready. Hurry up about it."

Cole found the captain already at the airlock when he arrived with the gear he needed for the repair. To his surprise the Old Man was suited up. "Explain to me what I'm to do," he ordered Bill.

"You're not going out, sir?" The captain simply nodded.

Bill took a look at his captain's waist line, or where his waist line used to be. Why, the Old Man must be thirty-five if he were a day! "I'm afraid I can't explain too clearly. I had expected to make the repair myself."

"I've never asked a man to do a job I wouldn't do myself. Explain it to me."

"Excuse me, sir—but can you chin yourself with one hand?"

"What's that got to do with it?"

"Well, we've got forty-eight passengers, sir, and—"

"Shut up!"

Sandburg and he, both in space suits, helped the Old Man down the hole after the inner door of the lock was closed and the air exhausted. The space beyond the lock was a vast, starflecked emptiness. With spin still on the ship, every direction outward was "down," down for millions of uncounted miles. They put a safety line on him, of course—nevertheless it gave him a sinking feeling to see the captain's head disappear in the bottomless, black hole.

The line paid out steadily for several feet, then stopped. When it had been stopped for several minutes, Bill leaned over and touched his helmet against Sandburg's. "Hang on to my feet. I'm going to take a look."

He hung his head down out the lock and looked around. The captain was stopped, hanging by both hands, nowhere near the antenna fixture. He scrambled back up and reversed himself. "I'm going out."

It was no great trick, he found, to hang by his hands and swing himself along to where the captain was stalled. The *Valkyrie* was a space-to-space ship, not like the sleek-sided jobs we see around earthports; she was covered with handholds for the convenience of repairmen at the terminals. Once he reached him, it was possible, by grasping the same steel rung that the captain clung to, to aid him in swinging back to the last one he had quitted. Five minutes later Sandburg was pulling the Old Man up through the hole and Bill was scrambling after him.

He began at once to unbuckle the repair gear from the captain's suit and transfer it to his own. He lowered himself back down the hole and was on his way before the older man had recovered enough to object, if he still intended to.

Swinging out to where the antenna must be replaced was not too hard, though he had all eternity under his toes. The suit impeded him a little—the gloves were clumsy—but he was used to spacesuits. He was a little winded from helping the captain, but he could not stop to think about that. The increased spin bothered him somewhat; the airlock was nearer the axis of spin than was the antenna—he felt heavier as he moved out.

Getting the replacement antenna shipped was another matter. It was neither large nor heavy, but he found it imposible to fasten it into place. He needed one hand to cling by, one to hold the antenna, and one to handle the wrench. That left him shy one hand, no matter how he tried it.

Finally, he jerked his safety line to signal Sandburg for more slack. Then he unshackled it from his waist, working with one hand, passed the end twice through a handhold and knotted it; he left about six feet of it hanging free. The shackle on the free end he fastened to another handhold. The result was a loop, a bight, an improvised bosun's chair, which would support his weight while he man-handled the antenna into place. The job went fairly quickly then.

He was almost through. There remained one bolt to fasten on the far side, away from where he swung. The antenna was already secured at two points and its circuit connection made. He decided he could manage it with one hand. He left his perch and swung over, monkey fashion.

The wrench slipped as he finished tightening the bolt; it slipped from his grasp, fell free. He watched it go, out and out and out, down and down and down, until it was so small he could no longer see it. It made him dizzy to watch it, bright in the sunlight against the deep black of space. He had been too busy to look down, up to now.

He shivered. "Good thing I was through with it," he said. "It would be a long walk to fetch it." He started to make his way back.

He found that he could not.

He had swung past the antenna to reach his present position, using a grip on his safety-line swing to give him a few inches more reach. Now the loop of line hung quietly, just out of reach. There was no way to reverse the process.

He hung by both hands and told himself not to get panicky—he must think his way out. Around the other side? No, the steel skin of the *Valkyrie* was smooth there—no handhold for more than six feet. Even if he were not tired—and he had to admit that he was, tired and getting a little cold— even if he were fresh, it was an impossible swing for anyone not a chimpanzee.

He looked down—and regretted it.

There was nothing below him but stars, down and down, endlessly. Stars, swinging past as the ship spun with him, emptiness of all time and blackness and cold.

He found himself trying to hoist himself bodily onto the single narrow rung he clung to, trying to reach it with his toes. It was a futile, strength-wasting excess. He quieted his panic sufficiently to stop it, then hung limp.

It was easier if he kept his eyes closed. But after a while he always had to open them and look. The Big Dipper would swing past and then, presently, Orion. He tried to compute the passing minutes in terms of the number of rotations the ship made, but his mind would not work clearly, and, after a while, he would have to shut his eyes.

His hands were becoming stiff—and cold. He tried to rest them by hanging by one hand at a time. He let go with his left hand, felt pins-and-needles course through it, and beat it against his side. Presently it seemed time to spell his right hand.

He could no longer reach up to the rung with his left hand. He did not have the power left in him to make the extra pull; he was fully extended and could not shorten himself enough to get his left hand up.

He could no longer feel his right hand at all.

He could see it slip. It was slipping—

The sudden release in tension let him know that he was falling . . . falling. The ship dropped away from him.

He came to with the captain bending over him. "Just keep quiet, Bill."

"Where—"

"Take it easy. The patrol from Deimos was already close by when you let go. They tracked you on the 'scope, matched orbits with you, and picked you up. First time in history, I guess. Now keep quiet. You're a sick man—you hung there more than two hours, Bill."

The meowing started up again, louder than ever. He got up on his knees and looked out over the windowsill. The kitten was still away to the left on the ledge. He thrust his head cautiously out a little further, remembering not to look at anything but the kitten and the ledge. "Here, kitty!" he called. "Here, kit-kit-kitty! Here, kitty, come kitty!"

The kitten stopped washing and managed to look puzzled.

"Come, kitty," he repeated softly. He let go of the windowsill with his right hand and gestured toward it invitingly. The kitten approached about three inches, then sat down. "Here, kitty," he pleaded and stretched his arm as far as possible.

The fluff ball promptly backed away again.

He withdrew his arm and thought about it. This was getting nowhere, he decided. If he were to slide over the edge and stand on the ledge, he could hang on with one arm and be perfectly safe. He knew that, he knew it would be safe—he needn't look down!

He drew himself back inside, reversed himself, and, with great caution, gripping the sill with both arms, let his legs slide down the face of the building. He focused his eyes carefully on the corner of the bed.

The ledge seemed to have been moved. He could not find it, and was beginning to be sure that he had reached past it, when he touched it with one toe—then he had both feet firmly planted on it. It seemed about six inches wide. He took a deep breath.

Letting go with his right arm, he turned and

faced the kitten. It seemed interested in the procedure but not disposed to investigate more closely. If he were to creep along the ledge, holding on with his left hand, he could just about reach it from the corner of the window—

He moved his feet one at a time, baby fashion, rather than pass one past the other. By bending his knees a trifle, and leaning, he could just manage to reach it. The kitten sniffed his groping fingers, then leaped backward. One tiny paw missed the edge; it scrambled and regained its footing. "You little idiot!" he said indignantly, "do you want to bash your brains out?"

"If any," he added. The situation looked hopeless now; the baby cat was too far away to be reached from his anchorage at the window, no matter how he stretched. He called "Kitty, kitty" rather hopelessly, then stopped to consider the matter.

He could give it up.

He could prepare himself to wait all night in the hope that the kitten would decide to come closer. Or he could go get it.

The ledge was wide enough to take his weight. If he made himself small, flat to the wall, no weight rested on his left arm. He moved slowly forward, retaining the grip on the window as long as possible, inching so gradually that he hardly seemed to move. When the window frame was finally out of reach, when his left hand was flat to smooth wall, he made the mistake of looking down, down, past the sheer wall at the glowing pavement far below.

He pulled his eyes back and fastened them on a

spot on the wall, level with his eyes and only a few feet away. He was still there!

And so was the kitten. Slowly he separated his feet, moving his right foot forward, and bent his knees. He stretched his right hand along the wall, until it was over and a little beyond the kitten.

He brought it down in a sudden swipe, as if to swat a fly. He found himself with a handful of scratching, biting fur.

He held perfectly still then, and made no attempt to check the minor outrages the kitten was giving him. Arms still outstretched, body flat to the wall, he started his return. He could not see where he was going and could not turn his head without losing some little of his margin of balance. It seemed a long way back, longer than he had come, when at last the fingertips of his left hand slipped into the window opening.

He backed up the rest of the way in a matter of seconds, slid both arms over the sill, then got his right knee over. He rested himself on the sill and took a deep breath. "Man!" he said aloud. "That was a tight squeeze. You're a menace to traffic, little cat."

He glanced down at the pavement. It was certainly a long way down—looked hard, too.

He looked up at the stars. Mighty nice they looked and mighty bright. He braced himself in the window frame, back against one side, foot pushed against the other, and looked at them. The kitten settled down in the cradle of his stomach and began to buzz. He stroked it absent-mindedly and reached for a cigarette. He would go out to the port and take his physical and his psycho tomorrow, he decided. He scratched the kitten's ears. "Little fluffhead," he said, "how would you like to take a long, long ride with me?"

The Green Hills of Earth

This is the story of Rhysling, the Blind Singer of the Spaceways—but not the official version. You sang his words in school:

> *"I pray for one last landing*
> *On the globe that gave me birth;*
> *Let me rest my eyes on the fleecy skies*
> *And the cool, green hills of Earth."*

Or perhaps you sang in French, or German. Or it might have been Esperanto, while Terra's rainbow banner rippled over your head.

The language does not matter—it was certainly an *Earth* tongue. No one has ever translated *"Green Hills"* into the lisping Venerian speech; no Martian ever croaked and whispered it in the dry corridors. This is ours. We of Earth have exported everything from Hollywood crawlies to synthetic radioactives, but this belongs solely to Terra, and to her sons and daughters wherever they may be.

We have all heard many stories of Rhysling. You may even be one of the many who have sought degrees, or acclaim, by scholarly evaluations of his published works—*Songs of the Spaceways, The Grand Canal, and other Poems, High and Far,* and *"UP SHIP!"*

Nevertheless, although you have sung his songs and read his verses, in school and out your whole life, it is at least an even money bet—unless you are a spaceman yourself—that you have never even heard of most of Rhysling's unpublished songs, such items as *Since the Pusher Met My Cousin, That Red-Headed Venusburg Gal, Keep Your Pants On, Skipper,* or *A Space Suit Built for Two.*

Nor can we quote them in a family magazine.

Rhysling's reputation was protected by a careful literary executor and by the happy chance that he was never interviewed. *Songs of the Spaceways* appeared the week he died; when it became a best seller, the publicity stories about him were pieced together from what people remembered about him plus the highly colored handouts from his publishers.

The resulting traditional picture of Rhysling is about as authentic as George Washington's hatchet or King Alfred's cakes.

In truth you would not have wanted him in your parlor; he was not socially acceptable. He had a permanent case of sun itch, which he scratched continually, adding nothing to his negligible beauty.

Van der Voort's portrait of him for the Harriman Centennial edition of his works shows a figure of high tragedy, a solemn mouth, sightless eyes concealed by black silk bandage. He was never solemn! His mouth was always open, singing, grinning, drinking, or eating. The bandage was any rag, usually dirty. After he lost his sight he became less and less neat about his person.

*   *   *

"Noisy" Rhysling was a jetman, second class, with eyes as good as yours, when he signed on for a loop trip to the Jovian asteroids in the R.S. *Goshawk*. The crew signed releases for everything in those days; a Lloyd's associate would have laughed in your face at the notion of insuring a spaceman. The Space Precautionary Act had never been heard of, and the Company was responsible only for wages, if and when. Half the ships that went further than Luna City never came back. Spacemen did not care; by preference they signed for shares, and any one of them would have bet you that he could jump from the 200th floor of Harriman Tower and ground safely, if you offered him three to two and allowed him rubber heels for the landing.

Jetmen were the most carefree of the lot and the meanest. Compared with them the masters, the radarmen, and the astrogators (there were no supers or stewards in those days) were gentle vegetarians. Jetmen knew too much. The others trusted the skill of the captain to get them down safely; jetmen knew that skill was useless against the blind and fitful devils chained inside their rocket motors.

The *Goshawk* was the first of Harriman's ships to be converted from chemical fuel to atomic power-piles—or rather the first that did not blow up. Rhysling knew her well; she was an old tub that had plied the Luna City run, Supra-New York space station to Leyport and back, before she was converted for deep space. He had worked the Luna run in her and had been along on the first deep space trip, Drywater on Mars—and back, to everyone's surprise.

He should have made chief engineer by the time he signed for the Jovian loop trip, but, after the Drywater pioneer trip, he had been fired, blacklisted, and grounded at Luna City for having spent his time writing a chorus and several verses at a time when he should have been watching his gauges. The song was the infamous *The Skipper is a Father to his Crew*, with the uproariously unprintable final couplet.

The blacklist did not bother him. He won an accordion from a Chinese barkeep in Luna City by cheating at one-thumb and thereafter kept going by singing to the miners for drinks and tips until the rapid attrition in spacemen caused the Company agent there to give him another chance. He kept his nose clean on the Luna run for a year or two, got back into deep space, helped give Venusburg its original ripe reputation, strolled the banks of the Grand Canal when a second colony was established at the ancient Martian capital, and froze his toes and ears on the second trip to Titan.

Things moved fast in those days. Once the power-pile drive was accepted the number of ships that put out from the Luna-Terra system was limited only by the availability of crews. Jetmen were scarce; the shielding was cut to a minimum to save weight and few married men cared to risk possible exposure to radioactivity. Rhysling did not want to be a father, so jobs were always open to him during the golden days of the claiming boom. He crossed and recrossed the system, singing the doggerel that boiled up in his head, chording it out on his accordion.

The master of the *Goshawk* knew him; Captain Hicks had been astrogator on Rhysling's first trip in her. "Welcome home, Noisy," Hicks had greeted him. "Are you sober, or shall I sign the book for you?"

"You can't get drunk on the bug juice they sell here, Skipper." He signed and went below, lugging his accordion.

Ten minutes later he was back. "Captain," he stated darkly, "that number two jet ain't fit. The cadmium dampers are warped."

"Why tell me? Tell the Chief."

"I did, but he says they will do. He's wrong."

The captain gestured at the book. "Scratch out your name and scram. We raise ship in thirty minutes."

Rhysling looked at him, shrugged, and went below again.

It is a long climb to the Jovian planetoids; a Hawk-class clunker had to blast for three watches before going into free flight. Rhysling had the second watch. Damping was done by hand then, with a multiplying vernier and a danger gauge. When the gauge showed red, he tried to correct it—no luck.

Jetmen don't wait; that's why they are jetmen. He slapped the emergency discover and fished at the hot stuff with the tongs. The lights went out, he went right ahead. A jetman has to know his power room the way your tongue knows the inside of your mouth.

He sneaked a quick look over the top of the lead baffle when the lights went out. The blue radioactive glow did not help him any; he jerked his head back and went on fishing by touch.

When he was done he called over the tube, "Number two jet out. And for crissake get me some light down here!"

There was light—the emergency circuit—but not for him. The blue radioactive glow was the last thing his optic nerve ever responded to.

II

*"As Time and Space come bending back to shape
this star-specked scene,
The tranquil tears of tragic joy still spread their
silver sheen;
Along the Grand Canal still soar the fragile Towers of Truth;
Their fairy grace defends this place of Beauty,
calm and couth.*

*"Bone-tired the race that raised the Towers, for-
gotten are their lores;
Long gone the gods who shed the tears that lap
these crystal shores.
Slow beats the time-worn heart of Mars beneath
this icy sky;
The thin air whispers voicelessly that all who live
must die—*

*"Yet still the lacy Spires of Truth sing Beauty's
madrigal
And she herself will ever dwell along the Grand
Canal!"*

—from *The Grand Canal*, by permission of
Lux Transcriptions, Ltd., London and Luna City

On the swing back they set Rhysling down on Mars at Drywater; the boys passed the hat and the skipper kicked in a half month's pay. That was all—*finis*—just another space bum who had not had the good fortune to finish it off when his luck ran out. He holed up with the prospectors and archeologists at How-Far? for a month or so, and could probably have stayed forever in exchange for his songs and his accordion playing. But spacemen die if they stay in one place; he hooked a crawler over to Drywater again and thence to Marsopolis.

The capital was well into its boom; the processing plants lined the Grand Canal on both sides and roiled the ancient waters with the filth of the run-off. This was before the Tri-Planet Treaty forbade disturbing cultural relics for commerce; half the slender, fairylike towers had been torn down, and others were disfigured to adapt them as pressurized buildings for Earthmen.

Now Rhysling had never seen any of these changes and no one described them to him; when he "saw" Marsopolis again, he visualized it as it had been, before it was rationalized for trade. His memory was good. He stood on the riparian esplanade where the ancient great of Mars had taken their ease and saw its beauty spreading out before his blinded eyes—ice blue plain of water unmoved by tide, untouched by breeze, and reflecting serenely the sharp, bright stars of the Martian sky, and beyond the water the lacy buttresses and flying towers of an architecture too delicate for our rumbling, heavy planet.

The result was *Grand Canal*.

The subtle change in his orientation which enabled him to see beauty at Marsopolis where beauty

was not now began to affect his whole life. All
women became beautiful to him. He knew them
by their voices and fitted their appearances to the
sounds. It is a mean spirit indeed who will speak
to a blind man other than in gentle friendliness;
scolds who had given their husbands no peace
sweetened their voices to Rhysling.

It populated his world with beautiful women
and gracious men. *Dark Star Passing, Berenice's
Hair, Death Song of a Wood's Colt*, and his
other love songs of the wanderers, the womenless
men of space, were the direct result of the fact that
his conceptions were unsullied by tawdry truths. It
mellowed his approach, changed his doggerel to
verse, and sometimes even to poetry.

He had plenty of time to think now, time to get
all the lovely words just so, and to worry a verse
until it sang true in his head. The monotonous
beat of *Jet Song*—

When the field is clear, the reports all seen,
When the lock sighs shut, when the lights wink
   green,
When the check-off's done, when it's time to pray,
When the Captain nods, when she blasts away—

   Hear the jets!
   Hear them snarl at your back
   When you're stretched on the rack;
   Feel your ribs clamp your chest,
   Feel your neck grind its rest.
   Feel the pain in your ship,
   Feel her strain in their grip,
   Feel her rise! Feel her drive!
   Straining steel, come alive,
   On her jets!

—came to him not while he himself was a jetman but later while he was hitchhiking from Mars to Venus and sitting out a watch with an old shipmate.

At Venusburg he sang his new songs and some of the old, in the bars. Someone would start a hat around for him; it would come back with a minstrel's usual take doubled or tripled in recognition of the gallant spirit behind the bandaged eyes.

It was an easy life. Any space port was his home and any ship his private carriage. No skipper cared to refuse to lift the extra mass of blind Rhysling and his squeeze box; he shuttled from Venusburg to Leyport to Drywater to New Shanghai, or back again, as the whim took him.

He never went closer to Earth than Supra-New York Space Station. Even when signing the contract for *Songs of the Spaceways* he made his mark in a cabin-class liner somewhere between Luna City and Ganymede. Horowitz, the original publisher, was aboard for a second honeymoon and heard Rhysling sing at a ship's party. Horowitz knew a good thing for the publishing trade when he heard it; the entire contents of *Songs* were sung directly into the tape in the communications room of the ship before he let Rhysling out of his sight. The next three volumes were squeezed out of Rhysling at Venusburg, where Horowitz had sent an agent to keep him liquored up until he had sung all he could remember.

UP SHIP! is certainly not authentic Rhysling throughout. Much of it is Rhysling's, no doubt, and *Jet Song* is unquestionably his, but most of the verses were collected after his death from people who had known him during his wanderings.

The Green Hills of Earth grew through twenty

years. The earliest form we know about was composed before Rhysling was blinded, during a drinking bout with some of the indentured men on Venus. The verses were concerned mostly with the things the labor clients intended to do back on Earth if and when they ever managed to pay their bounties and thereby be allowed to go home. Some of the stanzas were vulgar, some were not, but the chorus was recognizably that of *Green Hills*.

We know exactly where the final form of *Green Hills* came from, and when.

There was a ship in at Venus Ellis Isle which was scheduled for the direct jump from there to Great Lakes, Illinois. She was the old *Falcon*, youngest of the Hawk class and the first ship to apply the Harriman Trust's new policy of extra-fare express service between Earth cities and any colony with scheduled stops.

Rhysling decided to ride her back to Earth. Perhaps his own song had gotten under his skin—or perhaps he just hankered to see his native Ozarks one more time.

The Company no longer permitted deadheads; Rhysling knew this but it never occurred to him that the ruling might apply to him. He was getting old, for a spaceman, and just a little matter of fact about his privileges. Not senile—he simply knew that he was one of the landmarks in space, along with Halley's Comet, the Rings, and Brewster's Ridge. He walked in the crew's port, went below, and made himself at home in the first empty acceleration couch.

The Captain found him there while making a last minute tour of his ship. "What are you doing here?" he demanded.

"Dragging it back to Earth, Captain," Rhysling needed no eyes to see a skipper's four stripes.

"You can't drag in this ship; you know the rules. Shake a leg and get out of here. We raise ship at once." The Captain was young; he had come up after Rhysling's active time, but Rhysling knew the type—five years at Harriman Hall with only cadet practice trips instead of solid, deep space experience. The two men did not touch in background nor spirit; space was changing.

"Now, Captain, you wouldn't begrudge an old man a trip home."

The officer hesitated—several of the crew had stopped to listen. "I can't do it. 'Space Precautionary Act, Clause Six: No one shall enter space save as a licensed member of a crew of a chartered vessel, or as a paying passenger of such a vessel under such regulations as may be issued pursuant to this act.' Up you get and out you go."

Rhysling lolled back, his hands under his head. "If I've got to go, I'm damned if I'll walk. Carry me."

The Captain bit his lip and said, "Master-at-Arms! Have this man removed."

The ship's policeman fixed his eyes on the overhead struts. "Can't rightly do it, Captain. I've sprained my shoulder." The other crew members, present a moment before, had faded into the bulkhead paint.

"Well, get a working party!"

"Aye, aye, sir." He, too, went away.

Rhysling spoke again. "Now look, Skipper—let's not have any hard feelings about this. You've got an out to carry me if you want to—the 'Distressed Spaceman' clause."

" 'Distressed Spaceman,' my eye! You're no distressed spaceman; you're a space-lawyer. I know who you are; you've been bumming around the system for years. Well, you won't do it in my ship. That clause was intended to succor men who had missed their ships, not to let a man drag free all over space."

"Well, now, Captain, can you properly say I haven't missed my ship? I've never been back home since my last trip as a signed-on crew member. The law says I can have a trip back."

"But that was years ago. You've used up your chance."

"Have I now? The clause doesn't say a word about how soon a man has to take his trip back; it just says he's got it coming to him. Go look it up, Skipper. If I'm wrong, I'll not only walk out on my two legs, I'll beg your humble pardon in front of your crew. Go on—look it up. Be a sport."

Rhysling could feel the man's glare, but he turned and stomped out of the compartment. Rhysling knew that he had used his blindness to place the Captain in an impossible position, but this did not embarrass Rhysling—he rather enjoyed it.

Ten minutes later the siren sounded, he heard the orders on the bull horn for Up-Stations. When the soft sighing of the locks and the slight pressure change in his ears let him know that take-off was imminent he got up and shuffled down to the power room, as he wanted to be near the jets when they blasted off. He needed no one to guide him in any ship of the Hawk class.

Trouble started during the first watch. Rhysling had been lounging in the inspector's chair, fiddling with the keys of his accordion and trying out a new version of *Green Hills.*

> *"Let me breathe unrationed air again*
> *Where there's no lack nor dearth*

And something, something, something 'Earth' "— it would not come out right. He tried again.

> *"Let the sweet fresh breezes heal me*
> *As they rove around the girth*
> *Of our lovely mother planet,*
> *Of the cool green hills of Earth."*

That was better, he thought. "How do you like that, Archie?" he asked over the muted roar.

"Pretty good. Give out with the whole thing." Archie Macdougal, Chief Jetman, was an old friend, both spaceside and in bars; he had been an apprentice under Rhysling many years and millions of miles back.

Rhysling obliged, then said, "You youngsters have got it soft. Everything automatic. When I was twisting her tail you had to stay awake."

"You still have to stay awake." They fell to talking shop and Macdougal showed him the direct response damping rig which had replaced the manual vernier control which Rhysling had used. Rhysling felt out the controls and asked questions until he was familiar with the new installation. It was his conceit that he was still a jetman and that his present occupation as a troubadour was simply an expedient during one of the fusses with the company that any man could get into.

"I see you still have the old hand damping plates

installed," he remarked, his agile fingers flitting over the equipment.

"All except the links. I unshipped them because they obscure the dials."

"You ought to have them shipped. You might need them."

"Oh, I don't know. I think—" Rhysling never did find out what Macdougal thought for it was at that moment the trouble tore loose. Macdougal caught it square, a blast of radioactivity that burned him down where he stood.

Rhysling sensed what had happened. Automatic reflexes of old habit came out. He slapped the discover and rang the alarm to the control room simultaneously. Then he remembered the unshipped links. He had to grope until he found them, while trying to keep as low as he could to get maximum benefit from the baffles. Nothing but the links bothered him as to location. The place was as light to him as any place could be; he knew every spot, every control, the way he knew the keys of his accordion.

"Power room! Power room! What's the alarm?"

"Stay out!" Rhysling shouted. "The place is 'hot.'" He could feel it on his face and in his bones, like desert sunshine.

The links he got into place, after cursing someone, anyone, for having failed to rack the wrench he needed. Then he commenced trying to reduce the trouble by hand. It was a long job and ticklish. Presently he decided that the jet would have to be spilled, pile and all.

First he reported. "Control!"

"Control aye aye!"

"Spilling jet three—emergency."

"Is this Macdougal?"

"Macdougal is dead. This is Rhysling, on watch. Stand by to record."

There was no answer; dumbfounded the Skipper may have been, but he could not interfere in a power room emergency. He had the ship to consider, and the passengers and crew. The doors had to stay closed.

The Captain must have been still more surprised at what Rhysling sent for record. It was:

> *"We rot in the molds of Venus,*
> *We retch at her tainted breath.*
> *Foul are her flooded jungles,*
> *Crawling with unclean death."*

Rhysling went on cataloguing the Solar System as he worked, "—harsh bright soil of Luna—," "—Saturn's rainbow rings—," "—the frozen night of Titan—," all the while opening and spilling the jet and fishing it clean. He finished with an alternate chorus—

> *"We've tried each spinning space mote*
> *And reckoned its true worth:*
> *Take us back again to the homes of men*
> *On the cool, green hills of Earth."*

—then, almost absentmindedly remembered to tack on his revised first verse:

> *"The arching sky is calling*
> *Spacemen back to their trade.*
> *All hands! Stand by! Free falling!*
> *And the lights below us fade.*

> *Out ride the sons of Terra,*
> *Far drives the thundering jet,*
> *Up leaps the race of Earthmen,*
> *Out, far, and onward yet—"*

The ship was safe now and ready to limp home shy one jet. As for himself, Rhysling was not so sure. That "sunburn" seemed sharp, he thought. He was unable to see the bright, rosy fog in which he worked but he knew it was there. He went on with the business of flushing the air out through the outer valve, repeating it several times to permit the level of radioaction to drop to something a man might stand under suitable armor. While he did this he sent one more chorus, the last bit of authentic Rhysling that ever could be:

> *"We pray for one last landing*
> *On the globe that gave us birth;*
> *Let us rest our eyes on fleecy skies*
> *And the cool, green hills of Earth."*

Logic of Empire

"Don't be a sentimental fool, Sam!"

"Sentimental, or not," Jones persisted, "I know human slavery when I see it. That's what you've got on Venus."

Humphrey Wingate snorted. "That's utterly ridiculous. The company's labor clients are employees, working under legal contracts, freely entered into."

Jones' eyebrows raised slightly. "So? What kind of a contract is it that throws a man into jail if he quits his job?"

"That's not the case. Any client can quit his job on the usual two weeks notice—I ought to know; I—"

"Yes, I know," agreed Jones in a tired voice. "You're a lawyer. You know all about contracts. But the trouble with you, you dunderheaded fool, is that all you understand is legal phrases. Free contract—nuts! What I'm talking about is *facts*, not legalisms. I don't care what the contract says— those people are slaves!"

Wingate emptied his glass and set it down. "So I'm a dunderheaded fool, am I? Well, I'll tell you what you are, Sam Houston Jones—you are a half-baked parlor pink. You've never had to work for a living in your life and you think it's just too dreadful that anyone else should have to. No, wait a minute," he continued, as Jones opened his mouth, "listen to me. The company's clients on Venus are a damn sight better off than most people of their own class here on earth. They are certain of a job, of food, and a place to sleep. If they get sick, they're certain of medical attention. The trouble with people of that class is that they don't want to work—"

"Who does?"

"Don't be funny. The trouble is, if they weren't under a fairly tight contract, they'd throw up a good job the minute they got bored with it and expect the company to give 'em a free ride back to Earth. Now it may not have occurred to your fine, free charitable mind, but the company has obligations to its stockholders—you, for instance!—and it can't afford to run an interplanetary ferry for the benefit of a class of people that feel that the world owes them a living."

"You got me that time, pal," Jones acknowledged with a wry face, "—that crack about me being a stockholder. I'm ashamed of it."

"Then why don't you sell?"

Jones looked disgusted. "What kind of a solution is that? Do you think I can avoid the responsibilty of *knowing* about it just unloading my stock?"

"Oh, the devil with it," said Wingate. "Drink up."

"Righto," agreed Jones. It was his first night

aground after a practice cruise as a reserve officer; he needed to catch up on his drinking. Too bad, thought Wingate, that the cruise should have touched at Venus—

"All out! All out! Up *aaaall* you idlers! Show a leg there! Show a leg and grab a sock!" The raucous voice sawed its way through Wingate's aching head. He opened his eyes, was blinded by raw white light, and shut them hastily. But the voice would not let him alone. "Ten minutes till breakfast," it rasped. "Come and get it, or we'll throw it out!"

He opened his eyes again, and with trembling willpower forced them to track. Legs moved past his eyes, denim clad legs mostly, though some were bare—repulsive hairy nakedness. A confusion of male voices, from which he could catch words but not sentences, was accompanied by an obligato of metallic sounds, muffled but pervasive—shrrg, shrrg, thump! Shrrg, shrrg, thump! The thump with which the cycle was completed hurt his aching head but was not as nerve stretching as another noise, a toneless whirring sibilance which he could neither locate nor escape.

The air was full of the odor of human beings, too many of them in too small a space. There was nothing so distinct as to be fairly termed a stench, nor was the supply of oxygen inadequate. But the room was filled with the warm, slightly musky smell of bodies still heated by bedclothes, bodies not dirty but not freshly washed. It was oppressive and unappetizing—in his present state almost nauseating.

He began to have some appreciation of the nature of his surroundings; he was in a bunkroom of some sort. It was crowded with men, men getting up, shuffling about, pulling on clothes. He lay on the bottom-most of a tier of four narrow bunks. Through the interstices between the legs which crowded around him and moved past his face he could see other such tiers around the walls and away from the walls, stacked floor to ceiling and supported by stanchions.

Someone sat down on the foot of Wingate's bunk, crowding his broad fundament against Wingate's ankles while he drew on his socks. Wingate squirmed his feet away from the intrusion. The stranger turned his face toward him. "Did I crowd 'ja, bud? Sorry." Then he added, not unkindly, "Better rustle out of there. The Master-at-Arms'll be riding you to get them bunks up." He yawned hugely, and started to get up, quite evidently having dismissed Wingate and Wingate's affairs from his mind.

"Wait a minute!" Wingate demanded hastily.

"Huh?"

"Where am I? In jail?"

The stranger studied Wingate's bloodshot eyes and puffy, unwashed face with detached but unmalicious interest. "Boy, oh boy, you must 'a' done a good job of drinking up your bounty money."

"Bounty money? What the hell are you talking about?"

"Honest to God, don't you know where you are?"

"No."

"Well . . ." The other seemed reluctant to proclaim a truth made silly by its self-evidence until

Wingate's expression convinced him that he really wanted to know. "Well, you're in the *Evening Star*, headed for Venus."

A couple of minutes later the stranger touched him on the arm. "Don't take it so hard, bud. There's nothing to get excited about."

Wingate took his hands from his face and pressed them against his temples. "It's not real," he said, speaking more to himself than to the other. "It can't be real—"

"Stow it. Come and get your breakfast."

"I couldn't eat anything."

"Nuts. Know how you feel . . . felt that way sometimes myself. Food is just the ticket." The Master-at-Arms settled the issue by coming up and prodding Wingate in the ribs with his truncheon.

"What d'yuh think this is—sickbay, or first class? Get those bunks hooked up."

"Easy, mate, easy," Wingate's new acquaintance conciliated, "our pal's not himself this morning." As he spoke he dragged Wingate to his feet with one massive hand, then with the other shoved the tier of bunks up and against the wall. Hooks clicked into their sockets, and the tier stayed up, flat to the wall.

"He'll be a damn sight less himself if he interferes with my routine," the petty officer predicted. But he moved on. Wingate stood barefooted on the floorplates, immobile and overcome by a feeling of helpless indecision which was reinforced by the fact that he was dressed only in his underwear. His champion studied him.

"You forgot your pillow. Here—" He reached down into the pocket formed by the lowest bunk and the wall and hauled out a flat package covered with transparent plastic. He broke the seal and shook out the contents, a single coverall garment of heavy denim. Wingate put it on gratefully. "You can get the squeezer to issue you a pair of slippers after breakfast," his friend added. "Right now we gotta eat."

The last of the queue had left the galley window by the time they reached it and the window was closed. Wingate's companion pounded on it. "Open up in there!"

It slammed open. "No seconds," a face announced.

The stranger prevented the descent of the window with his hand. "We don't want seconds, shipmate, we want firsts."

"Why the devil can't you show up on time?" the galley functionary groused. But he slapped two ration cartons down on the broad sill of the issuing window. The big fellow handed one to Wingate, and sat down on the floor-plates, his back supported by the galley bulkhead.

"What's your name, bud?" he inquired, as he skinned the cover off his ration. "Mine's Hartley— 'Satchel' Hartley."

"Mine is Humphrey Wingate."

"Okay, Hump. Pleased to meet 'cha. Now what's all this song and dance you been giving me?" He spooned up an impossible bite of baked eggs and sucked coffee from the end of his carton.

"Well," said Wingate, his face twisted with worry, "I guess I've been shanghaied." He tried to emulate Hartley's method of drinking, and got the brown liquid over his face.

"Here—that's no way to do," Hartley said hastily. "Put the nipple in your mouth, then don't

squeeze any harder than you suck. Like this." He
illustrated. "Your theory don't seem very sound to
me. The company don't need crimps when there's
plenty of guys standing in line for a chance to sign
up. What happened? Can't you remember?"

Wingate tried. "The last thing I recall," he
said, "is arguing with a gyro driver over his fare."

Hartley nodded. "They'll gyp you every time.
D'you think he put the slug on you?"

"Well . . . no, I guess not. I seem to be all
right, except for the damndest hangover you can
imagine."

"You'll feel better. You ought to be glad the
Evening Star is a high-gravity ship instead of a
trajectory job. Then you'd really be sick, and no
foolin'."

"How's that?"

"I mean that she accelerates or decelerates her
whole run. Has to, because she carries cabin passengers. If we had been sent by a freighter, it'd be
a different story. They gun 'em into the right
trajectory, then go weightless for the rest of the
trip. Man, how the new chums do suffer!" He
chuckled.

Wingate was in no condition to dwell on the
hardships of space sickness. "What I can't figure
out," he said, "is how I landed here. Do you
suppose they could have brought me aboard by
mistake, thinking I was somebody else?"

"Can't say. Say, aren't you going to finish your
breakfast?"

"I've had all I want." Hartley took his statement
as an invitation and quickly finished off Wingate's
ration. Then he stood up, crumpled the two car-

tons into a ball, stuffed them down a disposal chute, and said,

"What are you going to do about it?"

"What am I going to do about it?" A look of decision came over Wingate's face. "I'm going to march right straight up to the Captain and demand an explanation, that's what I'm going to do!"

"I'd take that by easy stages, Hump," Hartley commented doubtfully.

"Easy stages, hell!" He stood up quickly. "Ow! My head!"

The Master-at-Arms referred them to the Chief Master-at-Arms in order to get rid of them. Hartley waited with Wingate outside the stateroom of the Chief Master-at-Arms to keep him company. "Better sell 'em your bill of goods pretty pronto," he advised.

"Why?"

"We'll ground on the Moon in a few hours. The stop to refuel at Luna City for deep space will be your last chance to get out, unless you want to walk back."

"I hadn't thought of that," Wingate agreed delightedly. "I thought I'd have to make the round trip in any case."

"Shouldn't be surprised but what you could pick up the *Morning Star* in a week or two. If it's their mistake, they'll have to return you."

"I can beat that," said Wingate eagerly. "I'll go right straight to the bank at Luna City, have them arrange a letter of credit with my bank, and buy a ticket on the Earth-Moon shuttle."

Hartley's manner underwent a subtle change. He had never in his life "arranged a letter of credit." Perhaps such a man *could* walk up to the Captain and lay down the law.

The Chief Master-at-Arms listened to Wingate's story with obvious impatience, and interrupted him in the middle of it to consult his roster of emigrants. He thumbed through it to the Ws, and pointed to a line. Wingate read it with a sinking feeling. There was his own name, correctly spelled. "Now get out," ordered the official, "and quit wasting my time."

But Wingate stood up to him. "You have no authority in this matter—none whatsoever. I insist that you take me to the Captain."

"Why, you—" Wingate thought momentarily that the man was going to strike him. He interrupted.

"Be careful what you do. You are apparently the victim of an honest mistake—but your legal position will be very shaky indeed, if you disregard the requirements of spacewise law under which this vessel is licensed. I don't think your Captain would be pleased to have to explain such actions on your part in federal court."

That he had gotten the man angry was evident. But a man does not get to be chief police officer of a major transport by jeopardizing his superior officers. His jaw muscles twitched but he pressed a button, saying nothing. A junior master-at-arms appeared. "Take this man to the Purser." He turned his back in dismissal and dialed a number on the ship's intercommunication system.

Wingate was let in to see the Purser, ex-officio company business agent, after only a short wait. "What's this all about?" that officer demanded. "If you have a complaint, why can't you present it at the morning hearings in the regular order?"

Wingate explained his predicament as clearly, convincingly, and persuasively as he knew how. "And so you see," he concluded, "I want to be put aground at Luna City. I've no desire to cause the company any embarrassment over what was undoubtedly an unintentional mishap—particularly as I am forced to admit that I had been celebrating rather freely and, perhaps, in some manner, contributed to the mistake."

The Purser, who had listened noncommittally to his recital, made no answer. He shuffled through a high stack of file folders which rested on one corner of his desk, selected one, and opened it. It contained a sheaf of legal-size papers clipped together at the top. These he studied leisurely for several minutes, while Wingate stood waiting.

The Purser breathed with an asthmatic noisiness while he read, and, from time to time, drummed on his bared teeth with his fingernails. Wingate had about decided, in his none too steady nervous condition, that if the man approached his hand to his mouth just once more that he, Wingate, would scream and start throwing things. At this point the Purser chucked the dossier across the desk toward Wingate. "Better have a look at these," he said.

Wingate did so. The main exhibit he found to be a contract, duly entered into, between Humphrey Wingate and the Venus Development Company for six years of indentured labor on the planet Venus.

"That your signature?" asked the Purser.

Wingate's professional caution stood him in good stead. He studied the signature closely in order to gain time while he tried to collect his wits. "Well," he said at last, "I will stipulate that it looks very much like my signature, but I will not concede that it is my signature—I'm not a handwriting expert."

The Purser brushed aside the objection with an air of annoyance. "I haven't time to quibble with you. Let's check the thumbprint. Here." He shoved an impression pad across his desk. For a moment Wingate considered standing on his legal rights by refusing, but no, that would prejudice his case. He had nothing to lose; it *couldn't* be his thumbprint on the contract. Unless—

But it was. Even his untrained eye could see that the two prints matched. He fought back a surge of panic. This was probably a nightmare, inspired by his argument last night with Jones. Or, if by some wild chance it were real, it was a frameup in which he must find the flaw. Men of his sort were not framed; the whole thing was ridiculous. He marshalled his words carefully.

"I won't dispute your position, my dear sir. In some fashion both you and I have been made the victims of a rather sorry joke. It seems hardly necessary to point out that a man who is unconscious, as I must have been last night, may have his thumbprint taken without his knowledge. Superficially this contract is valid and I assume naturally your good faith in the matter. But, in fact, the instrument lacks one necessary element of a contract."

"Which is?"

"The intention on the part of both parties to enter into a contractual relationship. Notwithstanding signature and thumbprint I had no intention of contracting which can easily be shown by other factors. I am a successful lawyer with a good practice, as my tax returns will show. It is not reasonable to believe—and no court *will* believe—that I voluntarily gave up my accustomed life for six years of indenture at a much lower income."

"So you're a lawyer, eh? Perhaps there has been chicanery—on your part. How does it happen that you represent yourself here as a radio technician?"

Wingate again had to steady himself at this unexpected flank attack. He was in truth a radio expert—it was his cherished hobby—but how had they known? Shut up, he told himself. Don't admit anything. "The whole thing is ridiculous," he protested. "I insist that I be taken to see the Captain—I can break that contract in ten minutes time."

The Purser waited before replying. "Are you through speaking your piece?"

"Yes."

"Very well. You've had your say, now I'll have mine. You listen to me, Mister Spacelawyer. The contract was drawn up by some of the shrewdest legal minds in two planets. They had specifically in mind that worthless bums would sign it, drink up their bounty money, and then decide that they didn't want to go to work after all. That contract has been subjected to every sort of attack possible and revised so that it can't be broken by the devil himself.

"You're not peddling your curbstone law to another stumble-bum in this case; you are talking to a man who knows just where he stands, legally. As for seeing the Captain—if you think the commanding officer of a major vessel has nothing more to do than listen to the *rhira*-dreams of a self-appointed word artist, you've got another think coming! Return to your quarters!"

Wingate started to speak, thought better of it, and turned to go. This would require some thought. The Purser stopped him. "Wait. Here's your copy of the contract." He chucked it, the flimsy white sheets riffled to the deck. Wingate picked them up and left silently.

Hartley was waiting for him in the passageway. "How d'ja make out, Hump?"

"Not so well. No, I don't want to talk about it. I've got to think." They walked silently back the way they had come toward the ladder which gave access to the lower decks. A figure ascended from the ladder and came toward them. Wingate noted it without interest.

He looked again. Suddenly the whole preposterous chain of events fell into place; he shouted in relief. "Sam!" he called out. "Sam—you cockeyed old so-and-so. I should have spotted your handiwork." It was all clear now; Sam had framed him with a phony shanghai. Probably the skipper was a pal of Sam's—a reserve officer, maybe—and they had cooked it up between them. It was a rough sort of a joke, but he was too relieved to be angry. Just the same he would make Jones pay for his fun, somehow, on the jump back from Luna City.

It was then that he noticed that Jones was not laughing.

Furthermore he was dressed—most unreasonably—in the same blue denim that the contract laborers were. "Hump," he was saying, "are you still drunk?"

"Me? No. What's the i—"

"Don't you realize we're in a jam?"

"Oh hell, Sam, a joke's a joke, but don't keep it

up any longer. I've caught on, I tell you. I don't mind—it was a good gag."

"Gag, eh?" said Jones bitterly. "I suppose it was just a gag when you talked me into signing up."

"*I* persuaded *you* to sign up?"

"You certainly did. You were so damn sure you knew what you were talking about. You claimed that we could sign up, spend a month or so on Venus, and come home. You wanted to bet on it. So we went around to the docks and signed up. It seemed like a good idea then—the only way to settle the argument."

Wingate whistled softly. "Well, I'll be—Sam, I haven't the slightest recollection of it. I must have drawn a blank before I passed out."

"Yeah, I guess so. Too bad you didn't pass out sooner. Not that I'm blaming you; you didn't drag me. Anyhow, I'm on my way up to try to straighten it out."

"Better wait a minute till you hear what happened to me. Oh yes—Sam, this is, uh, Satchel Hartley. Good sort." Hartley had been waiting uncertainly near them; he stepped forward and shook hands.

Wingate brought Jones up to date, and added, "So you see your reception isn't likely to be too friendly. I guess I muffed it. But we are sure to break the contract as soon as we can get a hearing on time alone."

"How do you mean?"

"We were signed up less than twelve hours before ship lifting. That's contrary to the Space Precautionary Act."

"Yes—yes, I see what you mean. The Moon's in her last quarter; they would lift ship some time

after midnight to take advantage of favorable
earthswing. I wonder what time it was when we
signed on?"

Wingate took out his contract copy. The notary's
stamp showed a time of eleven thirty-two. "Great
Day!" he shouted. "I knew there would be a flaw in
it somewhere. This contract is invalid on its face.
The ship's log will prove it."

Jones studied it. "Look again," he said. Wingate
did so. The stamp showed eleven thirty-two, but
A.M., not P.M.

"But that's impossible," he protested.

"Of course it is. But it's official. I think we will
find that the story is that we were signed on in the
morning, paid our bounty money, and had one last
glorious luau before we were carried aboard. I
seem to recollect some trouble in getting the re-
cruiter to sign us up. Maybe we convinced him by
kicking in our bounty money."

"But we *didn't* sign up in the morning. It's not
true and I can prove it."

"Sure you can prove it—*but how can you prove
it without going back to Earth first!*"

"So you see it's this way," Jones decided after
some minutes of somewhat fruitless discussion,
"there is no sense in trying to break our contracts
here and now; they'll laugh at us. The thing to do
is to make money talk, and talk loud. The only
way I can see to get us off at Luna City is to post
non-performance bonds with the company bank
there—cash, and damn big ones, too."

"How big?"

"Twenty thousand credits, at least, I should
guess."

"But that's not equitable—it's all out of proportion."

"Quit worrying about equity, will you? Can't you realize that they've got us where the hair is short? This won't be a bond set by a court ruling; it's got to be big enough to make a minor company official take a chance on doing something that's not in the book."

"I can't raise such a bond."

"Don't worry about that. I'll take care of it."

Wingate wanted to argue the point, but did not. There are times when it is very convenient to have a wealthy friend.

"I've got to get a radiogram off to my sister," Jones went on, "to get this done—"

"Why your sister? Why not your family firm?"

"Because we need fast action, that's why. The lawyers that handle our family finances would fiddle and fume around trying to confirm the message. They'd send a message back to the Captain, asking if Sam Houston Jones were really aboard, and he would answer 'No,' as I'm signed up as Sam Jones. I had some silly idea of staying out of the news broadcasts, on account of the family."

"You can't blame them," protested Wingate, feeling an obscure clannish loyalty to his colleagues in law, "they're handling other peoples' money."

"I'm not blaming them. But I've got to have fast action and Sis'll do what I ask her. I'll phrase the message so she'll know it's me. The only hurdle now is to persuade the Purser to let me send a message on tick."

He was gone for a long time on this mission. Hartley waited with Wingate, both to keep him company and because of a strong human interest in unusual events. When Jones finally appeared he wore a look of tight-lipped annoyance. Wingate, seeing the expression, felt a sudden, chilling apprehension. "Couldn't you send it? Wouldn't he let you?"

"Oh, he let me—finally," Jones admitted, "but that Purser—man, is he tight!"

Even without the alarm gongs Wingate would have been acutely aware of the grounding at Luna City. The sudden change from the high gravity deceleration of their approach to the weak surface gravity—one-sixth earth normal—of the Moon took immediate toll on his abused stomach. It was well that he had not eaten much. Both Hartley and Jones were deepspace men and regarded enough acceleration to permit normal swallowing as adequate for any purpose. There is a curious lack of sympathy between those who are subject to spacesickness and those who are immune to it. Why the spectacle of a man regurgitating, choked, eyes streaming with tears, stomach knotted with pain, should seem funny is difficult to see, but there it is. It divides the human race into two distinct and antipathetic groups—amused contempt on one side, helpless murderous hatred on the other.

Neither Hartley nor Jones had the inherent sadism which is too frequently evident on such occasions—for example the great wit who suggests salt pork as a remedy—but, feeling no discomfort themselves, they were simply unable to comprehend (having forgotten the soul-twisting intensity of their own experience as new chums) that Wingate was literally suffering "a fate worse than death" —much worse, for it was stretched into a sensible eternity by a distortion of the time sense known only to sufferers from spacesicknesses, seasicknesses, and (we are told) smokers of hashish.

As a matter of fact, the stop on the Moon was less than four hours long. Toward the end of the wait Wingate had quieted down sufficiently again to take an interest in the expected reply to Jones' message, particularly after Jones had assured him that he would be able to spend the expected lay-over under bond at Luna City in a hotel equipped with a centrifuge.

But the answer was delayed. Jones had expected to hear from his sister within an hour, perhaps before the *Evening Star* grounded at the Luna City docks. As the hours stretched out he managed to make himself very unpopular at the radio room by his repeated inquiries. An over-worked clerk had sent him brusquely about his business for the seventeenth time when he heard the alarm sound preparatory to raising ship; he went back and admitted to Wingate that his scheme had apparently failed.

"Of course, we've got ten minutes yet," he finished unhopefully, "if the message should arrive before they raise ship, the Captain could still put us aground at the last minute. We'll go back and haunt 'em some more right up to the last. But it looks like a thin chance."

"Ten minutes—" said Wingate, "couldn't we manage somehow to slip outside and run for it?"

Jones looked exasperated. "Have you ever tried running in a total vacuum?"

Wingate had very little time in which to fret on the passage from Luna City to Venus. He learned a great deal about the care and cleaning of washrooms, and spent ten hours a day perfecting his new skill. Masters-at-Arms have long memories.

The *Evening Star* passed beyond the limits of ship-to-Terra radio communication shortly after leaving Luna City; there was nothing to do but wait until arrival at Adonis, port of the north polar colony. The company radio there was strong enough to remain in communication at all times except for the sixty days bracketing superior conjunction and a shorter period of solar interference at inferior conjunction. "They will probably be waiting for us with a release order when we ground," Jones assured Wingate, "and we'll go back on the return trip of the *Evening Star*—first class, this time. Or, at the very worst, we'll have to wait over for the *Morning Star*. That wouldn't be so bad, once I get some credit transferred; we could spend it at Venusburg."

"I suppose you went there on your cruise," Wingate said, curiosity showing in his voice. He was no Sybarite, but the lurid reputation of the most infamous, or famous—depending on one's evaluations—pleasure city of three planets was enough to stir the imagination of the least hedonistic.

"No—worse luck!" Jones denied. "I was on a hull inspection board the whole time. Some of my messmates went, though . . . boy!" He whistled softly and shook his head.

But there was no one awaiting their arrival, nor was there any message. Again they stood around the communication office until told sharply and officially to get on back to their quarters and stand by to disembark, "—and be quick about it!"

"I'll see you in the receiving barracks, Hump,"

were Jones' last words before he hurried off to his own compartment.

The Master-at-Arms responsible for the compartment in which Hartley and Wingate were billeted lined his charges up in a rough column of two's and, when ordered to do so by the metallic bray of the ship's loudspeaker, conducted them through the central passageway and down four decks to the lower passenger port. It stood open; they shuffled through the lock and out of the ship— not into the free air of Venus, but into a sheetmetal tunnel which joined it, after some fifty yards, to a building.

The air within the tunnel was still acrid from the atomized antiseptic with which it had been flushed out, but to Wingate it was nevertheless fresh and stimulating after the stale flatness of the repeatedly reconditioned air of the transport. That, plus the surface gravity of Venus, five-sixths of earthnormal, strong enough to prevent nausea yet low enough to produce a feeling of lightness and strength—these things combined to give him an irrational optimism, an up-and-at-'em frame of mind.

The exit from the tunnel gave into a moderately large room, windowless but brilliantly and glarelessly lighted from concealed sources. It contained no furniture.

"Squaaad—HALT!" called out the Master-at-Arms, and handed papers to a slight, clerkish-appearing man who stood near an inner doorway. The man glanced at the papers, counted the detachment, then signed one sheet, which he handed back to the ship's petty officer who accepted it and returned through the tunnel.

The clerkish man turned to the immigrants. He

was dressed, Wingate noted, in nothing but the briefest of shorts, hardly more than a strap, and his entire body, even his feet, was a smooth mellow tan. "Now men," he said in a mild voice, "strip off your clothes and put them in the hopper." He indicated a fixture set in one wall.

"Why?" asked Wingate. His manner was uncontentious but he made no move to comply.

"Come now," he was answered, still mildly but with a note of annoyance, "don't argue. It's for your own protection. We can't afford to import disease."

Wingate checked a reply and unzipped his coverall. Several who had paused to hear the outcome followed his example. Suits, shoes, underclothing, socks, they all went into the hopper. "Follow me," said their guide.

In the next room the naked herd were confronted by four "barbers" armed with electric clippers and rubber gloves who proceeded to clip them smooth. Again Wingate felt disposed to argue, but decided the issue was not worth it. But he wondered if the female labor clients were required to submit to such drastic quarantine precautions. It would be a shame, it seemed to him, to sacrifice a beautiful head of hair that had been twenty years in growing.

The succeeding room was a shower room. A curtain of warm spray completely blocked passage through the room. Wingate entered it unreluctantly, even eagerly, and fairly wallowed in the first decent bath he had been able to take since leaving Earth. They were plentifully supplied with liquid green soap, strong and smelly, but which lathered freely. Half a dozen attendants, dressed as skimpily as their guide, stood on the far side of the wall of water and saw to it that the squad remained under the shower a fixed time and scrubbed. In some cases they made highly personal suggestions to insure thoroughness. Each of them wore a red cross on a white field affixed to his belt which lent justification to their officiousness.

Blasts of warm air in the exit passageway dried them quickly and completely.

"Hold still." Wingate complied, the bored hospital orderly who had spoken dabbed at Wingate's upper arm with a swab which felt cold to touch, then scratched the spot. "That's all, move on." Wingate added himself to the queue at the next table. The experience was repeated on the other arm. By the time he had worked down to the far end of the room the outer sides of each arm were covered with little red scratches, more than twenty of them.

"What's this all about?" he asked the hospital clerk at the end of the line, who had counted his scratches and checked his name off a list.

"Skin tests . . . to check your resistances and immunities."

"Resistance to what?"

"Anything. Both terrestrial and Venerian diseases. Fungoids, the Venus ones are, mostly. Move on, you're holding up the line." He heard more about it later. It took from two to three weeks to recondition the ordinary terrestrial to Venus conditions. Until that reconditioning was complete and immunity was established to the new hazards of another planet it was literally death to an Earth man to expose his skin and particularly his mucous membranes to the ravenous invisible parasites of the surface of Venus.

The ceaseless fight of life against life which is the dominant characteristic of life anywhere proceeds with especial intensity, under conditions of high metabolism, in the steamy jungles of Venus. The general bacteriophage which has so nearly eliminated disease caused by pathogenic microorganisms on Earth was found capable of a subtle modification which made it potent against the analogous but different diseases of Venus. The hungry fungi were another matter.

Imagine the worst of the fungoid-type skin diseases you have ever encountered—ringworn, dhobie itch, athlete's foot, Chinese rot, saltwater itch, seven year itch. Add to that your conception of mold, of damp rot, of scale, of toadstools feeding on decay. Then conceive them speeded up in their processes, visibly crawling as you watch—picture them attacking your eyeballs, your armpits, the soft wet tissues inside your mouth, working down into your lungs.

The first Venus expedition was lost entirely. The second had a surgeon with sufficient imagination to provide what seemed a liberal supply of salicylic acid and mercury salicylate as well as a small ultraviolet radiator. Three of them returned.

But permanent colonization depends on adaptation to environment, not insulating against it. Luna City might be cited as a case which denies this proposition but it is only superficially so. While it is true that the "lunatics" are absolutely dependent on their citywide hermetically-sealed air bubble, Luna City is not a self-sustaining colony; it is an outpost, useful as a mining station, as an observatory, as a refueling stop beyond the densest portion of Terra's gravitational field.

Venus is a colony. The colonists breathe the air of Venus, eat its food, and expose their skins to its climate and natural hazards. Only the cold polar regions—approximately equivalent in weather conditions to an Amazonian jungle on a hot day in the rainy season—are tenable by terrestrials, but here they slop barefooted on the marshy soil in a true ecological balance.

Wingate ate the meal that was offered him—satisfactory but roughly served and dull, except for Venus sweet-sour melon, the portion of which he ate would have fetched a price in a Chicago gourmets' restaurant equivalent to the food budget for a week of a middle-class family—and located his assigned sleeping billet. Thereafter he attempted to locate Sam Houston Jones. He could find no sign of him among the other labor clients, nor any one who remembered having seen him. He was advised by one of the permanent staff of the conditioning station to enquire of the factor's clerk. This he did, in the ingratiating manner he had learned it was wise to use in dealing with minor functionaries.

"Come back in the morning. The lists will be posted."

"Thank you, sir. Sorry to have bothered you, but I can't find him and I was afraid he might have taken sick or something. Could you tell me if he is on the sick list?"

"Oh, well—Wait a minute." The clerk thumbed through his records. "Hmmm . . . you say he was in the *Evening Star?*"

"Yes, sir."

"Well, he's not . . . Mmmm, no—Oh, yes, here he is. He didn't disembark here."

"What did you say?"

"He went on with the *Evening Star* to New Auckland, South Pole. He's stamped in as a machinist's helper. If you had told me that, I'd 'a' known. All the metal workers in this consignment were sent to work on the new South Power Station."

After a moment Wingate pulled himself together enough to murmur, "Thanks for your trouble."

" 'S all right. Don't mention it." The clerk turned away.

South Pole Colony! He muttered it to himself. South Pole Colony, his only friend twelve thousand miles away. At last Wingate felt alone, alone and trapped, abandoned. During the short interval between waking up aboard the transport and finding Jones also aboard he had not had time fully to appreciate his predicament, nor had he, then, lost his upper class arrogance, the innate conviction that it could not be serious—such things just don't happen to people, not to people one *knows!*

But in the meantime he had suffered such assaults to his human dignity (the Chief Master-at-Arms had seen to some of it) that he was no longer certain of his essential inviolability from unjust or arbitrary treatment. But now, shaved and bathed without his consent, stripped of his clothing and attired in a harnesslike breechclout, transported millions of miles from his social matrix, subject to the orders of persons indifferent to his feelings and who claimed legal control over his person and actions, and now, most bitterly, cut off from the one human contact which had given him support and courage and hope, he realized at last with chilling thoroughness that anything could happen to him, to *him*, Humphrey Belmont Wingate, successful attorney-at-law and member of all the right clubs.

"Wingate!"

"That's you, Jack. Go on in, don't keep them waiting." Wingate pushed through the doorway and found himself in a fairly crowded room. Thirty-odd men were seated around the sides of the room. Near the door a clerk sat at a desk, busy with papers. One brisk-mannered individual stood in the cleared space between the chairs near a low platform on which all the illumination of the room was concentrated. The clerk at the door looked up to say, "Step up where they can see you." He pointed a stylus at the platform.

Wingate moved forward and did as he was bade, blinking at the brilliant light. "Contract number 482-23-06," read the clerk, "client Humphrey Wingate, six years, radio technician non-certified, pay grade six-D, contract now available for assignment." Three weeks it had taken them to condition him, three weeks with no word from Jones. He had passed his exposure test without infection; he was about to enter the active period of his indenture. The brisk man spoke up close on the last words of the clerk:

"Now here, patrons, if you please—we have an exceptionally promising man. I hardly dare tell you the ratings he received on his intelligence, adaptability, and general information tests. In fact I won't, except to tell you that Administration has put in a protective offer of a thousand credits. But it would be a shame to use any such client for the routine work of administration when we need good men so badly to wrest wealth from the wilderness. I venture to predict that the lucky bidder who obtains the services of this client will be using him as a foreman within a month. But look him over for yourselves, talk to him, and see for yourselves."

The clerk whispered something to the speaker. He nodded and added, "I am required to notify you, gentlemen and patrons, that this client has given the usual legal notice of two weeks, subject of course to liens of record." He laughed jovially, and cocked one eyebrow as if there were some huge joke behind his remarks. No one paid attention to the announcement; to a limited extent Wingate appreciated wryly the nature of the jest. He had given notice the day after he found out that Jones had been sent to South Pole Colony, and had discovered that while he was free theoretically to quit, it was freedom to starve on Venus, unless he first worked out his bounty, and his passage both ways.

Several of the patrons gathered around the platform and looked him over, discussing him as they did so. "Not too well muscled." "I'm not overeager to bid on these smart boys; they're trouble-makers." "No, but a stupid client isn't worth his keep." "What can he *do?* I'm going to have a look at his record." They drifted over to the clerk's desk and scrutinized the results of the many tests and examinations that Wingate had undergone during his period of quarantine. All but one beady-eyed individual who sidled up closer to Wingate, and, resting one foot on the platform so that he could bring his face nearer, spoke in confidential tones.

"I'm not interested in those phony puff-sheets, bub. Tell me about yourself."

"There's not much to tell."

"Loosen up. You'll like my place. Just like a home—I run a free crock to Venusburg for my boys. Had any experience handling niggers?"

"No."

"Well, the native ain't niggers anyhow, except in a manner of speaking. You look like you could boss a gang. Had any experience?"

"Not much."

"Well . . . maybe you're modest. I like a man who keeps his mouth shut. And my boys like me. I never let my pusher take kickbacks."

"No," put in another patron who had returned to the side of the platform, "you save that for yourself, Rigsbee."

"You stay out o' this, Van Huysen!"

The newcomer, a heavy-set, middle-aged man, ignored the other and addressed Wingate himself. "You have given notice. Why?"

"The whole thing was a mistake. I was drunk."

"Will you do honest work in the meantime?"

Wingate considered this. "Yes," he said finally. The heavy-set man nodded and walked heavily back to his chair, settling his broad girth with care and giving his harness a hitch.

When the others were seated the spokesman announced cheerfully, "Now, gentlemen, if you are quite through— Let's hear an opening offer for this contract. I wish I could afford to bid him in as my assistant, by George, I do! Now . . . do I hear an offer?"

"Six hundred."

"Please, patrons! Did you not hear me mention a protection of one thousand?"

"I don't think you mean it. He's a sleeper."

The company agent raised his eyebrows. "I'm sorry. I'll have to ask the client to step down from the platform."

But before Wingate could do so another voice said, "One thousand."

"Now that's better!" exclaimed the agent. "I should have known that you gentlemen wouldn't let a real opportunity escape you. But a ship can't fly on one jet. Do I hear eleven hundred? Come, patrons, you can't make your fortunes without clients. Do I hear—"

"Eleven hundred."

"Eleven hundred from Patron Rigsbee! And a bargain it would be at that price. But I doubt if you will get it. Do I hear twelve?"

The heavy-set man flicked a thumb upward. "Twelve hundred from Patron van Huysen. I see I've made a mistake and am wasting your time; the intervals should be not less than two hundred. Do I hear fourteen? Do I hear fourteen? Going once for twelve . . . going twi—"

"Fourteen," Rigsbee said sullenly.

"Seventeen," Van Huysen added at once.

"Eighteen," snapped Rigsbee.

"Nooo," said the agent, "no interval of less than two, please."

"All right, dammit, nineteen!"

"Nineteen I hear. It's a hard number to write; who'll make it twenty-one?" Van Huysen's thumb flicked again. "Twenty-one it is. It takes money to make money. What do I hear? What do I hear?" He paused. "Going once for twenty-one . . . going twice for twenty-one. Are you giving up so easily, Patron Rigsbee?"

"Van Huysen is a—" The rest was muttered too indistinctly to hear.

"One more chance, gentlemen. Going, going, . . . GONE!—" He smacked his palms sharply together. "—and sold to Patron van Huysen for twenty-one hundred credits. My congratulations, sir, on a shrewd deal."

Wingate followed his new master out the far door. They were stopped in the passageway by Rigsbee. "All right, Van, you've had your fun. I'll cut your losses for two thousand."

"Out of my way."

"Don't be a fool. He's no bargain. You don't know how to sweat a man—I do." Van Huysen ignored him, pushing on past. Wingate followed him out into warm winter drizzle to the parking lot where steel crocodiles were drawn up in parallel rows. Van Huysen paused beside a thirty-foot Remington. "Get in."

The long boxlike body of the crock was stowed to its load line with supplies Van Huysen had purchased at the base. Sprawled on the tarpaulin which covered the cargo were half a dozen men. One of them stirred as Wingate climbed over the side. "Hump! Oh, Hump!"

It was Hartley. Wingate was surprised at his own surge of emotion. He gripped Hartley's hand and exchanged friendly insults. "Chums," said Hartley, "meet Hump Wingate. He's a right guy. Hump, meet the gang. That's Jimmie right behind you. He rassles this velocipede."

The man designated gave Wingate a bright nod and moved forward into the operator's seat. At a wave from Van Huysen, who had seated his bulk in the little sheltered cabin aft, he pulled back on both control levers and the crocodile crawled away, its caterpillar treads clanking and chunking through the mud.

Three of the six were old-timers, including Jimmie, the driver. They had come along to handle cargo, the ranch products which the patron had brought in to market and the supplies he had purchased to take back. Van Huysen had bought the contracts of two other clients in addition to Wingate and Satchel Hartley. Wingate recognized them as men he had known casually in the *Evening Star* and at the assignment and conditioning station. They looked a little woebegone, which Wingate could thoroughly understand, but the men from the ranch seemed to be enjoying themselves. They appeared to regard the opportunity to ride a load to and from town as an outing. They sprawled on the tarpaulin and passed the time gossiping and getting acquainted with the new chums.

But they asked no personal questions. No labor client on Venus ever asked anything about what he had been before he shipped with the company unless he first volunteered information. It "wasn't done."

Shortly after leaving the outskirts of Adonis the car slithered down a sloping piece of ground, teetered over a low bank, and splashed logily into water. Van Huysen threw up a window in the bulkhead which separated the cabin from the hold and shouted, "Dumkopf! How many times do I tell you to take those launchings slowly?"

"Sorry, Boss," Jimmie answered. "I missed it."

"You keep your eyes peeled, or I get me a new

crocker!" He slammed the port. Jimmie glanced around and gave the other clients a sly wink. He had his hands full; the marsh they were traversing looked like solid ground, so heavily was it over-grown with rank vegetation. The crocodile now functioned as a boat, the broad flanges of the treads acting as paddle wheels. The wedge-shaped prow pushed shrubs and marsh grass aside, or struck and ground down small trees. Occasionally the lugs would bite into the mud of a shoal bottom, and, crawling over a bar, return temporarily to the status of a land vehicle. Jimmie's slender, nervous hands moved constantly over the controls, avoiding large trees and continually seeking the easiest, most nearly direct route, while he split his attention between the terrain and the craft's compass.

Presently the conversation lagged and one of the ranch hands started to sing. He had a passable tenor voice and was soon joined by others. Wingate found himself singing the choruses as fast as he learned them. They sang *Pay Book* and *Since the Pusher Met My Cousin* and a mournful thing called *They Found Him in the Bush*. But this was followed by a light number, *The Night the Rain Stopped*, which seemed to have an endless string of verses recounting various unlikely happenings which occurred on that occasion. ("The Squeezer bought a round-a-drinks—")

Jimmie drew applause and enthusiastic support in the choruses with a ditty entitled *That Red-headed Venusburg Gal*, but Wingate considered it inexcusably vulgar. He did not have time to dwell on the matter; it was followed by a song which drove it out of his mind.

The tenor started it, slowly and softly. The others sang the refrains while he rested—all but Wingate; he was silent and thoughtful throughout. In the triplet of the second verse the tenor dropped out and the others sang in his place.

"Oh, you stamp your paper and you sign your name,
   (*"Come away! Come away!"*)
"They pay your bounty and you drown your shame.
   (*"Rue the day! Rue the day!"*)
"They land you down at Ellis Isle and put you in a pen;
"There you see what happens to the Six-Year men—
"They haven't paid their bounty and they sign 'em up again!
   (*"Here to stay! Here to stay!"*)
"But me I'll save my bounty and a ticket on the ship,
   (*"So you say! So you say!"*)
"And then you'll see me leavin' on the very next trip.
   (*"Come the day! Come the day!"*)
"Oh, we've heard that kinda story just a thousand times and one.
"Now we wouldn't say you're lyin' but we'd like to see it done.
"We'll see you next at Venusburg apayin' for your fun!
   [Spoken slowly] *"And you'll never meet your bounty on this hitch!*
   (*"Come away!"*)*

It left Wingate with a feeling of depression not entirely accounted for by the tepid drizzle, the unappetizing landscape, nor by the blanket of pale mist which is the invariable Venerian substitute for the open sky. He withdrew to one corner of the hold and kept to himself, until, much later, Jimmie shouted, "Lights ahead!"

Wingate leaned out and peered eagerly toward his new home.

Four weeks and no word from Sam Houston Jones. Venus had turned once on its axis, the fortnight long Venerian "winter" had given way to an equally short "summer"—indistinguishable from "winter" except that the rain was a trifle heavier and a little hotter—and now it was "winter" again. Van Huysens' ranch, being near the pole, was, like most of the tenable area of Venus, never in darkness. The miles-thick, everpresent layer of clouds tempered the light of the low-hanging sun during the long day, and, equally, held the heat and diffused the light from a sun just below the horizon to produce a continuing twilight during the two-week periods which were officially "night," or "winter."

Four weeks and no word. Four weeks and no sun, no moon, no stars, no dawn. No clean crisp breath of morning air, no life-quickening beat of noonday sun, no welcome evening shadows, nothing, nothing at all to distinguish one sultry, sticky hour from the next but the treadmill routine of sleep and work and food and sleep again—nothing but the gathering ache in his heart for the cool blue skies of Terra.

He had acceded to the invariable custom that new men should provide a celebration for the other clients and had signed the Squeezer's chits to obtain happywater—*rhira*—for the purpose—to discover, when first he signed the pay book, that his gesture of fellowship had cost him another four months of delay before he could legally quit his "job." Thereupon he had resolved never again to sign a chit, had foresworn the prospect of brief holidays at Venusburg, had promised himself to save every possible credit against his bounty and transportation liens.

Whereupon he discovered that the mild alcoholic drink was neither a vice nor a luxury, but a necessity, as necessary to human life on Venus as the ultraviolet factor present in all colonial illuminating systems. It produces, not drunkenness, but lightness of heart, freedom from worry, and without it he could not *get to sleep*. Three nights of self-recrimination and fretting, three days of fatigue-drugged uselessness under the unfriendly eye of the Pusher, and he had signed for his bottle with the rest, even though dully aware that the price of the bottle had washed out more than half of the day's microscopic progress toward freedom.

Nor had he been assigned to radio operation. Van Huysen had an operator. Wingate, although listed on the books as standby operator, went to the swamps with the rest. He discovered on re-reading his contract a clause which permitted his patron to do this, and he admitted with half his mind—the detached judicial and legalistic half—that the clause was reasonable and proper, not inequitable.

He went to the swamps. He learned to wheedle and bully the little, mild amphibian people into harvesting the bulbous underwater growth of *Hyacinthus veneris johnsoni*—Venus swamproot—and to bribe the cooperation of their matriarchs with promises of bonuses in the form of "thigarek", a term which meant not only cigarette, but tobacco in any form, the staple medium in trade when dealing with the natives.

He took his turn in the chopping sheds and learned, clumsily and slowly, to cut and strip the spongy outer husk from the pea-sized kernel which alone had commercial value and which must be removed intact, without scratch or bruise. The juice from the pods made his hands raw and the odor made him cough and stung his eyes, but he enjoyed it more than the work in the marshes, for it threw him into the company of the female labor clients. Women were quicker at the work than men and their smaller fingers more dextrous in removing the valuable, easily damaged capsule. Men were used for such work only when accumulated crops required extra help.

He learned his new trade from a motherly old person whom the other women addressed as Hazel. She talked as she worked, her gnarled old hands moving steadily and without apparent direction or skill. He could close his eyes and imagine that he was back on earth and a boy again, hanging around his grandmother's kitchen while she shelled peas and rambled on. "Don't you fret yourself, boy," Hazel told him. "Do your work and shame the devil. There's a great day coming."

"What kind of a great day, Hazel?"

"The day when the Angels of the Lord will rise up and smite the powers of evil. The day when the Prince of Darkness will be cast down into the pit and the Prophet shall reign over the children of Heaven. So don't you worry; it doesn't matter whether you are here or back home when the great day comes; the only thing that matters is your state of grace."

"Are you sure we will live long enough to see that day?"

She glanced around, then leaned over confidentially. "The day is almost upon us. Even now the Prophet moves up and down the land gathering his forces. Out of the clean farm country of the Mississippi Valley there comes the Man, known in this world"—she lowered her voice still more—"as *Nehemiah Scudder!*"

Wingate hoped that his start of surprise and amusement did not show externally. He recalled the name. It was that of a pipsqueak, backwoods evangelist, an unimportant nuisance back on Earth, the butt of an occasional guying news story, but a man of no possible consequence.

The chopping shed Pusher moved up to their bench. "Keep your eyes on your work, you! You're way behind now." Wingate hastened to comply, but Hazel came to his aid.

"You leave him be, Joe Tompson. It takes time to learn chopping."

"Okay, Mom," answered the Pusher with a grin, "but keep him pluggin'. See?"

"I will. You worry about the rest of the shed. This bench'll have its quota." Wingate had been docked two days running for spoilage. Hazel was lending him poundage now and the Pusher knew it, but everybody liked her, even pushers, who are reputed to like no one, not even themselves.

Wingate stood just outside the gate of the bachelors' compound. There was yet fifteen minutes before lock-up roll call; he had walked out in a subconscious attempt to rid himself of the pervading feeling of claustrophobia which he had had throughout his stay. The attempt was futile; there was no "outdoorness" about the outdoors on Venus, the bush crowded the clearing in on itself, the leaden misty sky pressed down on his head, and the steamy heat on his bare chest. Still, it was better than the bunkroom in spite of the dehydrators.

He had not yet obtained his evening ration of *rhira* and felt, consequently, nervous and despondent, yet residual self-respect caused him to cherish a few minutes' clear thinking before he gave in to the cheerful soporific. It's getting me, he thought, in a few more months I'll be taking every chance to get to Venusburg, or, worse yet, signing a chit for married quarters and condemning myself and my kids to a life-sentence. When he first arrived the women clients, with their uniformly dull minds and usually commonplace faces, had seemed entirely unattractive. Now, he realized with dismay, he was no longer so fussy. Why, he was even beginning to lisp, as the other clients did, in unconscious imitation of the amphibians.

Early, he had observed that the clients could be divided roughly into two categories, the child of nature and the broken men. The first were those of little imagination and simple standards. In all probability they had known nothing better back on earth; they saw in the colonial culture, not slavery, but freedom from responsibility, security, and an occasional spree. The others were the broken men, the outcasts, they who had once been somebody, but through some defect of character, or some accident, had lost their places in society. Perhaps the judge had said, "Sentence suspended if you ship for the colonies."

He realized with sudden panic that his own status was crystallizing; he was becoming one of the broken men. His background on Earth was becoming dim in his mind; he had put off for the last three days the labor of writing another letter to Jones; he had spent all the last shift rationalizing the necessity for taking a couple of days holiday at Venusburg. Face it, son, face it, he told himself. You're slipping, you're letting your mind relax into slave psychology. You've unloaded the problem of getting out of this mess onto Jones—how do you know he *can* help you? For all you know he may be dead. Out of the dimness of his memory he recaptured a phrase which he had read somewhere, some philosopher of history: "No slave is ever freed, *save he free himself.*"

All right, all right—pull up your socks, old son. Take a brace. No more *rhira*—no, that wasn't practical; a man had to have sleep. Very well, then, no *rhira* until lights-out, keep your mind clear in the evenings and *plan.* Keep your eyes open, find out all you can, cultivate friendships, and watch for a chance.

Through the gloom he saw a human figure approaching the gate of the compound. As it approached he saw that it was a woman and supposed it to be one of the female clients. She came closer, he saw that he was mistaken. It was Annek van Huysen, daughter of the patron.

She was a husky, overgrown blonde girl with unhappy eyes. He had seen her many times, watching the clients as they returned from their labor, or wandering alone around the ranch clearing. She was neither unsightly, nor in anywise attractive; her heavy adolescent figure needed more to flatter it than the harness which all colonists wore as the maximum tolerable garment.

She stopped before him, and, unzipping the pouch at her waist which served in lieu of pockets, took out a package of cigarettes. "I found this back there. Did you lose it?"

He knew that she lied; she had picked up nothing since she had come into sight. And the brand was one smoked on Earth and by patrons; no client could afford such. What was she up to?

He noted the eagerness in her face and the rapidity of her breathing, and realized, with confusion, that this girl was trying indirectly to make him a present. Why?

Wingate was not particularly conceited about his own physical beauty, or charm, nor had he any reason to be. But what he had not realized was that among the common run of the clients he stood out like a cock pheasant in a barnyard. But that Annek found him pleasing he was forced to admit; there could be no other explanation for her trumped-up story and her pathetic little present.

His first impulse was to snub her. He wanted nothing of her and resented the invasion of his privacy, and he was vaguely aware that the situation could be awkward, even dangerous to him, involving, as it did, violations of custom which jeopardized the whole social and economic structure. From the viewpoint of the patrons, labor clients were almost as much beyond the pale as the amphibians. A liaison between a labor client and one of the womenfolk of the patrons could easily wake up old Judge Lynch.

But he had not the heart to be brusque with her. He could see the dumb adoration in her eyes; it would have required cold heartlessness to have repulsed her. Besides, there was nothing coy or provocative in her attitude; her manner was naive, almost childlike in its unsophistication. He recalled his determination to make friends; here was friendship offered, a dangerous friendship, but one which might prove useful in winning free.

He felt a momentary wave of shame that he should be weighing the potential usefulness of this defenseless child, but he suppressed it by affirming to himself that he would do her no harm, and, anyhow, there was the old saw about the vindictiveness of a woman scorned.

"Why, perhaps I did lose it," he evaded, then added, "It's my favorite brand."

"Is it?" she said happily. "Then do take it, in any case."

"Thank you. Will you smoke one with me? No, I guess that wouldn't do; your father would not want you to stay here that long."

"Oh, he's busy with his accounts. I saw that before I came out," she answered, and seemed unaware that she had given away her pitiful little deception. "But go ahead, I—I hardly ever smoke."

"Perhaps you prefer a meerschaum pipe, like your father."

She laughed more than the poor witticism deserved. After that they talked aimlessly, both agreeing that the crop was coming in nicely, that the weather seemed a little cooler than last week, and that there was nothing like a little fresh air after supper.

"Do you ever walk for exercise after supper?" she asked.

He did not say that a long day in the swamps offered more than enough exercise, but agreed that he did.

"So do I," she blurted out. "Lots of times up near the water tower."

He looked at her. "Is that so? I'll remember that." The signal for roll call gave him a welcome excuse to get away; three more minutes, he thought, and I would have had to make a date with her.

Wingate found himself called for swamp work the next day, the rush in the chopping sheds having abated. The crock lumbered and splashed its way around the long, meandering circuit, leaving one or more Earthmen at each supervision station. The car was down to four occupants, Wingate, Satchel, the Pusher, and Jimmie the Crocker, when the Pusher signalled for another stop. The flat, bright-eyed heads of amphibian natives broke water on three sides as soon as they were halted. "All right, Satchel," ordered the Pusher, "this is your billet. Over the side."

Satchel looked around. "Where's my skiff?" The ranchers used small flat-bottomed duralumin skiffs in which to collect their day's harvest. There was not one left in the crock.

"You won't need one. You goin' to clean this field for planting."

"That's okay. Still—I don't see nobody around, and I don't see no solid ground." The skiffs had a double purpose; if a man were working out of contact with other Earthmen and at some distance from safe dry ground, the skiff became his life boat. If the crocodile which was supposed to collect him broke down, or if for any other reason he had need to sit down or lie down while on station, the skiff gave him a place to do so. The older clients told grim stories of men who had stood in eighteen inches of water for twenty-four, forty-eight, seventy-two hours, and then drowned horribly, out of their heads from sheer fatigue.

"There's dry ground right over there." The Pusher waved his hand in the general direction of a clump of trees which lay perhaps a quarter of a mile away.

"Maybe so," answered Satchel equably. "Let's go see." He glanced at Jimmie, who turned to the Pusher for instructions.

"Damnation! Don't argue with me! Get over the side!"

"Not," said Satchel, "until I've seen something better than two feet of slime to squat on in a pinch."

The little water people had been following the argument with acute interest. They clucked and lisped in their own language; those who knew some pidgin English appeared to be giving newsy and undoubtedly distorted explanations of the events to their less sophisticated brethren. Fuming as he was, this seemed to add to the Pusher's anger.

"For the last time—get out there!"

"Well," said Satchel, settling his gross frame more comfortably on the floorplates, "I'm glad we've finished with that subject."

Wingate was behind the Pusher. This circumstance probably saved Satchel Hartley at least a scalp wound, for he caught the arm of the Pusher as he struck. Hartley closed in at once; the three wrestled for a few seconds on the bottom of the craft.

Hartley sat on the Pusher's chest while Wingate pried a blackjack away from the clenched fingers of the Pusher's right fist. "Glad you saw him reach for that, Hump," Satchel acknowledged, "or I'd be needin' an aspirin about now."

"Yeah, I guess so," Wingate answered, and threw the weapon as far as he could out into the marshy waste. Several of the amphibians streaked after it and dived. "I guess you can let him up now."

The Pusher said nothing to them as he brushed himself off, but he turned to the Crocker who had remained quietly in his saddle at the controls the whole time. "Why the hell didn't you help me?"

"I supposed you could take care of yourself, Boss," Jimmie answered noncommittally.

Wingate and Hartley finished that work period as helpers to labor clients already stationed. The Pusher had completely ignored them except for curt orders necessary to station them. But while they were washing up for supper back at the compound they received word to report to the Big House.

When they were ushered into the Patron's office they found the Pusher already there with his employer and wearing a self-satisfied smirk while Van Huysen's expression was black indeed.

"What's this I hear about you two?" he burst out. "Refusing work. Jumping my foreman. By Joe, I'll show you a thing or two!"

"Just a moment, Patron van Huysen," began Wingate quietly, suddenly at home in the atmosphere of a trial court, "no one refused duty. Hartley simply protested doing dangerous work without

reasonable safeguards. As for the fracas, your foreman attacked us; we acted simply in self-defense,
and desisted as soon as we had disarmed him."

The Pusher leaned over Van Huysen and whispered in his ear. The Patron looked more angry
than before. "You did this with natives watching.
Natives! You know colonial law? I could send you
to the mines for this."

"No," Wingate denied, "your foreman did it in
the presence of natives. Our role was passive and
defensive throughout—"

"You call jumping my foreman peaceful? Now
you listen to me—Your job here is to work. My
foreman's job is to tell you where and how to
work. He's not such a dummy as to lose me my
investment in a man. He judges what work is
dangerous, not you." The Pusher whispered again
to his chief. Van Huysen shook his head. The
other persisted, but the Patron cut him off with a
gesture, and turned back to the two labor clients.

"See here—I give every dog one bite, but not
two. For you, no supper tonight and no *rhira*.
Tomorrow we see how you behave."

"But Patron van Huys—"

"That's all. Get to your quarters."

At lights out Wingate found, on crawling into
his bunk, that someone had hidden therein a
foodbar. He munched it gratefully in the dark and
wondered who his friend could be. The food stayed
the complaints of his stomach but was not sufficient,
in the absence of *rhira*, to permit him to go to
sleep. He lay there, staring into the oppressive
blackness of the bunkroom and listening to the
assorted irritating noises that men can make while
sleeping, and considered his position. It had been

bad enough but barely tolerable before; now, he was logically certain, it would be as near hell as a vindictive overseer could make it. He was prepared to believe, from what he had seen and the tales he had heard, that it would be very near indeed!

He had been nursing his troubles for perhaps an hour when he felt a hand touch his side. "Hump! Hump!" came a whisper, "come outside. Something's up." It was Jimmie.

He felt his way cautiously through the stacks of bunks and slipped out the door after Jimmie. Satchel was already outside and with him a fourth figure.

It was Annek van Huysen. He wondered how she had been able to get into the locked compound. Her eyes were puffy, as if she had been crying.

Jimmie started to speak at once, in cautious, low tones. "The kid tells us that I am scheduled to haul you two lugs back into Adonis tomorrow."

"What for?"

"She doesn't know. But she's afraid it's to sell you South. That doesn't seem likely. The Old Man has never sold anyone South—but then nobody ever jumped his pusher before. I don't know."

They wasted some minutes in fruitless discussion, then, after a bemused silence, Wingate asked Jimmie, "Do you know where they keep the keys to the crock?"

"No. Why do y—"

"I could get them for you," offered Annek eagerly.

"You can't drive a crock."

"I've watched you for some weeks."

"Well, suppose you can," Jimmie continued to protest, "suppose you run for it in the crock. You'd be lost in ten miles. If you weren't caught, you'd starve."

Wingate shrugged. "I'm not going to be sold South."

"Nor am I," Hartley added.

"Wait a minute."

"Well, I don't see any bet—"

"Wait a minute," Jimmie reiterated snappishly. "Can't you see I'm trying to think?"

The other three kept silent for several long moments. At last Jimmie said, "Okay. Kid, you'd better run along and let us talk. The less you know about this the better for you." Annek looked hurt, but complied docilely to the extent of withdrawing out of earshot. The three men conferred for some minutes. At last Wingate motioned for her to rejoin them.

"That's all, Annek," he told her. "Thanks a lot for everything you've done. We've figured a way out." He stopped, and then said awkwardly, "Well, good night."

She looked up at him.

Wingate wondered what to do or say next. Finally he led her around the corner of the barracks and bade her good night again. He returned very quickly, looking shame-faced. They re-entered the barracks.

Patron van Huysen also was having trouble getting to sleep. He hated having to discipline his people. By damn, why couldn't they all be good boys and leave him in peace? Not but what there was precious little peace for a rancher these days. It cost more to make a crop than the crop fetched in Adonis—at least it did after the interest was paid.

He had turned his attention to his accounts after dinner that night to try to get the unpleasantness out of his mind, but he found it hard to concentrate on his figures. That man Wingate, now . . . he had bought him as much to keep him away from that slavedriver Rigsbee as to get another hand. He had too much money invested in hands as it was in spite of his foreman always complaining about being short of labor. He would either have to sell some, or ask the bank to refinance the mortgage again.

Hands weren't worth their keep any more. You didn't get the kind of men on Venus that used to come when he was a boy. He bent over his books again. If the market went up even a little, the bank should be willing to discount his paper for a little more than last season. Maybe that would do it.

He had been interrupted by a visit from his daughter. Annek he was always glad to see, but this time what she had to say, what she finally blurted out, had only served to make him angry. She, preoccupied with her own thoughts, could not know that she hurt her father's heart, with a pain that was actually physical.

But that had settled the matter insofar as Wingate was concerned. He would get rid of the trouble-maker. Van Huysen ordered his daughter to bed with a roughness he had never before used on her.

Of course it was all his own fault, he told himself after he had gone to bed. A ranch on Venus was no place to raise a motherless girl. His

Annekchen was almost a grown woman now; how was she to find a husband here in these outlands? What would she do if he should die? She did not know it, but there would be nothing left, nothing, not even a ticket to Terra. No, she would not become a labor client's vrouw; no, not while there was a breath left in his old tired body.

Well, Wingate would have to go, and the one they called Satchel, too. But he would not sell them South. No, he had never done that to one of his people. He thought with distaste of the great, factorylike plantations a few hundred miles further from the pole, where the temperature was always twenty to thirty degrees higher than it was in his marshes and mortality among labor clients was a standard item in cost accounting. No, he would take them in and trade them at the assignment station; what happened to them at auction there would be none of his business. But he would not sell them directly South.

That gave him an idea; he did a little computing in his head and estimated that he might be able to get enough credit on the two unexpired labor contracts to buy Annek a ticket to Earth. He was quite sure that his sister would take her in, reasonably sure anyway, even though she had quarreled with him over marrying Annek's mother. He could send her a little money from time to time. And perhaps she could learn to be a secretary, or one of those other fine jobs a girl could get on Earth.

But what would the ranch be like without Annekchen?

He was so immersed in his own troubles that he

did not hear his daughter slip out of her room and go outside.

Wingate and Hartley tried to appear surprised when they were left behind at muster for work. Jimmie was told to report to the Big House; they saw him a few minutes later, backing the big Remington out of its shed. He picked them up, then trundled back to the Big House and waited for the Patron to appear. Van Huysen came out shortly and climbed into his cabin with neither word nor look for anyone.

The crocodile started toward Adonis, lumbering a steady ten miles an hour. Wingate and Satchel conversed in subdued voices, waiting, and wondered. After an interminable time the crock stopped. The cabin window flew open. "What's the matter?" Van Huysen demanded. "Your engine acting up?"

Jimmie grinned at him. "No, I stopped it."

"For what?"

"Better come up here and find out."

"By damn, I do!" The window slammed; presently Van Huysen reappeared, warping his ponderous bulk around the side of the little cabin. "Now what this monkeyshines?"

"Better get out and walk, Patron. This is the end of the line."

Van Huysen seemed to have no remark suitable in answer, but his expression spoke for him.

"No, I mean it," Jimmie went on. "This is the end of the line for you. I've stuck to solid ground the whole way, so you could walk back. You'll be able to follow the trail I broke; you ought to be able to make it in three or four hours, fat as you are."

The Patron looked from Jimmie to the others. Wingate and Satchel closed in slightly, eyes unfriendly. "Better get goin', Fatty," Satchel said softly, "before you get chucked out headfirst."

Van Huysen pressed back against the rail of the crock, his hands gripping it. "I won't get out of my own crock," he said tightly.

Satchel spat in the palm of one hand, then rubbed the two together. "Okay, Hump. He asked for it—"

"Just a second." Wingate addressed Van Huysen, "See here, Patron van Huysen—we don't want to rough you up unless we have to. But there are three of us and we are determined. Better climb out quietly."

The older man's face was dripping with sweat which was not entirely due to the muggy heat. His chest heaved, he seemed about to defy them. Then something went out inside him. His figure sagged, the defiant lines in his face gave way to a whipped expression which was not good to see.

A moment later he climbed quietly, listlessly, over the side into the ankle-deep mud and stood there, stooped, his legs slightly bent at the knees.

When they were out of sight of the place where they had dropped their patron Jimmie turned the crock off in a new direction. "Do you suppose he'll make it?" asked Wingate.

"Who?" asked Jimmie. "Van Huysen? Oh, sure, he'll make it—probably." He was very busy now with his driving; the crock crawled down a slope and lunged into navigable water. In a few minutes the marsh grass gave way to open water. Wingate saw that they were in a broad lake whose further shores were lost in the mist. Jimmie set a compass course.

The far shore was no more than a strand; it concealed an overgrown bayou. Jimmie followed it a short distance, stopped the crock, and said, "This must be just about the place," in an uncertain voice. He dug under the tarpaulin folded up in one corner of the empty hold and drew out a broad flat paddle. He took this to the rail, and, leaning out, he smacked the water loudly with the blade: Slap! . . . slap, slap. . . . Slap!

He waited.

The flat head of an amphibian broke water near the side; it studied Jimmie with bright, merry eyes. "Hello," said Jimmie.

It answered in its own language. Jimmie replied in the same tongue, stretching his mouth to reproduce the uncouth clucking syllables. The native listened, then slid underwater again.

He—or, more probably, she—was back in a few minutes, another with her. "Thigarek?" the newcomer said hopefully.

"Thigarek when we get there, old girl," Jimmie temporized. "Here . . . climb aboard." He held out a hand, which the native accepted and wriggled gracefully inboard. It perched its unhuman, yet oddly pleasing little figure on the rail near the driver's seat. Jimmie got the car underway.

How long they were guided by their little pilot Wingate did not know, as the timepiece on the control panel was out of order, but his stomach informed him that it was too long. He rummaged through the cabin and dug out an iron ration which he shared with Satchel and Jimmie. He offered some to the native, but she smelled at it and drew her head away.

Shortly after that there was a sharp hissing noise and a column of steam rose up ten yards ahead of them. Jimmie halted the crock at once. "Cease firing!" he called out. "It's just us chickens."

"Who are you?" came a disembodied voice.

"Fellow travelers."

"Climb out where we can see you."

"Okay."

The native poked Jimmie in the ribs. "Thigarek," she stated positively.

"Huh? Oh, sure." He parceled out trade tobacco until she acknowledged the total, then added one more package for good will. She withdrew a piece of string from her left cheek pouch, tied up her pay, and slid over the side. They saw her swimming away, her prize carried high out of the water.

"Hurry up and show yourself!"

"Coming!" They climbed out into waist-deep water and advanced holding their hands overhead. A squad of four broke cover and looked them over, their weapons lowered but ready. The leader searched their harness pouches and sent one of his men on to look over the crocodile.

"You keep a close watch," remarked Wingate.

The leader glanced at him. "Yes," he said, "and no. The little people told us you were coming. They're worth all the watch dogs that were ever littered."

They got underway again with one of the scouting party driving. Their captors were not unfriendly but not disposed to talk. "Wait till you see the Governor," they said.

Their destination turned out to be a wide stretch of moderately high ground. Wingate was amazed at the number of buildings and the numerous population. "How in the world can they keep a place like this a secret?" he asked Jimmie.

"If the state of Texas were covered with fog and had only the population of Waukegan, Illinois, you could hide quite a lot of things."

"But wouldn't it show on a map?"

"How well mapped do you think Venus is? Don't be a dope."

On the basis of the few words he had had with Jimmie beforehand Wingate had expected no more than a camp where fugitive clients lurked in the bush while squeezing a precarious living from the country. What he found was a culture and a government. True, it was a rough frontier culture and a simple government with few laws and an unwritten constitution, but a framework of customs was in actual operation and its gross offenders were punished—with no higher degree of injustice than one finds anywhere.

It surprised Humphrey Wingate that fugitive slaves, the scum of Earth, were able to develop an integrated society. It had surprised his ancestors that the transported criminals of Botany Bay should develop a high civilization in Australia. Not that Wingate found the phenomenon of Botany Bay surprising—that was history, and history is never surprising—after it happens.

The success of the colony was more credible to Wingate when he came to know more of the character of the Governor, who was also generalissimo, and administrator of the low and middle justice. (High justice was voted on by the whole community, a procedure that Wingate considered outrageously sloppy, but which seemed to satisfy the community.) As magistrate the Governor handed out decisions with a casual contempt for rules or evidence and legal theory that reminded Wingate of stories he had heard of the apocryphal Old Judge Bean, "The Law West of Pecos," but again the people seemed to like it.

The great shortage of women in the community (men outnumbered them three to one) caused incidents which more than anything else required the decisions of the Governor. Here, Wingate was forced to admit, was a situation in which traditional custom would have been nothing but a source of trouble; he admired the shrewd common sense and understanding of human nature with which the Governor sorted out conflicting strong human passions and suggested *modus operandi* for getting along together. A man who could maintain a working degree of peace in such matters did not need a legal education.

The Governor held office by election and was advised by an elected council. It was Wingate's private opinion that the Governor would have risen to the top in any society. The man had boundless energy, great gusto for living, a ready thunderous laugh—and the courage and capacity for making decisions. He was a "natural."

The three runaways were given a couple of weeks in which to get their bearings and find some job in which they could make themselves useful and self-supporting. Jimmie stayed with his crock, now confiscated for the community, but which still required a driver. There were other crockers available who probably would have liked the job, but there was tacit consent that the man who brought it in should drive it, if he wished. Satchel found a billet in the fields, doing much the same work he had done for Van Huysen. He told Wingate that he was actually having to work harder; nevertheless he liked it better because the conditions were, as he put it, "looser."

Wingate detested the idea of going back to agricultural work. He had no rational excuse, it was simply that he hated it. His radio experience at last stood him in good stead. The community had a jury-rigged, low-power radio on which a constant listening watch was kept, but which was rarely used for transmission, because of the danger of detection. Earlier runaway slave camps had been wiped out by the company police through careless use of radio. Nowadays they hardly dared use it, except in extreme emergency.

But they needed radio. The grapevine telegraph maintained through the somewhat slap-happy help of the little people enabled them to keep some contact with the other fugitive communities with which they were loosely confederated, but it was not really fast, and any but the simplest of messages were distorted out of recognition.

Wingate was assigned to the community radio when it was discovered that he had appropriate technical knowledge. The previous operator had been lost in the bush. His opposite number was a pleasant old codger, known as Doc, who could listen for signals but who knew nothing of upkeep and repair.

Wingate threw himself into the job of overhauling the antiquated installation. The problems presented by lack of equipment, the necessity for "making do," gave him a degree of happiness he had not known since he was a boy, but he was not aware of it.

He was intrigued by the problem of safety in radio communication. An idea, derived from some account of the pioneer days in radio, gave him a lead. His installation, like all others, communicated by frequency modulation. Somewhere he had seen a diagram for a totally obsolete type of transmitter, an amplitude modulator. He did not have much to go on, but he worked out a circuit which he believed would oscillate in that fashion and which could be hooked up from the gear at hand.

He asked the Governor for permission to attempt to build it. "Why not? Why not?" the Governor roared at him. "I haven't the slightest idea what you are talking about, son, but if you think you can build a radio that the company can't detect, go right ahead. You don't have to ask me; it's your pidgin."

"I'll have to put the station out of commission for sending."

"Why not?"

The problem had more knots in it than he had thought. But he labored at it with the clumsy but willing assistance of Doc. His first hookup failed; his forty-third attempt five weeks later worked. Doc, stationed some miles out in the bush, reported himself able to hear the broadcast via a small receiver constructed for the purpose, whereas Wingate picked up nothing whatsoever on the conventional receiver located in the same room with the experimental transmitter.

In the meantime he worked on his book.

Why he was writing a book he could not have told you. Back on earth it could have been termed a political pamphlet against the colonial system. Here there was no one to convince of his thesis, nor had he any expectation of ever being able to present it to a reading public. Venus was his home. He knew that there was no chance for him ever to return; the only way lay through Adonis, and there, waiting for him, were warrants for half the crimes in the calendar, contract-jumping, theft, kidnapping, criminal abandonment, conspiracy, subverting government. If the company police ever laid hands on him, they would jail him and lose the key.

No, the book arose, not from any expectation of publication, but from a half-subconscious need to arrange his thoughts. He had suffered a complete upsetting of all the evaluations by which he had lived; for his mental health it was necessary that he formulate new ones. It was natural to his orderly, if somewhat unimaginative, mind that he set his reasons and conclusions forth in writing.

Somewhat diffidently he offered the manuscript to Doc. He had learned that the nickname title had derived from the man's former occupation on Earth; he had been a professor of economics and philosophy in one of the smaller universities. Doc had even offered a partial explanation of his presence on Venus. "A little matter involving one of my women students," he confided. "My wife took an unsympathetic view of the matter and so did the board of regents. The board had long considered my opinions a little too radical."

"Were they?"

"Heavens, no! I was rockbound conservative.

But I had an unfortunate tendency to express conservative principles in realistic rather than allegorical language"

"I suppose you're a radical now."

Doc's eyebrows lifted slightly. "Not at all. Radical and conservative are terms for emotional attitudes, not sociological opinions."

Doc accepted the manuscript, read it through, and returned it without comment. But Wingate pressed him for an opinion. "Well, my boy, if you insist—"

"I do."

"—I would say that you have fallen into the commonest fallacy of all in dealing with social and economic subjects—the 'devil theory.' "

"Huh?"

"You have attributed conditions to villainy that simply result from stupidity. Colonial slavery is nothing new; it is the inevitable result of imperial expansion, the automatic result of an antiquated financial structure—"

"I pointed out the part the banks played in my book."

"No, no, no! You think bankers are scoundrels. They are not. Nor are company officials, nor patrons, nor the governing classes back on earth. Men are constrained by necessity and build up rationalizations to account for their acts. It is not even cupidity. Slavery is economically unsound, non-productive, but men drift into it whenever the circumstances compel it. A different financial system—But that's another story."

"I still think it's rooted in human cussedness," Wingate said stubbornly.

"Not cussedness—simple stupidity. I can't prove it to you, but you will learn."

The success of the "silent radio" caused the Governor to send Wingate on a long swing around the other camps of the free federation to help them rig new equipment and to teach them how to use it. He spent four hard-working and soul-satisfying weeks, and finished with the warm knowledge that he had done more to consolidate the position of the free men against their enemies than could be done by winning a pitched battle.

When he returned to his home community, he found Sam Houston Jones waiting there.

Wingate broke into a run. "Sam!" he shouted, "Sam! *Sam!*" He grabbed his hand, pounded him on the back, and yelled at him the affectionate insults that sentimental men use in attempting to cover up their weakness. "Sam, you old scoundrel! When did you get here? How did you escape? And how the devil did you manage to come all the way from the South Pole? Were you transferred before you escaped?"

"Howdy, Hump," said Sam. "Now one at a time, and not so fast."

But Wingate bubbled on. "My, but it's good to see your ugly face, fellow. And am I glad you came here—this is a great place. We've got the most up-and-coming little state in the whole federation. You'll like it. They're a great bunch—"

"What are you?" Jones asked, eyeing him. "President of the local chamber of commerce?"

Wingate looked at him, and then laughed. "I get it. But seriously, you will like it. Of course, it's a lot different from what you were used to back on Earth—but that's all past and done with. No use crying over spilt milk, eh?"

"Wait a minute. You are under a misapprehension, Hump. Listen. I'm not an escaped slave. *I'm here to take you back.*"

Wingate opened his mouth, closed it, then opened it again. "But Sam," he said, "that's impossible. You don't know."

"I think I do."

"But you don't. There's no going back for me. If I did, I'd have to face trial, and they've got me dead to rights. Even if I threw myself on the mercy of the court and managed to get off with a light sentence, it would be twenty years before I'd be a free man. No, Sam, it's impossible. You don't know the things I'm charged with."

"I don't, eh? It's cost me a nice piece of change to clear them up."

"Huh?"

"I know how you escaped. I know you stole a crock and kidnapped your patron and got two other clients to run with you. It took my best blarney and plenty of folding money to fix it. So help me, Hump—why didn't you pull something mild, like murder, or rape, or robbing a post office?"

"Well, now, Sam—I didn't do any of those things to cause you trouble. I had counted you out of my calculations. I was on my own. I'm sorry about the money."

"Forget it. Money isn't an item with me. I'm filthy with the stuff. You know that. It comes from exercising care in the choice of parents. I was just pulling your leg and it came off in my hand."

"Okay. Sorry." Wingate's grin was a little forced.

Nobody likes charity. "But tell me what happened. I'm still in the dark."

"Right." Jones had been as much surprised and distressed at being separated from Wingate on grounding as Wingate had been. But there had been nothing for him to do about it until he received assistance from Earth. He had spent long weeks as a metal worker at South Pole, waiting and wondering why his sister did not answer his call for help. He had written letters to her to supplement his first radiogram, that being the only type of communication he could afford, but the days crept past with no answer.

When a message did arrive from her the mystery was cleared up. She had not received his radio to Earth promptly, because she too, was aboard the *Evening Star*—in the first class cabin, traveling, as was her custom, in a stateroom listed under her maid's name. "It was the family habit of avoiding publicity that stymied us," Jones explained. "If I hadn't sent the radio to her rather than to the family lawyers, or if she had been known by name to the purser, we would have gotten together the first day."

The message had not been relayed to her on Venus because the bright planet had by that time crawled to superior opposition on the far side of the sun from the Earth. For a matter of sixty earth days there was no communication, Earth to Venus. The message had rested, recorded but still scrambled, in the hands of the family firm, until she could be reached.

When she received it, she started a small tornado. Jones had been released, the liens against his contract paid, and ample credit posted to his name on Venus, in less than twenty-four hours. "So that was that," concluded Jones, "except that I've got to explain to big sister when I get home how I got into this mess. She'll burn my ears."

Jones had chartered a rocket for North Pole and had gotten on Wingate's trail at once. "If you had held on one more day, I would have picked you up. We retrieved your ex-patron about a mile from his gates."

"So the old villain made it. I'm glad of that."

"And a good job, too. If he hadn't I might never have been able to square you. He was pretty well done in, and his heart was kicking up plenty. Do you know that abandonment is a capital offense on this planet—with a mandatory death sentence if the victim dies?"

Wingate nodded. "Yeah, I know. Not that I ever heard of a patron being gassed for it, if the corpse was a client. But that's beside the point. Go ahead."

"Well, he was plenty sore. I don't blame him, though I don't blame you, either. Nobody wants to be sold South, and I gather that was what you expected. Well, I paid him for his crock, and I paid him for your contract—take a look at me, I'm your new owner!—and I paid for the contracts of your two friends as well. Still he wasn't satisfied. I finally had to throw in a first-class passage for his daughter back to Earth, and promise to find her a job. She's a big dumb ox, but I guess the family can stand another retainer. Anyhow, old son, you're a free man. The only remaining question is whether or not the Governor will let us leave here. It seems it's not done."

"No, that's a point. Which reminds me—how did you locate the place?"

"A spot of detective work too long to go into now. That's what took me so long. Slaves don't like to talk. Anyhow, we've a date to talk to the Governor tomorrow."

Wingate took a long time to get to sleep. After his first burst of jubilation he began to wonder. Did he want to go back? To return to the law, to citing technicalities in the interest of whichever side employed him, to meaningless social engagements, to the empty, sterile, bunkum-fed life of the fat and prosperous class he had moved among and served—did he want that, he, who had fought and worked with *men?* It seemed to him that his anachronistic little "invention" in radio had been of more worth than all he had ever done on Earth.

Then he recalled his book.

Perhaps he could get it published. Perhaps he could expose this disgraceful, inhuman system which sold men into legal slavery. He was really wide awake now. *There* was a thing to do! That was his job—to go back to Earth and plead the cause of the colonists. Maybe there was destiny that shapes men's lives after all. He was just the man to do it, the right social background, the proper training. *He* could make himself heard.

He fell asleep, and dreamt of cool, dry breezes, of clear blue sky. Of moonlight. . . .

Satchel and Jimmie decided to stay, even though Jones had been able to fix it up with the Governor. "It's like this," said Satchel. "There's nothing for us back on Earth, or we wouldn't have shipped in the first place. And you can't undertake to support a couple of deadheads. And this isn't such a bad place. It's going to be something someday. We'll stay and grow up with it."

They handled the crock which carried Jones and Wingate to Adonis. There was no hazard in it, as Jones was now officially their patron. What the authorities did not know they could not act on. The crock returned to the refugee community loaded with a cargo which Jones insisted on calling their ransom. As a matter of fact, the opportunity to send an agent to obtain badly needed supplies— one who could do so safely and without arousing the suspicions of the company authorities—had been the determining factor in the Governor's unprecedent decision to risk compromising the secrets of his constituency. He had been frankly not interested in Wingate's plans to agitate for the abolishment of the slave trade.

Saying goodbye to Satchel and Jimmie was something Wingate found embarrassing and unexpectedly depressing.

For the first two weeks after grounding on Earth both Wingate and Jones were too busy to see much of each other. Wingate had gotten his manuscript in shape on the return trip and had spent the time getting acquained with the waiting rooms of publishers. Only one had shown any interest beyond a form letter of rejection.

"I'm sorry, old man," that one had told him. "I'd like to publish your book, in spite of its controversial nature, if it stood any chance at all of success. But it doesn't. Frankly, it has no literary merit whatsoever. I would as soon read a brief."

"I think I understand," Wingate answered sullenly. "A big publishing house can't afford to print anything which might offend the powers-that-be."

The publisher took his cigar from his mouth and looked at the younger man before replying. "I suppose I should resent that," he said quietly, "but I won't. That's a popular misconception. The powers-that-be, as you call them, do not resort to suppression in this country. We publish what the public will buy. We're in business for that purpose.

"I was about to suggest, if you will listen, a means of making your book salable. You need a collaborator, somebody that knows the writing game and can put some guts in it."

Jones called the day that Wingate got his revised manuscript back from his ghost writer. "Listen to this, Sam," he pleaded. "Look what the dirty so-and-so has done to my book. Look. '—I heard again the crack of the overseer's whip. The frail body of my mate shook under the lash. He gave one cough and slid slowly under the waist-deep water, dragged down by his chains.' Honest, Sam, did you ever see such drivel? And look at the new title: '*I Was a Slave on Venus*.' It sounds like a confession magazine."

Jones nodded without replying. "And listen to this," Wingate went on, " '—crowded like cattle in the enclosure, their naked bodies gleaming with sweat, the women slaves shrank from the—' Oh, hell, I can't go on!"

"Well, they did wear nothing but harnesses."

"Yes, yes—but that has nothing to do with the case. Venus costume is a necessary concomitant of the weather. There's no excuse to leer about it. He's turned my book into a damned sex show.

And he had the nerve to defend his actions. He claimed that social pamphleteering is dependent on extravagant language."

"Well, maybe he's got something. *Gulliver's Travels* certainly has some racy passages, and the whipping scenes in *Uncle Tom's Cabin* aren't anything to hand a kid to read. Not to mention *Grapes of Wrath*."

"Well, I'm damned if I'll resort to that kind of cheap sensationalism. I've got a perfectly straightforward case that anyone can understand."

"Have you now?" Jones took his pipe out of his mouth. "I've been wondering how long it would take you to get your eyes opened. What is your case? It's nothing new; it happened in the Old South, it happened again in California, in Mexico, in Australia, in South Africa. Why? Because in any expanding free enterprise economy which does not have a money system designed to fit its requirements, the use of mother-country capital to develop the colony inevitably results in subsistence-level wages at home and slave labor in the colonies. The rich get richer and the poor get poorer, and all the good will in the world on the part of the so-called ruling class won't change it, because the basic problem is one requiring scientific analysis and a mathematical mind. Do you think you can explain those issues to the general public?"

"I can try."

"How far did I get when I tried to explain them to you—before you had seen the results? And you are a smart hombre. No, Hump, these things are too difficult to explain to people and too abstract to interest them. You spoke before a women's club the other day, didn't you?"

"Yes."

"How did you make out?"

"Well . . . the chairwoman called me up beforehand and asked me to hold my talk down to ten minutes, as their national president was to be there and they would be crowded for time."

"Hmm . . . you see where your great social message rates in competition. But never mind. Ten minutes is long enough to explain the issue to a person if they have the capacity to understand it. Did you sell anybody?"

"Well . . . I'm not sure."

"You're darn tootin' you're not sure. Maybe they clapped for you but how many of them came up afterwards and wanted to sign checks? No, Hump, sweet reasonableness won't get you anywhere in this racket. To make yourself heard you have to be a demagogue, or a rabble-rousing political preacher like this fellow Nehemiah Scudder. We're going merrily to hell and it won't stop until it winds up in a crash."

"But— Oh, the devil! What can we *do* about it?"

"Nothing. Things are bound to get a whole lot worse before they can get any better. Let's have a drink."

DAVID WEBER

<u>The Honor Harrington series:</u> *(cont.)*

Field of Dishonor
Honor goes home to Manticore—and fights for her life on a battlefield she never trained for, in a private war that offers just two choices: death—or a "victory" that can end only in dishonor and the loss of all she loves....

Flag in Exile
Hounded into retirement and disgrace by political enemies, Honor Harrington has retreated to planet Grayson, where powerful men plot to reverse the changes she has brought to their world. And for their plans to succeed, Honor Harrington must die!

Honor Among Enemies
Offered a chance to end her exile and again command a ship, Honor Harrington must use a crew drawn from the dregs of the service to stop pirates who are plundering commerce. Her enemies have chosen the mission carefully, thinking that either she will stop the raiders or they will kill her . . . and either way, her enemies will win....

In Enemy Hands
After being ambushed, Honor finds herself aboard an enemy cruiser, bound for her scheduled execution. But one lesson Honor has never learned is how to give up!

Echoes of Honor
"Brilliant! Brilliant! Brilliant!"—*Anne McCaffrey*

continued

THE SHIP WHO SANG IS NOT ALONE!

Anne McCaffrey, with Mercedes Lackey, S.M. Stirling, and Jody Lynn Nye, explores the universe she created with her ground-breaking novel, The Ship Who Sang.

THE SHIP WHO SEARCHED
by Anne McCaffrey & Mercedes Lackey

Tia, a bright and spunky seven-year-old accompanying her exo-archaeologist parents on a dig, is afflicted by a paralyzing alien virus. Tia won't be satisfied to glide through life like a ghost in a machine. Like her predecessor Helva, *The Ship Who Sang*, she would rather strap on a spaceship!

THE CITY WHO FOUGHT
by Anne McCaffrey & S.M. Stirling

Simeon was the "brain" running a peaceful space station—but when the invaders arrived, his only hope of protecting his crew and himself was to become *The City Who Fought*.

THE SHIP WHO WON
by Anne McCaffrey & Jody Lynn Nye

"The brainship Carialle and her brawn, Keff, find a habitable planet inhabited by an apparent mix of races and cultures and dominated by an elite of apparent magicians. Appearances are deceiving, however ... a brisk, well-told often amusing tale.... Fans of either author, or both, will have fun with this book."　　　　　　　　　　　　—*Booklist*